Acclaim for Stanley G. West's
Until They Bring the Streetcars Back

"Stanley West, an extraordinary novelist and storyteller who writes with searing beauty and truth, has written a lyrical and moving novel . . . a story that pierces to the core of life . . . compelling reading for people of all times and places. . . ."
—*Richard Wheeler, winner of the Golden Spur Award, author of some thirty novels*

". . . the story is so universal, so honest in its challenges and themes, so compelling, that readers anywhere can relate to and feel for the protagonist. . . ."
—*Sue Hart, Professor of English, Montana State University-Billings*

"It's a charming and engaging book."
—*John Moore, retired President, Columbia University Press*

"One of the most gripping books I read all year."
—*Marjorie Smith,* Bozeman Daily Chronicle

"West has again captured an often untold yet important part of the human story . . . encouraging for all who may feel it's too late to make a change. . . ."
—*Brad Walton, The Brad Walton Show, WCCO Radio*

"It is about people who are trapped . . . about heroism and losing something you cannot get back."
—*Don Boxmeyer,* Saint Paul Pioneer Press

"It shows that questions of morality are still the stuff of which great stories are made."
—*Gary Svee,* Billings Gazette

Stanley Gordon West

FINDING LAURA BUGGS

Stanley West was born in Saint Paul, the third in a family of
four children. He grew up during the Great Depression and
the World War II years, attending the city's public schools
and getting around riding the streetcars. He graduated from
Central High School in 1950. He attended Macalester
College and the University of Minnesota, earning a degree in
history and geology in 1955. He moved from the Midwest to
Montana in 1964 where he raised a large family and he has
lived there ever since. His novel *Amos* was produced as a
CBS Movie of the Week starring Kirk Douglas, Elizabeth
Montgomery and Dorothy McGuire and was nominated for
four Emmys.

Also By Stanley G. West

Amos
Until They Bring the Streetcars Back

FINDING
Laura Buggs

Stanley Gordon West

LEXINGTON-MARSHALL PUBLISHING
BOZEMAN, MONTANA

Published in the United States by Lexington•Marshall Publishing
P.O. Box 388, Shakopee, Minnesota 55379.

Library of Congress Catalog Card Number: 99-094302
ISBN 0-9656247-7-3

Book design by Richard Krogstad
Book production by Peregrine Graphics Services
Author photograph © Linda Richmond
Printed in the United States by McNaughton & Gunn, Inc.

7 9 10 8 6

Second Printing: February 2001
Third Printing: March 2003
Fourth Printing: March 2004
Sixth Printing: October 2006

Dedicated to all abandoned children,
disowned, betrayed,
lost in the shuffle,
in search of your family and self.

In memory of
Peter Eagle Lightfoot
who finally found home

Hope is the thing with feathers
That perches in the soul,
And sings the tune without the words,
And never stops at all . . .
—Emily Dickinson (1891)

Sometimes
　　to very fortunate people
the spark of authenticity
　　is struck in their innermost being.

The glowing ember
　　seems terribly fragile
　　　　　and

In fear of loss,
　　that the newborn flame
　　will be smothered by
　　family, friends, teachers
　　who seem to want to impose their visions

You rebel and argue and strike out
Such senseless hurt
For from the beginning
　　only you can dim yourself
　　　　　—Bruce Patrick

FINDING LAURA BUGGS

Chapter 1

Come out, come out, wherever you are! I was playing hide-and-seek with sudden death and I didn't want to play. I had no choice. My life measured from heartbeat to heartbeat, from one breath to the next. Any moment he might open the door and my life would be over. In a rage at finding me there, crouched in that ridiculous broom closet, he'd surely strangle me while I was helpless to move.

The trouble was I'd covered my trail, no one would be looking for me. I'd been careless, stupidly careless. Despite Clara's blaring old bugle he'd surprised me, giving me a split-second to duck into that stifling coffin. He was there, in the kitchen, inches from the narrow door that stood open a crack. I could hear him muttering to himself. He'd said I was a persistent girl and I'd taken it as a compliment, proud of my stubbornness. But it had all gone wrong and my stubbornness would be the end of me.

Why hadn't I left well enough alone, accepted my life for what it was? It was a good life, I had everything to live for, full of promise. People would sadly shake their heads when they'd see she was only seventeen on my tombstone. Only I'd never have a tombstone. If he opened that broom closet door, I knew I'd dug my own grave in his fruit cellar floor and I'd join my mother and father, disappearing as they had, in that unmarked family plot.

It was terrifying comedy; there I was, squatting on a pail, tangled with a broom handle and mop and dustpan, expecting him to find me second by second. Drenched in sweat and afraid I'd cough or sneeze, I didn't dare move a muscle, didn't dare twitch. My breath echoed loudly in my skull. Desperately fighting the panic welling up in my throat, struggling to calm myself, I thought back to how I ever got into that deadly mess.

The trouble began on my twelfth birthday when my parents told me I was adopted. Actually it was my mother who did the dirty work while my father awkwardly stood by. Awkward was pretty normal in our family, just me and the two of them. As far back as I could remember I always felt an uneasiness between us, even before they spilled the beans. I don't know why they told me, as if the law required them to come clean, but maybe they felt I was grown up enough to take it.

Happy Birthday, Sandy, you're not our kid.

I don't want to sound mean or anything, they were doing what they thought was the right thing, but it didn't make for a rip-roaring birthday. It felt like a total eclipse of my heart, all light sucked from the life I knew. I wandered around in a daze for a while, trying to catch my breath. Like a can of food whose label had come off, you couldn't tell who I was. My world turned topsy-turvy, birds flew upside-down, compass needles pointed true west, and two plus two was seven.

This was the deal: my mother wasn't my mother! I'd gotten it wrong for twelve years. I thought of running away with the circus or hitchhiking to Duluth and stowing away on an ocean-going freighter. I didn't tell any of my friends for over two years and then one night at Jean Daley's slumber party, as if I were announcing I had leprosy, I told them. Judas Priest, they looked at me as though I'd been hatched from an egg in some tropical swamp. By that time I'd already started scrutinizing women who would be about my mother's age to see if I could detect any resemblance.

It was a relief in some ways because I'd always felt I was oddly different from my parents, like we weren't from the same deck of cards. I often felt like a stranger in my own home and one day when I asked my mother why I didn't have any sisters or brothers she only said they thought one child was enough to raise. She was pretty frail and sick a lot and it made sense to me at the time.

The only time my father and I really talked was at the dinner table. It seemed he never could think of anything to say with me and I was the same with him and it was always slightly strained between us unless I could come up with something about plumbing and heating or he could come up with something about school, but he never talked about his days at school or when he was a boy. We both were relieved when we came up with a common subject like the mating call of the short-tailed albatross or irregular verb forms of the Sino-Tibetan language.

So this was the deal: I didn't know who my real parents were, didn't know if they were dead or alive, and I didn't know who that made me. Some kids are adopted and never know it, and some who know it don't give a rip who their real parents were, but I had to know, it was driving me crazy. I really tried to forget about it for almost five years, just push it out of my mind, and sometimes I wished they hadn't told me. But when I started my senior year at Saint Paul Central High School I realized that when you're adopted there are two questions you can't bury or outrun. *Why didn't they keep me?* and *Who were they?* I vowed I'd find out before I graduated or I'd just die.

If I'd imagined the horror I'd uncover and the danger I'd face, I might not've dared to start down that path into the forest, might've chosen the safety of the sunlit meadow and been satisfied to be Sandy Meyer. But I never could've known where it would lead, never wanted to hurt anyone, just find out who I was and my given name, the name my real mother gave me the day I was born, because I'd heard that's the name God knows you by. I'd tried to let it lie but it had become a part of my heartbeat, in every breath I took, and something I couldn't name drew me like an unheard voice just below the surface.

It really started that Friday afternoon, the first week of school. I had to stay an hour after school because the kids in

Whalmen's study hall set marbles on the slanted auditorium floor and scared the daylights out of her when they came roaring down where she was sitting at her little table. Gosh, she jumped up and started hop-scotching around like she had hornets in her girdle and we were falling out of our seats, laughing so hard it hurt. When she figured out what was going on she was really burned. Kids called her the Prussian General and none of us could believe we'd dared to do it.

Jerry Douglas, one of the senior wheels, passed out the marbles in front hall just before study hall. I was usually chicken when it came to doing something that took nerve, but I took one. When the big clock beside the stage clicked to one twenty I held my breath and tried to set my marble on the wood floor but I couldn't. My fingers wouldn't let go and I clung to the marble with my sweaty fist and my chicken heart. All through the hour of detention I berated myself for chickening out and I felt like a traitor, acting as if I'd been a part of it with the marble still in my skirt pocket.

Anyway, I was late getting home. My mother had been in the hospital for almost two weeks in August and I wanted to see that she was all right. Jean and I were going to the football game that night and I wouldn't be home long. I ran the half block from the Randolph-Hazel Park streetcar to our house on Bayard and found my mother in her bedroom, sitting in her rocker with an Afghan over her lap. She appeared pale and weak, but she looked that way a lot and I had worried growing up that she would die.

She was gazing at the picture of Amelia Earhart that sat framed on the dresser, the woman aviator who disappeared in 1937 in the South Pacific while attempting to fly around the world. People told my mother that she looked like Amelia, and there was a resemblance, but my mother was a lot skinnier. Amelia was her hero and she was certain the Japs were holding her captive in some hidden dungeon. She wrote letters to the President and congressmen and the FBI and the Navy, urging them to continue the search and rescue Amelia. It was one of my mother's quirks.

"How are you, Mom?"

"I'm just fine," she said.

My mother had a way of saying she was fine that made you feel guilty for not seeing that she obviously wasn't.

"Can I get you anything?"

"I want you to come and sit down for a minute," she said.

I sat on the bed and felt something sticky in the air. The look on her gaunt face scared me and I was afraid she was about to tell me she was dying.

"Sandy, I know how important it is for you to know who your real parents were."

Golly, she knocked the wind out of me. I'd done every-thing I could to never let on. Right from the start I told them it didn't make any difference because I didn't want to hurt them and make them think I didn't love them.

"I don't care about that, Mom."

"You hush now and listen to me. I realized had I died in the hospital, you'd never know. Your father would never tell you; he's too ashamed."

"You don't have to—"

"Hush." She held up her hand as if she were stopping traffic. "Let me say what I want to say while I have the gumption."

She looked at me with such anguish my throat went dry.

"Your father was arrested and went to jail when he was a young man. He stole from the man he worked for. His family disowned him publicly, put a notice in the *Pioneer Press*. His parents and two brothers never spoke to him again, the fami-ly black sheep. When he got out of jail he joined the Army but after he'd been in boot camp for several months they found out he'd been in jail and kicked him out. When we met he told me all about it and I could tell he'd learned his lesson. He was ashamed to have missed fighting in Europe with some of his friends."

Her voice broke and she took a drink of water from the glass on the bedstand.

"It doesn't matter, Mom, I just—"

"Let me get this out because I may never have the chance again."

She took my hand and hers felt cold and clammy and she had the look on her face she had the day she told me about the curse.

"After we were married, your father started out digging ditches with a pick and shovel, sewer lines and water lines, because no one else would hire him. We tried to have a baby for several years with no luck. Finally, the doctor told me I could never conceive, that we'd have to adopt if we wanted a family. But we knew no adoptive agency would accept your father; he was a felon. Just when we'd given up all hope, we found a lawyer who knew of a man who had an eleven-month-old baby girl whose mother was deathly ill. He was looking for a good home for the child, needed $970 to pay his wife's medical bills. We had to borrow some of the money."

"I was a black-market baby?"

"Not really," she said. She let go of my hand and waved hers lightly in the air. "We just didn't go through a normal adoption agency."

"What was the family's name?"

"We never were told; it was all kept secret on both sides. Only the lawyer knew who they were and he never told them who we were so there could never be any trouble."

"Did my mother die?"

"We don't know anything more than that. We took you home and loved you as much as anyone has ever loved their child, loved you as if I'd borne you with my own body and blood. You were the joy of my life. I'd take you for long walks in your buggy just so I could show you off to neighbors and strangers and everyone would tell me they never saw a more beautiful little girl."

She tilted her head slightly and looked at me as if I were still that pretty little girl.

"Why I remember once when you were about three, I had you in pigtails and a pretty little dress at the Como Zoo and in front of the bear cage a man asked if he could take your picture, a perfect stranger, said he'd never seen such an adorable child. I was so proud I almost burst."

"A snapshot of me?" I said.

"Yes, people on the street were taken by you, I was so delighted. Your father kept saying that in a few years the boys'd be lining up at the front door."

My dad didn't get that one right.

My mother sighed. "That's all I can tell you, except one more thing. The name of the lawyer was Arnold Shapiro, an older man; I'd guess he'd be seventy or more by now, but I have no idea if he's still alive."

My head felt like it was spinning. I squeezed my mother's hand and stood up. My throat was filling and I was getting all emotional.

"I gotta get ready for the game."

I started out of the room. My chest felt like it had a truck parked on it but I managed to smile.

"Thanks for telling me, Mom, but it really doesn't matter, I have *my* mom and dad."

I could tell by her face how that pleased her, how I'd said the words she was hoping I'd say.

"One more thing," she said. "Don't ever tell your father I told you, *never*. He still carries the shame of it all. It would hurt him a great deal if he knew I told you."

"Don't worry, I won't tell anyone."

I bolted down the hall to my room and shut the door. I dove onto the bed and buried my face in the pillow and bawled. I don't know why, but I really bawled. And then suddenly I stopped and rolled over. I stared at the blurry ceiling. How would I ever find an old fuddy-duddy named Arnold Shapiro? I slipped my hand into my skirt pocket and found the marble, a reminder of my chickenheart.

Where would I find the courage to go searching for my lost family?

Chapter 2

My father carted home several steaming cartons of Chinese food and we ate dinner at the kitchen table, something we did a lot when my mother was sick. Usually we ate in the dining room, but my father and I conspired to make things as easy as we could for her, foregoing the linen napkins, tablecloth and serving dishes.

While he helped set the table and dish up I tried to imagine him in jail, or stealing money from his boss. I couldn't. Howard Meyer had worked hard from the bottom up and now owned St. Clair Plumbing & Heating and he was the most law abiding citizen I'd ever heard of. I remembered how I admired him when he was an Air Raid Warden during the war and how he did everything he could to help the war effort: volunteered for the war bond drive, the scrap metal drive, the Red Cross blood drive. He caught me scrutinizing him out of the corner of my eye and I blushed, as if somehow he could tell I knew his secret.

While I helped with supper I had a hard time hiding my excitement and felt guilty for being so hopeful when my mother was sick. I was repeating a rhyme to myself with the lawyer's name, over and over, so I wouldn't forget it.

Arnold Shapiro, you're my hero,
If I never find you, I'll be a zero.

Since I was a little kid I'd always make up a rhyme about something I didn't want to forget. It was kind of drippy and the rhymes were corny, but I'd remember stuff forever that way.

We started our meal as always, with bowed heads and folded hands, reciting the table prayer in unison.

Heavenly Father, we thank you for this food. May it nourish us
to be a blessing to others and good neighbors to all. Amen.

Once when I asked my mother why we didn't ever use a different prayer, she said it had been her family prayer when she was a girl. I always figured if it had been up to my dad we'd have gone ahead without that routine nod to the Almighty.

"Who are you going with tonight?" my mother said as we passed the cartons around.

"Jean . . . most of the boys I like play on the team."

"Mutt and Jeff," my dad said.

He called us Mutt and Jeff because I was thin and kind of tall and Jean, my best friend, was real short and a little plump.

"I'm glad you're going out with lots of boys," my mother said. "You're much too young to be getting serious."

Serious! heck, I was serious with all of them. I really liked boys and I'd had a whole slug of boyfriends, although some times they didn't know they *were* my boyfriend. My mother's opinion of boys wasn't too hot. When I was thirteen she gave me about a ten-minute lecture on sex and her voice was different, the way it was when I was twelve and she told me I was adopted. I didn't like to think about what might be coming when I was fourteen. About the only thing I remembered from her talk was that boys have their minds in their pants and later Jean had to explain to me what that meant.

"I think Scott McFarland is swell," I said. "I'm in two of his classes."

"I know his father," my dad said. "He's an executive with First National Bank. A good family."

I never told my folks that the selection process I used to pick my classes for my senior year, since I had already fulfilled the required subjects to graduate, was to pick classes that were mostly all boys. Physics, wood shop, trigonometry, speech, and of course English, which we had to take all four years. I was the only girl in wood shop. It was peachy. And I managed to get in trouble fairly often and get seventh period because that was usually all boys, too.

This was the deal: my father and I would inconspicuously keep track of how much my mother ate. We'd learned we could tell how she was doing by her appetite. My mother's name was Gladys and she was a slight, dainty woman. I had always thought I was doomed to be skinny like her until she told me I was adopted. For my body that was good news, but I still checked my breasts in the mirror every morning to see if they'd shown up. They were stunted or ingrown or got lost on the way. All my girlfriends were growing breasts as if they slept in a greenhouse and all I had was two thimbles, little tiny thimbles, without even a hint of swelling. I needed a bra as much as the football team. I was sure they'd never grow and no boy would ever be attracted to me; I was just a bone. Maybe that's why I bit my fingernails all the time, even though I tried my darnedest to stop.

I met Jean Daley where we always met on the corner of Cleveland and Hartford, halfway between my house and hers, and we caught a streetcar to the game. Jean was a swell friend and I told her everything and I couldn't wait to tell her about the lawyer Arnold Shapiro and how my parents got me. She was as excited as I was and we laughed as we repeated the rhyme together.

Arnold Shapiro, you're my hero,
If I never find you, I'll be a zero.

"And they just bought you like a loaf of bread?" Jean said.

"Yeah . . . $970."

"How can we find the lawyer?" she said as we transferred onto a Snelling streetcar.

"I looked in the Saint Paul phone book. Mom thinks he might be dead."

"Oh, golly, I never thought of that," Jean said. "What if he is?"

"I'll die, I'll just die."

Jean and I went everywhere together, unless one of us had a date. She had a round, pretty face and looked like

Susan Hayward with freckles and bangs, and I knew she'd go through fire for me and I'd do the same for her.

Jean and Dave Neuberg were in love but their parents got together and broke them up. Her parents didn't want her going with a Jewish boy and his parents didn't want him going with a Catholic girl. It was really hard on both of them and they tried to see each other in secret but Jean's father told her he'd pull her out of Central and send her to Derham Hall and the rule of the nuns if she didn't break it off and that sounded worse than crucifixion.

Jean tried to have fun with other boys but I knew how much she loved Dave and most people would never guess because she was always smiling and loads of fun when she was with other kids. She didn't want to do anything to hurt her parents. Her oldest brother Don joined the Army in 1943 and a year later he was killed during the landing in Normandy and it seemed that Jean's mother was doing her best to shore up a gaping hole in her heart.

When we popped off the streetcar at Selby there wasn't another in sight heading towards school so we ducked in the Rexall Drug Store on the corner and I called Minneapolis information.

"No Arnold Shapiro," I said when I hung up, "not in Saint Paul, not in Minneapolis."

We crossed the street and caught a Selby-Lake.

"What if he's dead and buried?" Jean said as we slid onto the bench seat up front.

"He can't be, I just know I'll find him."

"Yeah, with a shovel in a graveyard," Jean said and then she bit her lip.

Everybody was at the game. We were playing Johnson and even though I didn't understand football very well I could tell we were beating them by the cheering Central fans. I yelled and screamed with them but I could never tell who

had the ball. Jean and I walked around the track at halftime
to see if we could meet any neat boys from Johnson and it
occurred to me that one of those kids could be my brother
or sister. We bumped into Steve Holland, a nifty senior at
Central, and he asked us if we'd like to get something to eat
after the game. We jumped at the chance.

Steve was really swell but he was kind of wild and you
never knew what he'd do. He had polio when he was in
grade school and it shriveled one of his legs and he kind of
limped but no one seemed to notice. I knew that it really
bothered him that he couldn't play football. He never had a
steady girlfriend and I had a crush on him when we were
juniors.

We went to the Flat Top Drive-in on Lake Street and the
old Chevy was jammed with kids as usual. Jerry and Sally
and Lola and Tom were in the back seat and I was shoved
up against Steve in front with my good friend Cal Gant, with
Jean on his lap, beside me. Everybody was feeling happy
because we beat Johnson 26 to 7.

After we stuffed ourselves with fries and hamburgers and
malts, Steve drove backwards down the River Boulevard,
scaring the wits out of us, and then he parked in a dark spot
near Minnehaha Falls. He was so nice to pay for my fries and
malt when we weren't even on a date. I had a malt whenever
I could, hoping it would put some flesh on my bones,
especially on my dormant breasts. I had heard that malts
would increase the size of your breasts and I had one every
chance I got.

The four in the back seat were steady couples and they
were necking like minks while the four of us in the front
seat just sat there like stumps and talked and listened to the
radio, trying to ignore the passion oozing out of the back
seat. I leaned up against Steve and hoped he'd at least put
his arm around me but he and Cal were talking and Jean
was laughing and the kids in the back seat were having all
the fun.

Frank Sinatra was singing "Till The End of Time" on the radio and I'd always get all queasy listening to him singing love songs and all of a sudden I started thinking about my real mother. Had she died? Where was my real father? Did I have any brothers or sisters? If I couldn't find Arnold Shapiro I'd never know, *ever.* It was scary. How in this great big world would I ever find them?

I was starting to feel kind of blue and I wished Steve would put his arm around me. Then Lola came up for air and said she had to get home.

Arnold Shapiro, you're my hero,
If I never find you, I'll be a zero.

Chapter 3

Saturday afternoon, when I was done with my housework, I hiked down to the river. When I was in sixth grade we'd moved from a house on Lincoln, near Ramsey Grade School, to the house we lived in on Bayard, across from Horace Mann. I never knew why we moved, my parents never told me, but before I'd made any new friends, I explored the inviting woods and cliffs along the Mississippi River, only six blocks from the house.

I guess I was a tomboy of sorts, being the only child of my father, who had hinted from time to time that he'd been an athlete in his boyhood days. He'd even been a wing walker on barnstorming airplanes, but to get him to talk about the time he was young was like trying to extract eye teeth with a bottle opener, and since my mother's bombshell, I finally understood why. Not that my father and I spent a lot of time together, but on occasion, at the lake or on a picnic, he'd challenge me, push me, to climb a tree or swim a distance underwater, and when I'd chicken out he'd call me a scaredy cat or worse, sissyskin. As I grew up I came to believe he was right, I was a sissyskin about daring things, but I could climb a tree like a squirrel.

One spring afternoon, by accident, I discovered a small cave near Hidden Falls while I was climbing trees and crawling around on the bedrock bluffs. The cave was oval shaped, about ten feet deep on the face of a sandstone cliff. You had to come down to it from above, using a narrow crevice for handholds and footholds. Inside I could curl up like a rabbit in a nest. I felt warm and safe there like no other place I'd ever been, and I'd daydream I was in my real father's arms or my real mother's belly and sometimes I could hear the heartbeat of the earth. I'd fall asleep some days and wake an hour later. I could sit with my legs over the ledge and look down a hundred feet to the trees and brush along the river, content to be there for hours.

A couple years after I discovered the cave I prayed to God. I told Him I knew he was my real father, that He made me, so if I didn't know who my human father was, it was okay, because He loved me and He'd never give me away. Then I prayed real hard and I asked, if it wasn't too much trouble, to please let me *hear* Him, somehow, to make some kind of sound so I knew He was there. Then I held my breath and listened. For several minutes the world around my cave was perfectly silent, not a sound. I strained my ears.

Suddenly, a flock of crows came swooping in and invaded the trees below me in a noisy, raucous flurry, cawing loudly back and forth, a black-feathered racket. I was delighted with this response, although I thought it was a strange way for God to talk. A crow's call wasn't what I expected for the voice of God, that wild, mysterious, lonely cry, but I believed with my whole heart that it *was* God talking to me! Every time I saw or heard a crow after that I figured it was God reminding me that He was around.

When I reached the river bluffs Saturday afternoon I climbed down the face of the cliff and into my welcoming cave. Someone told me that bedrock was called the St. Peter sandstone. I thought that was a good name for the rock that wrapped its arms around me and sheltered me from the world. I curled up inside the warm sandstone and thought about what my mother had told me.

My only link with my real parents was a man named Arnold Shapiro. What if I did find him? Did I want to know why my parents didn't keep me? Did I want to find out who my mother was? I shivered with the thought of it. She could be an imbecile or the Buffalo Woman in the freak show at the State Fair. I understood I was starting something I might one day wish I hadn't and I could hear my chickenheart whispering in my ear. But then a crow called somewhere along the river, *caw-caw-caw.*

   That did it. I vowed that if Arnold Shapiro wasn't already
dead I would find him. I knew it would be hard, and I
didn't know where to start, but I was determined to do
whatever it would take.

All that next week I called every law firm and lawyer in Saint
Paul and Minneapolis, never dreaming there were so many. It
seemed there was a lawyer for every man, woman and dog
on earth. But not one of them knew of an Arnold Shapiro,
and I was losing hope fast.
   I used the phone mostly at Jean's house after school. Her
mom worked a lot for the Red Cross and Community Chest
and stuff like that so she wasn't around much. It seemed as
if she were trying to do enough good in the world to bring
her son back and they kept his red, white and blue service
star in their front window as if they expected him to come
walking through the door any day.
   I didn't want my mother to know I was looking for my
real parents; it would break her heart. I'd never want to hurt
either of my parents. After all, they were the ones who raised
me and gave me everything I needed and changed my
diapers and gave me a nice home to live in and fed me all
those years. I don't know why I couldn't just forget about
Arnold Shapiro, but I couldn't.

Tuesday night I was at the Deb meeting at Geraldine Park's
and a lot of the nifty boys from Central showed up. All the
sororities and Hi-Ys and fraternities had their meetings on
Tuesday night at different kids' houses and when they were
over all the boys would pile into cars and crash the sorority
meetings. It was oodles of fun and exciting because you
might get to flirt with a nifty boy or get asked out for the
coming weekend or offered a ride home.
   When the boys poured in the front door of Geraldine's
house, Steve came bounding over to me like a puppy.

"Hi, Sandy, would you like to go to the dance on Friday night?"

Gosh, I thought he was kidding for a second, the way he'd always fool around. The Minute Men Club was putting on the Fall Fantasy at the Saint Paul Hotel, the first dance of the year. I was hoping Scott would ask me, but Steve was a panic and always loads of fun. I stood there for a second with my mouth half open and remembered my father's favorite saying: You don't look a gift horse in the mouth.

"Yes, thank you, I'd love to," I said.

"We'll double with Jerry and Sally," he said.

"That sounds peachy, Steve. I'll talk to Sally about what she's wearing."

"Yeah, and I'll check to see what toothpaste Jerry's going to use," he said and then sprayed the room with his raucous laugh.

Steve had no more than wandered into the kitchen in the middle of fifty or sixty kids when Scott came up to me shyly and said hello. That was a major move for Scott, a tall blond boyish-looking senior who invented bashful and polite. Then I felt it in the pit of my stomach, what I'd been hoping for for weeks.

"I suppose you're already going to the dance Friday with someone," he said while looking at the carpet.

"Oh, yeah, I am. I'm sorry, Scott."

"That's okay," he said, glancing into my face for a moment. He seemed relieved. "Maybe some other time."

"Yes, some other time, please ask me again."

So often it seemed I got a date for a dance at the last hour or went stag with Jean or my other girlfriends, and now, in a matter of twenty seconds, I had invitations from two swell boys for the same dance. What a waste. I couldn't wait to tell Jean. Steve and Scott were fighting over me.

On Wednesday I couldn't wait to tell Jean what happened in English. Though late September, it felt like summer and we

were out on the lawn eating our bag lunches with loads of
other kids.

"I think Jerry may be in big trouble," I said.

"What happened?" Jean said.

"By the end of the hour we were all bored out of our
minds, reading out loud from *The Taming of the Shrew*. Kids
stammered along, a page each, and some kids read so slow I
was falling asleep. Then, when it was Jerry's turn, he reads
about one word a minute, like a dimwit."

I started laughing all over again.

"What did Bellows do?" Jean said.

"She kept saying Faster please, faster please, and every
time she said it Jerry slowed down. 'When . . . wouldest . . .
thou . . ?' He was driving her nuts. Finally she told Sue
Schwartz to read when Jerry had only finished about two
sentences and the look she gave him could've peeled varnish
off his desk."

"I wish I had English with you guys," Jean said.

"Wait, wait, there's more. When we were done and there
were a few minutes before the bell, she opened a book on
her desk. 'I want to read you a lovely poem,' she said in her
highfalutin voice. She looked around the room, into our
faces, just staring at us for a long time. I wondered what was
wrong. Then she closed the book. 'No, no,' she said, 'it would
be like casting pearls before swine.'"

"She *said* that?" Jean said.

"Yeah, pearls before swine, and then Jerry starts softly
oinking. He doesn't move his lips or change his expression
and he looks right at Bellows and she can't figure out where
it's coming from. Then someone else started oinking, I think
it was Cal, and then more oinking from all over the room.
The bell rang and by the time we hit the hall we were all
oinking and Bellows just stood in the doorway with her arms
folded, looking daggers at us."

Jean rolled back on the lawn laughing. "You have all the
fun in your classes. Mine are so normal." Then she popped

back up to a sitting position and stared into my face, wide-eyed.

"What?" I said.

"Jerry's father!"

"So?"

"He's a lawyer!" she said.

"We called them all, we must have hit his."

"Douglas?"

"I don't remember, but we called every attorney and law firm on earth."

"Well, I figure they're not going to give a hoot over the phone like that. Ask Jerry to have his father try," Jean said, "someone who gives a darn."

"What could I tell him why I want to find Arnold Shapiro?"

"Lots of reasons, an old neighbor, a friend of the family you've lost contact with, make something up. Jerry will do it. If he knows it's important to you, Jerry will do it."

I went back to my next class with a tuna fish sandwich in my stomach, washed down with a little hope.

Chapter 4

The dance Friday night was loads of fun. Everybody was there and Chet Harris and His Merry Men of Rhythm played all my favorite songs. Steve and I danced a lot and during one dance I talked him into cutting in on Jerry and Sally. They just stood there speechless, wondering what we were doing, and I grabbed Jerry and danced off with him, laughing. They were neat about it and I had Jerry alone for a minute. I hadn't been able to catch up to him since Wednesday and I didn't want a lot of kids knowing I was looking for some old lawyer. I told him I was looking for a family friend who'd been a lawyer and we couldn't find an address for him and would his dad see if he could find out what happened to him.

"He was a lawyer in the late thirties and into the forties but then we lost track of him," I said as we one-stepped around the floor.

"Sure, I can do that. Maybe my dad will know what happened to him. Sometimes the police help my dad find someone."

"That would be swell," I said and I bounced a little on my toes.

After the dance we ate at the Flat-Top even though Sally and I had dressy dresses and hoped we might go to the Rainbow. When we finished with the fries, burgers and malts, Steve pulled out on Lake Street and headed into Minneapolis. When I was hoping for a little romance along the River Boulevard I got drag racing on Lake Street.

Everyone knew that if you wanted to test your car, as well as your nerve, you could always find a challenger on Lake Street. After nine o'clock all you had to do was show up and before you knew it a kid would pull alongside and rev his engine. We found several.

His father's dull-gray '39 Chevy became like a healthy
right leg, and if the polio kept Steve from playing football,
doggone it, he'd win by outdriving other kids in their dads'
hot shot cars. Soon we were streaking past storefronts with
the speedometer bouncing around forty-five. A popular disc
jockey was playing "Bonaparte's Retreat" and Steve, wild and
cocky, enjoyed curling the hairs on our eyeballs.

I held my breath and hung onto my seat as we hurtled
past grocery stores, used-car lots, and sleazy bars across
Minneapolis.

Then, when I thought we would survive the night
unmaimed and still breathing, a polished black '46 four-door
Ford pulled alongside on the boulevard around Lake
Calhoun.

"Where you from?" a smart-aleck-looking kid shouted
from the front passenger seat.

"St. Paul Central!" Steve shouted.

"You know how to play Rotation?" a heavy, pimple-faced
boy called from the back seat.

"Yeah," Jerry shouted.

"No," I shouted, "do we look crazy?"

"Maybe you Central sissies are too chicken!" the four boys
in the Ford taunted.

"I'm not playing Rotation," I said and I froze. They were
talking about *me*, as if the word had spread to Minneapolis
that I was afraid to do anything daring, anything that took
nerve. Up at the lake when I wouldn't jump off the high
board, my dad said I was a sissyskin and I wanted to cry and
I told him it was all right to be a sissy if you were a girl but
I really didn't believe that and in my heart I was ashamed.

Last summer, when my friends had so much fun jumping
off ledges into the St.Croix River, I couldn't do it and I
hated myself for being a sissy. I *was* a chickenheart. When
my parents first heard about Rotation they made me promise
I'd never do it and I wanted to laugh and assure them I'd
never have the backbone. But I wanted to break out and do

something daring, prove to myself I had nerve and courage, but I didn't know if I could.

This was the deal: in a Chinese fire drill you came to a stop and everyone in the car leaped out and ran around the car and piled back in and you drove away. Rotation was like that only you did it at forty or fifty miles an hour. Everyone followed the driver who went from the front seat out the driver-side door, onto the running board, into the the back seat, out the right-side back door, into the front seat, and as each person passed the steering wheel, it was his turn to drive.

"You can let me out first," Sally said.

The Ford kept pace beside us. I glanced at Sally, she was wide-eyed. I felt relieved, I wasn't the only chicken.

"Oh, they'd rather go play with their girlfriend's titties!" one of the boys shouted.

Now *that* was the kind of boy my mother had warned me about. I blushed and felt self-conscious in front of Steve and Jerry but I don't know why, they couldn't have been refer-ring to me.

Jerry grabbed the door handle. "Stop the car! Let me smash that kid in the mouth."

"Okay," I said, "let's beat them," and I swallowed my gum.

"Yeah," Sally said, "let's shut their smutty mouths."

Steve cranked the guffer's knob, wheeling a U-turn, fol-lowed closely by the Minneapolis braggarts. Sally and I took off our loafers and we all peeled off our coats. We drove to a stretch of Lake Street, idling the cars side by side at a red light. I checked my door and hoped I wouldn't have to use the clutch.

The arrogant delinquents smirked over at us and hollered, "Try not to wet your pants, you Saint Paul chickens. *Baawwwk, bawk, bawk, bawk.*"

That was the same squawking sound my dad used to make when I couldn't do something he dared me to.

"We can beat you any day of the week and twice on Sunday!" Jerry shouted, checking the back doors to see that they were unlocked.

I had a hard time breathing and my armpits were wet.

When the semaphore opened its green glass eye, the two cars squealed up the street like scalded cats. I slid next to Steve and jammed my foot on top of his as he rammed the Chevy into second gear. I held the accelerator down and took the steering wheel. In a heartbeat he was out the door and into the back seat where Sally had opened the door for him. Out the back door, Jerry swung into the front seat next to me. I was floorboarding it while side by side, our two cars careened along Lake Street with their doors flapping like wings as we lunatics conducted a Chinese fire drill at fifty-three miles an hour.

"Hurry, hurry!" Steve shouted as Jerry took the wheel from me. Through the blasting night air, I clung to the center column and swung out onto the running board. My dress and slip were blowing up around my waist and for a second covered my face. I was gasping and gulping down my terror and trying to dive into the back seat. The foul-mouthed boys were slightly ahead when Sally took the steering wheel from Jerry, narrowly missing parked cars along the curb and dangerously close to the speeding car beside us. When I dove into the front seat beside Steve, completing the rotation, we were all shouting at the top of our lungs and the Minneapolis car still had a kid out on the running board.

We hooted and honked and slowed down. We'd beaten them at the contest that should've been named Insanity. When we were back to a legal speed and the Ford pulled up alongside, Steve blasted them with both barrels.

"Where'd you get your driver's licenses, you Minneapolis morphadites, in a box of Cracker Jack?"

All of us chimed in, razzing the humbled Minneapolis boys until they turned off and disappeared up the side street of their humiliation.

When I was breathing normally again I felt proud of myself, I had done it, I could be daring, and, as insane as it was, I'd shed my sissyskin and chickenhood somewhere back along the streetcar tracks on Lake Street. I wanted to tell my father but I knew I couldn't and I felt a small remorse that I'd broken my promise to him.

I felt strangely close to my crazy friends, as if we'd gone to war together. I couldn't believe what we'd done and while I was out on the running board, staring sudden death in the face, my mind was shouting, Arnold Shapiro! Arnold Shapiro! I'll never find out who I am!

All week I pestered Jerry, wondering if his father had found out anything about Arnold Shapiro and on Friday he told me before English that his father knew of an Arnold Shapiro and that he thought he was dead. But he called some people and found out that Arnold Shapiro had a son living in Milwaukee. The son's name was Ivan. That's all he knew.

Holy cow, I didn't know how to feel, happy or sad. I knew where his son was but Arnold might be dead. Saturday, before the football game, Jean and I met on Cleveland and walked to the drugstore on Ford Parkway. I had over three dollars in change and I called information in Milwaukee. They gave me the number of an Ivan Shapiro. The operator dialed the number but no one answered. Gad, I was so jumpy I couldn't eat or sleep.

We beat Murray 27 to 12 and every chance I got over the weekend I tried the number. Scott asked me to the Homecoming Dance on Monday after second lunch and when he scampered up the stairs, I walked into a freshman English class and tried to find my desk.

On the way home from school, at the drugstore on Randolph and Snelling, Jean and I called the number and a man answered.

"Hello, I'm calling for Ivan Shapiro."

"Yes, this is Ivan Shapiro."

"Do you have a father named Arnold?" I said, pressing the phone to my ear.

"Yes, why do you ask?"

"He helped me a long time ago, back in 1933, and I want to ask him a few questions," I said and held my breath.

"Good luck."

"Is he dead?"

"Might as well be. He's living in a home for the aged in Minneapolis but he can't remember his own name."

"Oh . . . I'm sorry . . . that's terrible."

"Who is this?" he said.

"Jean Daley," I said, so my parents wouldn't find out what I was up to.

"He's in the Sunset Home For The Aged And Friendless on Sheridan near 40th Street, Jean, and I wish you luck. Last time I saw him he didn't know me."

"When was that, how long ago?"

"Ah . . . about a year ago, around Christmas. We think it would be a relief for everyone if he'd just go to sleep and not wake up."

Did he want his father to die? How cruel.

"I'm sorry to bother you," I said, "but thanks. I'll go see him."

"Better do it fast."

Chapter 5

Tuesday afternoon I left school in a dither, weaving in and out around the flow of kids along Dunlap, thinking my heart would pop right out of my chest. I piled into a streetcar and knew I had a long way to go and still get back for supper so I didn't have to lie about where I was.

I stayed on the Selby-Lake past Snelling, heading for Minneapolis, bouncing on the seat with anticipation when who comes over and sits next to me but Donny Cunningham.

"You always transfer at Snelling," he said. "Did you forget?"

"No, Donny, I'm going to see an old friend."

Donny Cunningham was the smallest boy at Central, a senior who looked like a grade schooler. Not quite five feet tall and less than a hundred pounds, he wore wire-rimmed glasses and was always smiling like he was getting a kick out of life. The first time I saw him in freshman English I thought someone had brought their little brother to school.

Since then, Donny had taken a shine to me, followed me around and talked to me every chance he got, a big nuisance to say the least. He never asked me out, as if even he realized how ridiculous we'd look together, but he hung around as though I were his long-lost sister.

Donny got his reputation when he was a sophomore. Smoking was against the law for anyone under eighteen and so it was forbidden on the school grounds. You could be expelled. Kids who smoked, mostly boys, went across Lexington Parkway to Bob's milk store and hung around there.

When he was a sophomore, Donny ducked into the girl's lavatory on the third floor and hid in the janitor's mainte-nance locker just before the bell ending third period. He planned to peek through the louvers in the door. When the lavatory quickly filled with girls, two of them leaned on the locker door and lit cigarettes. They took a drag and blew the smoke through the louvers into the locker in case a teacher showed up. Not only could Donny no longer see any girls in various states of undress, but he could no longer breathe.

The girls puffed away like locomotives steaming uphill, turning the maintenance locker into a smoke house, trying to finish a cigarette in the few minutes they had between classes. Donny began gasping for air, choking, his eyes watering, terrified at being caught yet no longer able to suck a breath of air into his lungs. Frantically, he tried to squat in the narrow locker to escape the smoke and in the process tipped a loosely-covered bottle of bleach into his lap, soaking the front of his pants. As the girls pumped smoke into the locker, Donny had to decide between living in utter humiliation for the rest of his life or dying of asphyxiation in the girl's toilet on the third floor of Central High School.

He exploded from the locker, coughing and gasping, driven from cover like a rat by two female exterminators. He scared the bobby pins off the girls and dashed down two flights of stairs. When he thought his days at Central had come to an abrupt end, all he got was an hour of seventh period for running in the halls. The kid on the traffic squad who caught him took one look at his brown pants, streaked white down both legs as if he'd peed in them, and asked him if he'd been drinking sulfuric acid. The girls never ratted on him because, if they did, it would come out that they were smoking.

Donny got off at Prior, and if anyone had told me then that Donny Cunningham would have anything to do with me finding my mother, I'd have told him to go have his head examined.

I grew more and more excited crossing the bridge into Minneapolis. The leaves were changing and I spotted a crow gliding above the trees. I rode down Lake Street, where I'd overcome my chickenhood ten days ago in Steve's Chevy, and I transferred onto a Como-Harriet car at Hennepin. I got off at the Lake Harriet station and walked up the hill two blocks and turned on Sheridan. The Sunset Home For The Aged And Friendless was a two-story brick apartment building someone had converted into a residence for old people. It had a large sign over the door and I stood there a minute trying to gather my gumption. Did you have to be friendless to get in the joint? How sad. I took a deep breath and charged up the steps and pulled open the heavy wood door.

A birdlike woman in a nurse's uniform perched behind a gray metal desk in a small lobby. She peered over her pink plastic glasses and, with her bony nose and almost no chin, she reminded me of a plump pigeon. As I stepped over to her desk I read her name tag. BETTY BAIN. I'd guess she was about my mother's age.

"Can I help you?" she said in a sing-song voice.

"I'm here to see Arnold Shapiro."

I could feel my knees wobbling.

"Arnold Shapiro?"

The tone of her voice gave me the impression she was shocked that anyone would come to visit Arnold Shapiro. What was so strange about that? Was he a leper?

"Yes, Mr. Arnold Shapiro," I said.

"Are you family?" she said and her eyes narrowed.

"Sort of. Our families have known each other forever and I just found out he was here and I want to see how he's doing."

"Well, we understood all of his relatives were in Milwaukee." She pulled out a folder and scanned it.

"Yes, well I'm kind of a distant niece."

"What's your name?"

"Sandy . . . Sandy Meyer."

She glanced up from the folder. "Where do you live?"

"Saint Paul, where Mr. Shapiro used to be a lawyer."

"How did you find out he was here?"

"Ivan, his son in Milwaukee, he's my second cousin or something."

I felt like I'd broken the law the way she was grilling me. Why were they so upset to have someone visit Mr. Shapiro? I thought they'd welcome visitors.

"Mr. Shapiro isn't doing very well; a visit might be too tiring for him."

Her voice was thick, she had trouble breathing, and she held one nostril closed and used a nasal spray up the other.

"I won't stay long, if I could just talk to him for a few minutes."

She stuck the nozzle up the other nostril and pumped a couple times.

"We watch over our lambs pretty carefully," she said. "Do you now have, or in the past two weeks have you had, a cold or flu or other illness?"

"No, I'm fine, I'm super healthy."

"We can't have anyone bringing in something contagious that could strike down one of our lambs."

Look who was talking.

"Oh, I wouldn't," I said and I thought I'd stumbled into a barnyard by mistake and expected to hear sheep bleating down the hallway.

"Very well, come this way, but only for a few minutes."

She left her perch and stepped briskly down a long hall in her starched white dress as if she didn't have time to waste. With her skinny legs scooting along below her plump body she even walked like a pigeon. I followed her and my mouth went dry. There were a few old people shuffling through the hall like orphans and another nurse down a ways. I glanced in rooms as I passed and my chickenheart was shouting at me to turn and run. It wasn't a happy place.

"He's hard of hearing," she said, "so you'll have to speak up."

She had white crepe-soled shoes that squeaked on the gleaming waxed floor and I had a hard time keeping up.

"I ought to warn you that he's quite flatulent."

"Pardon me?"

"He has quite a problem with gas," she said. "He's a bitter and cantankerous old man so don't expect much."

She stopped and waited for me at an open door.

Dreading what I was getting into, I followed her into a small bright room that smelled so strongly of ammonia it hurt my nostrils.

"Arny, you have a visitor, honey," she shouted, "isn't that nice?"

Slumped in a wheelchair in a soiled shirt, baggy pants, and the most haunting face I'd ever seen, sat Arnold Shapiro, my hero. I would have laughed if he weren't so pitiful, a decrepit old man who looked as if he were starving. His hollow face reminded me of those I'd seen from concentration camps in the newsreels. His head shook slightly, and his hands danced along his lap. He wore thick glasses that made his eyes look huge. He reminded me of Lionel Barrymore only a lot older and one hundred pounds lighter, a skeleton of a man with pale scaly skin. He didn't seem to hear the woman.

"Arny, sweetheart," she said louder, "you have a visitor."

"My son come for me?" he said with a froggy voice.

"No, you have a nice young lady to see you. She says she knows you."

He gazed up at me with his big watery eyes.

"You looking for a handout?" he said.

I moved my lips but my voice wouldn't work.

Betty Bain nodded for me to sit in a brown upholstered chair that had been stained and scrubbed a lot. I perched on the edge of it and I was scared out of my wits.

A hospital bed with side rails filled half the room. The other half was crowded with a bed table, dresser, a bookshelf cluttered with dog-eared *National Geographics* and *Reader's Digests*, and the upholstered chair. The walls were white and the floor an ugly green linoleum. A walker stood beside the wheelchair and photographs in old ornate frames lingered on the small dresser.

"You have a nice visit, now," she said and she hurried into the hall as if there were something highly contagious in the room.

Mr. Shapiro turned his head toward the photos on the dresser as if he were alone.

I sat there with that wreck of a man and I didn't know what to say or do. I started to choke up, tears came flooding out of nowhere and filled my eyes. I wiped my dripping face on my sleeve and stared at his scuffed-up leather slippers. I don't think I was crying because he looked incapable of helping me. I think I was crying because that rickety old man was unwanted. The most terrible thing that can happen to a person is to be unwanted. Did he wonder why someone didn't keep *him?* I felt foolish and I tried to stop crying and I kept saying to myself:

Arnold Shapiro, you're my hero,
If you can't help me, I'll be a zero.

Chapter 6

I'd *found* Arnold Shapiro and there I sat, like a simpleton. My father always said You have to take the bull by the horns and I knew I had to forget my sadness and fright and do something before Mr. Shapiro keeled over dead in my lap. I wiped my tears on the cuff of my blouse and squatted in front of his wheelchair, where I could look into his face and get him to look at me. With those huge magnified eyes and the way he hunched over in his chair, he reminded me of an owl, a big old owl who had lost a lot of feathers, and the thin gray hair barely covering his half-bald scalp looked like furry down.

What hope I had was pulling stakes and stampeding for the door when I realized how bad off the man was. And Betty Bain hadn't told the half of it with her warnings. Besides being hard of hearing, and having failing eyesight and a tough time breathing, Mr. Shapiro was generating gas as if something inside of him were dead.

He sat there loudly detonating, and I tried to ignore it. Far be it for me to blink or let on that I'd noticed. I was from a family that shamed me severely when I was in grade school for acknowledging such a bodily function, sternly instructed me that respectable people not only never uttered that word but never took notice of such a thing, that it was unladylike and rude and vulgar, and that was the last time in my home that breaking wind was ever acknowledged.

Squatting in front of Mr. Shapiro's wheelchair I took the bull by the horns and shouted, "Mr. Shapiro, I'm Sandy Meyer, you helped my mother and father in the spring of 1933, Howard Meyer, do you remember?"

He turned and said, "Who are *you?*" as if he saw me for the first time.

"I'm Sandy Meyer, you were a lawyer and you helped Howard and Gladys Meyer adopt a baby girl in 1933."

"What?" he said and his head shook as if he were perpetually denying any connection with the human race.

"You helped Howard and Gladys Meyer adopt a baby."

"Have we eaten yet?" he said.

Whew, Betty Bain hadn't warned me about everything, halitosis, holy Mosis!

"No . . . I don't think so," I half shouted.

"What do *you* want?" he said with a gravelly voice.

"I want to know the name of my father."

"Everyone wants something, scavengers, vultures."

He turned his gaze to the window. Down the hall someone was playing a horn, a saxophone, and they kept doing the scales, slowly, over and over, up and down, like they were taking lessons.

"Do you remember when you were a lawyer and helped people?"

It was hard to tell where his eyes were looking through his thick lenses but they came back to me out of his gently bobbing head.

"How's that?"

"Do you remember," I shouted, "when you were a lawyer?"

"Lawyered for forty-two years."

"Do you remember doing an adoption in 1933?"

"You ever play Chinese checkers?"

"Yes," I said, "sometimes."

I hated Chinese checkers and the way I was shouting I figured they could hear me at the Harriet Station.

"Do you know your name?" I said.

"What kind of a question is that? I lawyered for forty-two years. You think I don't know my own name?"

"It's just that your son said—"

"You're like all the rest, think we're all morons in here, that if you're old you've lost your marbles."

He wheezed from the exertion of his answer and his breath rattled in his scrawny chest.

"I don't think you've lost your . . . mind, it's just that your son said—"

"My son's coming to get me."

I realized I wasn't getting off to a very good start and I decided that was enough for a beginning. I could feel Betty Bain sitting out there with a stop watch.

"I'll come and see you again, Mr. Shapiro."

"What?" He picked at a scab on his cheek.

"I'll come and see you again."

"I doubt it," he said and his large watery eyes examined my face as if he were thinking. "Will you play Chinese checkers with me?"

"Okay, I'll come again and we'll play Chinese checkers."

I'd have agreed to play strip poker if it would get him to talk.

Betty Bain appeared in the doorway like an undertaker and tapped her wrist watch. I nodded and, still squatting in front of him, looked into Mr. Shapiro's fish-bowl eyes.

"Can I bring you something, some candy or a magazine?" I shouted.

"Rat poison."

"Rat poison?" I said.

"Don't mind him, he's always kidding around," Betty Bain said. "And we'd rather you didn't bring him anything. We provide him with all his needs." She tapped her wrist watch again. "Time's up." Then she hustled up the hall.

He didn't sound like he was kidding, but why would he want rat poison. Did he have mice or rats in his room?

I felt I couldn't just leave him like that. I slid forward onto one knee and awkwardly hugged him. He felt brittle and clammy and I caught a whiff of body odor and bad breath and something like sorrow. He seemed momentarily shocked that I hugged him as if it were a completely unfamiliar experience. When I stood and said good-bye he followed me to the door with his sad owl eyes. Someone was still doing the scales on a saxophone.

"You coming back?" he said.

"Yes, tomorrow."

"That's what they all said." He turned his face away as if he'd shut a door.

Out in the hall I flinched from the pop of a flashbulb. An adorable little white-haired woman in a flowered house-dress smiled from behind her camera.

"Good picture," she said and then like a mouse she scooted back into her room.

While I rode the streetcar home in the rush hour, a fiery afterglow painted buildings and clouds ruby red and made it feel as though something special was happening. I could hardly sit still. I'd *found* Arnold Shapiro. It was a miracle. But now I'd need another miracle to get the old man to remember. Somewhere in his fragile egglike skull was the information I wanted; my name, my parents' name, and maybe something about what happened to them. And he could die in his sleep that night or the next and my history would be buried with him!

Finally on the Randolph streetcar and almost home, I was bushed. I couldn't wait to tell Jean that in the big wide world I'd found Arnold Shapiro. I decided I'd visit him every day that I could get away. Then I remembered I was going to the Homecoming Dance with Scott. That would be a dream come true and I could hardly wait. I'd had my eye on him ever since Cal told me what Scott had done in Mr. Stern's gym class when we were freshmen.

Mr. Stern was running the boys through strength and endurance tests and he was taking it out on Billy Pratt. Mr. Stern had been in the Army and had the personality of a drill sergeant. They came to the rope climb, a knotted rope hanging from the gym ceiling that you climbed hand over hand. The boys were in a large circle around the rope and Mr. Stern picked Billy to be first. Billy was fat. Billy gripped the rope with his arms extended above his head and lifted his feet off the floor and tried to pull himself up. He couldn't. Mr. Stern goaded him.

"C'mon, Pratt, haul that fat prat up the rope!"

Billy struggled, his feet hit the floor, he tried again, sweating, but he couldn't lift his fat body an inch with his arms. Mr. Stern kept at him, shouting. Billy was trying not to cry. Finally Mr. Stern shouted, "As you were, Pratt, you fat little girl, make way for a man!"

He glanced around the circle and called on Scott McFarland, one of the strongest boys at Central. Scott took a hold of the rope and lifted his feet off the floor and strained to pull himself up the rope, hand over hand. He didn't move, just hung there, grunting. His feet hit the floor, he tried again, but he never moved higher than Billy had. Mr. Stern was steaming. When it was obvious that Scott couldn't do it, he called on Cal Gant and then Tom Bradford and Jerry Douglas, but none of them pulled himself any higher than Billy Pratt. Not one boy in the class.

Mr. Stern turned red when he realized what they were doing.

"All right, ladies, get those arms out, snap those fingers!" he shouted.

The boys, still in a circle, held their arms out straight in front of them and closed their fists and then snapped out their fingers repeatedly. It was a form of punishment and it didn't start to hurt until you did it for several minutes.

"Keep those arms up, snap those fingers," he said.

Arms were wavering, the agony was setting in, but Billy Pratt kept up with all of them. After about five minutes when most arms had sagged and their shoulders ached and faces reflected the pain, Mr. Stern shouted.

"All right, girls, hit the showers!"

Billy Pratt left the gym with a look of surprise in his eyes. No one ever knew the reason, but Mr. Stern wasn't on the faculty when we returned as sophomores.

I think I fell in love with Scott the day I heard that story. I hoped he would like me and maybe we could go together, even go steady, and if he didn't like me I'd just die. I didn't know what I'd wear to homecoming but I decided I'd have a chocolate malt every day that week.

The gym was really nifty and romantic, decorated in red and black and dimly lit for the Homecoming Dance, but Scott and I were sitting along the wall under the basket in folding chairs and I was the only girl in the row of stags. He was talking about the game with Jim Andre and Doug Rogers and they went on and on through the whole dance. We tied Monroe and the boys were pretty down about it. Cal Cant sat next to me, he didn't have a date, and if it hadn't been for him I'd have fallen asleep.

I'd made it over to The Sunset Home For The Aged And Friendless Wednesday and Thursday that week and by Thursday I think Mr. Shapiro remembered who I was. On Wednesday he was really grouchy and acted like he didn't want me bothering him and between the stench of his gas and awful breath I about died. His stomach sounded like water gurgling through sewer pipes in the wall.

He insisted we play Chinese checkers and I'd managed to get him to say my father's name and I kept telling him about the adoption. I figured if I repeated it over and over it would ring a bell somewhere in his foggy memory.

"You have a mother don't you?" he said.

"Yeah."

"Don't you like her, is she mean?"

"No, she's a good mother, she's just been sick a lot and I worry about her," I said.

"Then why in hell are you looking for your real mother?"

"Because . . . I want to know why they didn't keep me, I want to know who they are and if they're still alive."

He moved a marble several holes and someone started doing scales on the saxophone.

"What's wrong with your mother?"

"They don't seem to know. She has a lot of pain in her stomach, she gets nauseous and can't eat, throws up and has the runs. They took out her gall bladder but she's still sick."

"They give her pain pills?"

"Yeah."

"Sleeping pills?" he said.

"Yes, why?"

"Bring me some," he said and he looked at me with those huge marblelike eyes.

"What?"

"Pain pills, sleeping pills, bring me some."

"What for, do you have trouble sleeping?" I said.

"Yes, I keep waking up in this hell hole. Bring me some, please, as many as you can."

It finally hit me what Mr. Shapiro was talking about.

"Oh, Mr. Shapiro, I couldn't, I couldn't do that."

"Have mercy on me . . . *please.*"

He looked into my face with the most pitiful pleading I'd ever seen.

"You shouldn't even think like that, Mr. Shapiro, that's up to God when—"

"Wait till you're sitting here," he said and he didn't talk much after that.

Thursday he only mentioned the pills once and I really got excited when he kept saying my father's name, Howard Meyer . . . Howard Meyer . . . as if he were trying to remember. Then he started grumbling about how everyone was trying to steal his money and he'd scold me when I'd make a bad move with my marble and he was a smelly old grouch. When I left I didn't have much hope that he'd ever be able to help me.

"Why aren't you dancing?" Cal said.

"I don't know . . . we did dance once but *I* had to ask *him.*"

We watched the couples dancing and having fun while Scott jabbered with his buddies. I didn't think it was because he didn't like me. He was scared of me, afraid to be dancing so close and having to talk to me. He was really bashful.

"I'd dance with you if you weren't with Scott," Cal said.

"I know, Bean, it's okay."

Cal and I had gone to grade school at Ramsey together and I'd given him the nickname Bean in third grade when he got his tongue stuck to a metal fence one cold morning and I poured my Thermos of hot bean soup over his tongue to get it free. I was the only one who called him Bean and he was one of my best friends, but for some reason we'd never gone out together, more like a brother and sister.

I watched the kids dancing, and I thought of Arnold Shapiro sitting alone in that bleak little room. Those kids had their whole life ahead of them, me, with my whole life ahead of me, and his was over, just waiting to die. Did I need to find out who my real parents were, did I need to find out why they didn't keep me? Someday I'd be in a bleak little room and my life would be over. Was I wasting precious time chasing after my past, my family ghosts? Arnold would never go to a dance again, never have a girlfriend or romance or someone to love him. He must have been in high school once, gone to a dance, kissed a girl. Now he had nothing but memories, and maybe he'd even lost those.

"If you were adopted," I said to Cal, "would you try to find out who your real parents were?"

"Sometimes I think I *am* adopted."

"Be serious . . . would you?"

"I don't know, I never thought about it," he said as he watched the dancers.

The band paused and then started playing "Sentimental Journey."

"I think this is the last dance," Cal said.

"I know, don't remind me."

All of a sudden Scott turned to me like he'd just realized he was at a dance. "Would you like to dance?" he said with a frog in his throat.

"I'd love to," I said and we stepped out onto the dance floor.

Scott was not a good dancer, a little clumsy actually, but he was so tall and strong I thought it was heavenly moving across the beautiful gym in his arms. I smiled up at him and I knew I was really in love. I was scared that he wouldn't like me and I wanted him to so much but I knew I always had bad luck with boys. I put my head on his chest and closed my eyes and that one wonderful dance was worth sitting there all night with the stags.

After we ate at the Flat-Top, Tom dropped me off first. Tom and Lola and Jerry and Sally sat necking in Tom's Buick while Scott said good-night at my door. He went on and on about President Truman and Joe DiMaggio and his father's new Kaiser until I was about to fall down and go to sleep right there on my front step. I think he was trying to get up the nerve to kiss me and I was hoping he would and I patiently nodded and tried to stay standing as he shuffled his feet back and forth and examined the bricks on my house and looked at the sky as if he'd find some nerve in the bricks or stars. Finally, Tom started the car and revved the engine. Scott wound-down another five minutes but never found the nerve.

When I was lying in bed and praying that Scott would like me, I kept seeing that miserable old man in that dreary little room. He was my only hope to find my mother, to find myself, and there in the darkness he seemed like no hope at all. I prayed that before he died, or found a way to commit suicide, he'd remember who I was.

Chapter 7

After school on Thursday I rode the Selby-Lake streetcar across Minneapolis as I had several times a week for the past three weeks. I'd learned I had to work myself up for my visit with Mr. Shapiro. On the ride I tried to soak up all the good things in the world: the sun and clouds and happy people, the fresh air and music and puppy dogs, to fight off the gloom in Mr. Shapiro's room, to prepare myself for that swamp of sadness. I'd try to come with a light heart and a smile and cheer things up a bit, but it was like telling a joke in the city morgue; I was always overwhelmed by the gloom. But on the trip Thursday afternoon I felt optimistic and I dared to believe that some of my prayers were being answered.

First of all my mother was improving and getting stronger every day. She was back to cooking and taking care of the house and she looked so much better with some color in her face and she'd joke around and laugh. When she was having a hard time she'd say What would Amelia do? And then she'd stand up straight and lift her chin and do what she had to do, like Amelia Earhart.

Then there was Scott McFarland. I thought he might be falling in love with me, just a little, and he was so nifty it scared me that I dared to hope. The past two weeks we'd lost to Washington and Mechanic Arts, but this week, on Wednesday night, we beat Humboldt 14 to 0. After the game Scott invited me to go to the drive-in with a carload of couples and then took me home. I thought he might finally find his nerve somewhere in the slate rock of my front steps, but after gabbing and staring at his shoes for what seemed like endless time, it ended up the usual way with kids in the car calling that they had to get home. I thought I might have to kiss him some night to get things going and I started wondering if he'd ever kissed a girl.

The other part of my answered prayer was Mr. Shapiro. The second week I went to see him he was sitting in his room in his coat and hat with a suitcase beside his wheelchair.

"Where are you going?" I shouted.

He looked at me with those watery magnified eyes.

"I'm leaving; my son is picking me up." He wheezed. "I'm going to Milwaukee."

My heart sank; I couldn't go to Milwaukee, I'd lost him. I sat on the edge of the upholstered chair and fired questions at him about the adoption, but all I got back was stuff about his son coming to get him. He insisted that we start a game of Chinese checkers of all things, but I couldn't concentrate and I frantically tried to prime the pump of his memory.

When Betty Bain showed up like a flu bug, I told her I'd never get to talk to him again, that he was going to live with his son in Milwaukee. She laughed with a funny little cackle and told me he did that two or three times a week; packed his suitcase, pulled on his hat and coat, and waited for his son to show up. But darn it, it bothered me that she talked like that in front of him, as if he weren't in the room, especially when she said Mr. Shapiro's son would show up the day cows flew. But my prayers were answered; Mr. Shapiro wasn't going to Milwaukee after all, though he might've been going to the cemetery any minute.

That week he was dressed and packed one other time but I took it in stride. It only made me sad to see him languishing there in his overcoat and hat, waiting for a son who wouldn't show up until cows flew. We played Chinese checkers and I was surprised at how well he played, and he had his marbles across the board and home long before mine were even close. I hated Chinese checkers, but I couldn't help but notice that the more we played the more he talked.

I transferred at Hennepin and caught the Como-Harriet car and sat next to a big Negro woman. She was humming away and smiling like she was real happy.

"Where're you goin', child?" she said.

"I'm looking for my mother."

"Land sakes, is she lost?"

"No, I was adopted and I've found an old man who might be able to help me find her."

"Oh, Lordy, haven't you got a mama now?"

"Yes, the mother who adopted me."

"Child, you ought to be satisfied with the mama you got and not be pokin' into old things like that."

She pulled the cord and I stood in the aisle to let her squeeze by.

"Folks ought to just leave things be," she said and she waddled to the back of the car to get off.

Her words hung in the air like gloomy little clouds and I asked myself the same question: Why couldn't I let it be? I wished I hadn't told her, I was always doing things like that, telling strangers what I'm thinking or feeling and then getting the rug pulled out from under me. I had to learn to keep things to myself more and not blab to the world every thought that crossed my mind.

I settled by the window as we rolled by Lake Calhoun and headed through the woods, and I felt kind of blue. Most of the leaves had fallen and winter's bleakness was creeping up on me. But then I thought of all the keen dances and things coming up, and imagined going to them with Scott, and I felt lots better.

I thought I was getting to know Scott but he really surprised me in physics. About the middle of the hour it was getting chilly in the room and the teacher, D.B. Sandersen, asked Jim Kinsey, a big strong boy, to close one of the huge windows. I didn't know why all the windows at Central were so enormous but maybe it was because the gigantic building was built like a castle.

Jim hopped out of his seat and with both hands he grabbed a hold of the window frame, which was about shoulder high. He pulled and pulled until he was grunting, but it wouldn't budge.

D.B. Sandersen watched him for a minute and then, with a sigh of impatience, told Scott to give him a hand. Scott, a strapping six-foot-three football player, stepped over and grabbed a hold of the window frame with both hands and shoulder to shoulder they heaved and grunted but it didn't move. By now the class was snickering and enjoying a break in the tedious hour when D.B.'s patience evaporated. He came wheeling around the big counter he taught behind, hustled over to the window, and waved the boys aside. He grabbed the window frame with both hands and with all his might heaved. The window, which wasn't stuck at all, slammed down with such a concussion that it was a miracle the window didn't break and we weren't all blinded by flying glass.

The class roared and D.B. flushed with embarrassment, but as he slunk back behind his counter, duped again, I suppose he realized he couldn't punish the boys for being too weak to close a window. I didn't know what got into Scott, pulling something like that, always so polite and proper, but I hoped he was showing off a little for me.

I paused in front of the Sunset Home For The Aged And Friendless and I took a deep breath. I tried to inhale as much happiness and cheer as I could smuggle into that graveyard. Betty Bain, the pigeon woman in pink plastic glasses, escorted me down the hall when I checked in and she seemed a little suspicious of my showing up all the time.

"Have you been sick, any cold or flu?" she said.

"No, I'm fine."

"We have to protect our lambs, you know," she said as she walked beside me. "Why is it again that you're *so interested* in Arny, I mean Mr. Shapiro?"

"He was the lawyer who helped my family back in 1933. I'm trying to see if he remembers, I'm trying to find my mother."

"Oh . . . well, Mr. Shapiro has considerable money, you know, and his son warned us about those who would try to bilk him out of it."

"I don't want any money from him, just some answers."

She eyed me as though she didn't completely believe me.

"Does anyone else visit Mr. Shapiro?" I said.

"No . . . you're the only one."

Mr. Shapiro qualified for the place, he was friendless.

Then, just before we reached Mr. Shapiro's room, the little white-haired woman stepped out and popped a flashbulb in our faces. Betty Bain stopped in her tracks and smiled.

"Good picture, Elsie."

"Good picture," the woman said and she scurried into her room like a startled chipmunk.

"Who's that?" I said.

"That's just Elsie. Her family keeps her in flashbulbs and film, they hope it will help her remember them. They pin up her photos of them in her room but she doesn't remember who they are."

"Are her snapshots any good?" I said.

"She remembers how to use a camera but doesn't know her real name, only answers to Elsie. Her real name is Martha Swanson."

"We're alike then; I don't know my real name either."

Betty Bain gave me a drippy smile and pigeoned back up the hall. The saxophone was playing, but instead of scales a sorrowful rendition of "Someone To Watch Over Me" drifted softly down the hall. When I stepped into Mr. Shapiro's room, he looked ridiculous in his overcoat and hat. He gazed at me from his wheelchair.

"You back again," he said with his grouch voice.

I sat in the worn-down upholstered chair and smiled.

"Yep, you can't get rid of me."

"I'm leaving today," he said and he patted the suitcase beside his wheelchair as if it were a faithful old dog.

"That's nice," I said.

He nodded at the Chinese checkerboard on the bookcase. I got it and rolled the bed table between us and cranked it down a little so we could play. I set up the marbles, and I'd learned not to ask a lot of questions right off, like we had to warm up his engine first the way my father told me to warm up our Ford before driving away. Mr. Shapiro would break wind and I'd sit as far back as the chair would allow from the little cloud of halitosis that steamed from his mouth. We'd talk about the weather or my ride over from Saint Paul but eventually I'd try to steer him back to 1933.

"It was tough back then," he said. Slouched in his wheelchair over the checker board, he rubbed his forehead and little scales of skin rained down onto the board and marbles. "Right in the middle of the Depression and I had to take whatever work I could find, mostly penny-ante stuff, wills, contracts, lawsuits, trying to collect bad debts, now and then a divorce, any clients I could dig up."

"Do you still have records of the stuff you did?"

He thought a minute. "No, no . . . that's all gone. Just the documents that'd be at the courthouse."

"Would an adoption be recorded at the courthouse?"

"Probably . . . but those records are locked up, sealed."

"I've seen a copy of my birth certificate. It lists Howard Meyer as my father and Gladys Meyer as my mother! How can they do that?"

"The court does it, just like you'd been born to them, your real parents erased."

His stomach growled and the saxophone played "Someone To Watch Over Me" and I didn't understand how they could just erase the woman who gave me birth.

"Did you do many adoptions back then, around 1933?"

He didn't answer for a minute, studying the checkerboard.

"Don't remember . . . don't remember doing any adoptions."

I leaned close to his face and tried not to breathe.

"You did *one,* in the spring of 1933. Remember? Howard and Gladys Meyer."

He paused, as if he were thinking, and I didn't push him. Then he wheezed with a long sigh.

"You know," he said, "I wanted to live with my son, lived with him for a while, but he said I wasn't happy with him and his family, with all the kids and everything."

He broke wind, a staccato burst like a package of fire-crackers. I sat there like I never heard him.

"It was all right, I didn't mind the kids much. They said I needed to be taken care of. Only wet the bed twice."

He lifted his head and gazed into my eyes like a big owl.

"Do you know what this place is?"

"A rest home," I said.

"A rest home, ha! I don't need any more *rest.* This is a waiting room, the waiting room to the morgue."

He coughed and caught his breath.

"People don't want us around anymore, we remind them of what's down the line. My boy wouldn't be living high on the hog if I hadn't given him his start, given him an educa-tion, given him the money to get a foothold."

He coughed until I thought he'd choke, all worked up.

"And what does he do, he dumps me. Dumps me in this vestibule of the mortuary, and then has the gall to tell me I'll like it here, as if he's talking to some nincompoop."

He stopped talking and I knew there wasn't much chance to steer him back to 1933. Then he whispered so softly I could barely hear what he said.

"When people get what they want from you they dump you."

I never got him back to the adoption and on the trip home I found myself humming "Someone To Watch Over Me." I always felt down after being there and I thought of my parents and what I would do when they got as decrepit as Mr. Shapiro. And what about me? Would I end up in a pitiful little room like that, with no one who cared if I was dead or alive? When Mr. Shapiro was seventeen I was sure, in his wildest dreams, he never thought he'd end up in that place, deserted and friendless. I hugged him when I left but I felt lousy. He made me realize I was just one more person buttering him up to get something out of him.

Arnold Shapiro, it isn't fair,
They never told you, you'd end up in there.

Chapter 8

I was trying to forget Mr. Shapiro for a few hours and have some fun. School was going well and things between Scott and me were hunky-dory and so much was going on I lost track of the days.

Tuesday was our last football game and we beat Wilson 25 to 7. The senior boys really played well and everyone was celebrating after the game. We parked by the Highland Tower and in the backseat of Tom's car, crammed in next to Jerry and Sally, Scott had managed to creep his arm around my shoulders and I was praying that he'd find his nerve.

My mother was always subtly warning me about what boys wanted, and not so subtly.

"If a boy wants to park down by the river," she'd say, "you tell him you're not that kind of girl."

No, I was the kind of girl who picked boys who were afraid to park down by the river because their fathers had given them the same lecture my mother had given me. The only trouble was, my mother never gave me the other part of the story: how you get a boy to *want* to park down by the river with you!

Our parents and ministers alike were always preaching restraint and self-denial and we were like fresh young horses bridled by our upbringing and hobbled by religious rules that shouted Whoa at all those natural instincts we were told were nasty and sinful. When my mother took me aside and told me about sex, I got the impression it was dirty and dangerous, maybe more from her tone and expression than from what she actually said, but it sounded like something to avoid like amoebic dysentery.

The book she used to educate me showed what boys looked like down there and though my mother gave dire warnings, I thought that strange appendage looked kind of funny and completely harmless. The final word was that *it* was a sin unless you were married, in fact, *it* was the original sin, and if Adam and Eve hadn't done *it*, we'd all have been much happier. When I thought about that it didn't make sense because if Adam and Eve *hadn't* done it, none of us would be here to be happy. I thought about Adam figuring out *how* to do it and I thought *that* was original.

When my mother was through, I had a hard time believing what grave danger we were in when we were out with boys. Most girls wouldn't kiss a boy until they'd gone out two or three times. After several dates, necking was the fare for most of us, most of the time. French kissing came after lots of necking with the same person, and petting, which no one spoke of openly, meant fondling the breasts, usually over the clothing, but nothing below the waist. I wanted to tell my parents they had nothing to worry about. A boy would need a magnifying glass and a working knowledge of braille to pet with me.

At my door it was exasperating. Scott had just been smashing and bashing all those huge Wilson boys on the football field but he was scared stiff of a skinny knobby-kneed girl on her front doorstep. I'd never understand boys. When he failed again I started to wonder if I'd caught Mr. Shapiro's halitosis.

The next day, thanks to the MEA Teachers' Convention, we all went off to the house parties where the sororities would rent cabins out in the country and we'd all spend the three days of vacation playing and having fun. The Sokos and Debs had their house party together and we rented four cabins up at St. Croix Falls and it was oodles of fun.

The boys came up during the day and we played touch football and hiked through the woods and explored the caves along the river. We had big camp fires at night and roasted marshmallows and we ate all the time. When the mothers who were chaperoning shagged the boys and herded us in for the night, we'd sing and gab and play cards and eat until three or four in the morning and then sleep until noon or until enough boys had returned to wake us and coax us out of the cabin to start the next day.

I never forgot Mr. Shapiro and right in the middle of all the fun I'd think of him and repeat my rhyme to myself, *Mr. Shapiro, you're my hero,* and I worried about not seeing him for so long. We didn't go home until Sunday morning so I had to do my usual Saturday housework and I couldn't get away. On Saturdays I'd vacuum and dust and wash clothes and iron, depending on how my mother was feeling, so I knew it would be Monday before I could get over to see Mr. Shapiro.

At dinner my father explained how Russia had the atom bomb and that there wasn't much hope for the world, even though he'd just come from House of Hope Presbyterian.

"If it isn't one thing it's another," my mother said.

"Will you be an air raid warden again?" I asked my dad.

"I don't think that will do any good anymore," he said and he looked out the front window with worry in his face.

"Will we have more scrap metal drives?" I said.

When I was a twelve-year-old Girl Scout I won a contest for collecting the most scrap in my neighborhood, 267 pounds of pots and pans and iron frying pans and car parts. I was pretty proud and I got my picture in the *Saint Paul Dispatch*.

"I don't think a war will last long enough to have a scrap drive," my dad said.

"Next thing you know we'll be building bomb shelters," my mother said.

I tried not to dwell on those scary things but I couldn't help thinking that we might be bombed before I ever found out who I was.

They'd had their canasta group over on Saturday night, atom bomb or not, and there were several leftover pastries. During the rest of the day I ate them all as I did my chores. I couldn't help wondering if my breasts would start to grow when I found out who I was. Every night when I'd undress I'd check my body in my dresser mirror. I was thin, with long legs, kind of like a Varga girl, and they weren't bad, but not a sign of any growth on my chest. I'd ask my mirror, Mirror, mirror, on the wall, who's the flattest of them all? and the mirror would say *You* are!

Monday was Halloween and everyone was in a goofy mood and I was jittery. I couldn't concentrate on anything and the day dragged except for the two times I talked to Scott in the halls. I couldn't wait for school to end so I could be on the streetcar rolling across Minneapolis.

I ran into Jerry outside Miss Bellows English class. In a sweat, he had his nose buried in our red English handbook, frantically memorizing the assigned poem due the minute we stepped into the classroom. She'd been after him since the Oink Oink incident and he was in danger of failing her class and therefore not graduating.

"Are you ready?" I said.

"I think so," he said without taking his eyes off the poem.

"How long have you been working on it?"

"Since I left for school this morning."

"Jerry! you know she'll be after you."

The first bell rang and we moved towards the room.

"I've got it down cold," he said and he pulled a sheet of paper from his notebook. His name and the class and the date appeared in the upper right-hand corner as required and the poem was already written out. "I'll hand this in."

"That's cheating," I said.

"No, that's survival, that's graduating." He laughed and we found our desks.

Miss Bellows took attendance.

"Very well, class, if you'll take out a clean sheet of paper we have a few minutes to write out Emily Dickinson's poem."

The class hushed and we all began writing. I had no trouble with it because I loved it, I memorized it, I adopted it as my own. I wrote it quickly.

"Hope is the thing with feathers,
That perches in the soul,
And sings the tune without the words,
And never stops at all,"

Since I was a young girl talking to God in my cave, hope, "the thing with feathers," was a crow, God's sign to me.

As I wrote the other two verses I glanced over at Jerry and he was writing like crazy on a blank sheet of paper. When we finished we were to sit erect and look forward. After about five minutes, Miss Bellows stood and clapped her hands.

"Time's up, pass your papers forward."

With a sleight of hand, Jerry pulled the perfect paper from his desk and mixed it with the others coming over his shoulder from Joanne Kranz behind him. In the same motion, he slid the half-written paper into his desk. I had to smile.

Miss Bellows collected the papers from each row and sat at her desk thumbing through them and somehow I knew which one she was looking for. She studied a paper for a moment.

"Jerry Douglas, will you come up and recite the poem for the class?" she said with a self-satisfied smirk.

Jerry sprang from the desk with his compact athletic body and swaggered to the front of the room. He stood beside Miss Bellows's desk and faced the class, his warm wide smile dripping with confidence. It was Douglas against Bellows in a fifteen rounder and I was pulling for Douglas.

"Hope, by Emily Dickinson," he said with a strong voice.

He paused and stared out the windows behind us.

"Hope is the thing . . ."

He stood with his mouth half open. He put his hands in his pockets. So far he had four words. He gazed at the ceiling as if the poem might be written somewhere up there. His eyes went blank. Round one to Bellows.

He pulled his hands out of his pockets and began again.

"Hope is the thing . . . ah . . . the thing . . ."

An incoming surf of panic was eroding the shoreline of his memory as he shifted from foot to foot. Kids around me were fighting off major constriction of the diaphragm and the class held its collective breath, knowing the axe was about to fall. I opened my notebook and quickly printed the first two lines of the poem in large letters with my pencil. I tipped it up on my desk and cleared my throat in hopes of catching Jerry's eye but he was rapidly going down at sea.

He swallowed hard and tried again.

"Hope is the thing with . . . ah . . ." He had five words. "Ah . . . feathers . . ." Six. Round two to Bellows.

I coughed and fanned my notebook at him, trying not to be too conspicuous, but his eyes had become glazed marbles as if he were flipping through the blank pages in his mind. He wrung his hands with desperation and began again, trying to catch the right cog in his memory to spew by rote those evasive words he'd suspiciously written out perfectly on his paper only three minutes ago.

"Hope is the thing with feathers . . . ah, feathers . . ."

The final "feathers" was barely audible. The words petrified in his mouth and fell to the floor like thudding stones, the first pieces of his self-constructed tomb. Half the class was near appendectomy, even some of the more serious students. Engulfed in humiliation and defeat, Jerry abruptly walked to his desk and deflated.

Knockout, Bellows.

The room had become so quiet we could hear the pen scratch the paper in Miss Bellows grade book and no one had any doubt about what grade she penned.

"Miss Meyer, you will be enrolled in Mr. Kirschbach's seventh period for one full week. To aid a fellow student is an admirable motive, to do so during a test is cheating!"

I was shocked, she'd seen me. Mr. Shapiro! Another five days without seeing him.

In the hall after class Jerry was in the dark.

"What did you do?" he said.

"What did I *do?* I put up a billboard that could be seen in North Dakota."

"Jeez, I'm sorry, I didn't see it."

"You didn't look like you could see the wall."

"Thanks for trying to help, Bellows really nailed me."

"She nailed us both," I said and as we hoofed it down the front hall stairs I wanted to tell him I was afraid I'd blown my only chance to ever find my mother.

Chapter 9

That following week I almost blew a fuse in seventh period.
I'd sit there and agonize about Mr. Shapiro dying or killing
himself, catching myself gnawing on my fingernails like a
starving beaver. Ever since I could remember I was high
strung, fidgety, couldn't sit still for two minutes, just like my
mother. It was confusing. My mother was really smart, read a
lot, used big words, and I always found school easy, so I
assumed I inherited my brains from her. Until she told me I
was adopted. Then I didn't know where I got it, or the way I
was always antsy, restless to be doing something, going
somewhere. Maybe you learn that stuff from your parents
rather than having it in your blood. Whatever the reason, I
was doing some major bouncing off the walls after going
two weeks without seeing Mr. Shapiro.

On Wednesday Phyllis Storberg had her sister's Nash convertible and she let Jean and Dave sit in the backseat during
lunch hour in the parking lot. Jean didn't say much about it,
only that it was sad because they loved each other so much
and being together for a half hour almost made it worse.

Saturday night there was a powwow out at Sucker Lake
and it started feeling like Scott and I were a couple. I'd
never lasted with the same boy for more than a few weeks
and I couldn't figure out why because I always liked them a
lot and sometimes I wondered if boys could tell that I didn't
know who I was or that my parents didn't keep me. Cal was
taking Jean and I was really happy for her because she loved
Dave so madly and it was hard for her on weekends when
I'd be going out with Scott and she'd be sitting home.

When eight of us were crammed in Jerry's '41 Oldsmobile
he drove up Summit.

"I want to stop at my grandparents' for a minute," Scott
said and I felt a little thrill go up my spine. Was he stopping

to introduce *me* to his grandparents? Maybe he liked me a lot more than I hoped.

The traffic on Summit was divided by a wide boulevard of lawn and giant elm trees and when Jerry parked on the opposite side of the the street from the house, I thought it was strange. We romped across the wide boulevard, through the brisk night air, and I was feeling frisky. Up the steps of the banked yard, we laughed and goofed around on the way to a large brick house.

"How old is your grandpa?" Jean said.

"He's over eighty," Scott said. "He can't walk very well."

Jerry stifled a laugh as we moved up onto the large porch but I didn't see anything funny about a poor man who couldn't walk very well. There were a few lights on in the house behind heavy drapes and we crowded around the large wood door.

"Knock," Scott said. "Loud, he's hard of hearing."

I beat the other girls to the punch and knocked as loud as I could and the boys began horsing around, grabbing and shoving each other. Scott moved up and banged on the door as if he were trying to knock it down. It was so nifty, meeting his family like this. I prayed that they'd like me. I only had on jeans and my old blue jacket but all of us were dressed for a powwow.

Suddenly the door flew open and a short stocky man in shirtsleeves stood there. He didn't look eighty and he didn't look as if he could hardly walk.

"Run!" Jerry shouted and he leaped off the porch.

"He's a madman! Run!" Cal yelled and everybody flew off the porch and down the bank.

I didn't know what was going on. Why should we run from Scott's grandfather? Instinct threw me off the porch and I came down running. By the time I hit the sidewalk I could see that the man was after Cal. I ran a ways up the street and watched and when Cal swerved around one of the large elm trees on the boulevard the man didn't turn with him but came straight at me.

I started screaming and ran for my life and I wet my pants. I cut up Wheeler. I could run fast but he was gaining on me and I was scared out of my wits. Where was Scott? Wasn't he supposed to protect me? Across Portland, I turned up the alley, hoping I could hide in the darkness, but he was right on my heels.

Then, half-way down the alley, scaring the toenails off me, a huge dog charged out of the shadows and started chasing both of us. It sounded mean, snarling and growling. I think I wet my pants again. Just before we were going to cross Aldine I ducked around the corner of a garage and flattened up against the wall. The two of them went by me like gang-busters. The dog was at the seat of his pants and the man was sprinting for his life.

I still didn't know what was going on. Was that Scott's grandfather, was he mad about something? I sneaked back down the alley and in the quiet of the night I could hear the dog snarling a block away. I stayed in the alley all the way to Fairview and then crept behind tree trunks over to Summit. Thank goodness I hadn't wet my pants enough to show much.

In a few minutes Jerry's car came by slowly and they were calling my name out the windows. I stepped out from behind the tree and waved and Jerry stopped. When I jumped in the back next to Scott they were all laughing and enjoying the prank and I was sitting there holding off a heart attack.

Jerry headed for Sucker Lake and they asked me what happened but I was too mad to tell them.

"How did you get away?" Cal said.

I wouldn't talk until we were out on Rice Street. Mostly I was mad because I thought Scott was introducing me to his grandparents because he liked me. What a dope.

"Did *you* know what was happening?" I asked Jean.

"No, gosh, it scared the liver out of me. I'm glad he didn't chase me."

I looked at Scott who was acting pretty meek.

"Did *you* know about that man?"

He cleared his throat and said, "What?"

"You heard me," I said and tried to sound really mad.

"Well . . . ah . . . sort of," Scott said and everyone roared.

"You *knew* and you let him scare me to death?"

We were having our first fight in front of everyone.

"C'mon, Sandy," Cal said, "what happened, how did you get away?"

Then I told them and everybody in the car was splitting a gut and I couldn't help laughing too as we could imagine that poor man running for his life down some dark alley with a mad dog snapping at the seat of his pants.

Steve didn't know about the prank, that was the first time he'd been up on the porch, too, but the other boys said they'd been knocking on the Runner's door since they were in grade school, though they hadn't done it for a couple of years and weren't sure the guy would still chase them.

Way out Rice Street we shouted the Burma Shave signs we passed.

"Cheek to cheek . . . They meant to be . . . The lights went out . . . And so did he . . . He needed . . . Burma Shave!"

We laughed and hooted and I forgave them for scaring the daylights out of me. It *was* funny. I made up with Scott at the powwow and we sat around the fire and sang and ate hot dogs and he put his arm around me.

By the time the following Monday came around I was a nervous wreck, and I caught myself urging the streetcar along Lake Calhoun and into the woods. I was standing and hanging onto a strap near the back platform where men stood and smoked. Usually if there was a man sitting he would get up and give his seat to a woman, but the seats were all filled with women and I was so jittery I'd rather stand anyway.

The trip seemed like it took forever and I was trying to fill myself with joy and good cheer. When the streetcar stopped at the Lake Harriet Station I flew out the back doors and ran the four blocks to the rest home. Before I went in I stopped and caught my breath and straightened my skirt and brushed my hair back and looked at the beautiful world, but I couldn't get rid of the bad feeling in the pit of my stomach.

I pushed through the big door into that awful sadness and found a heavyset woman I hadn't seen before at the reception desk. She was on the phone and she nodded at me. I waited and noticed she wasn't in a nurse's uniform but wore a flowered dress and white crepe-soled shoes. She was young, with a pumpkin face and a terrible complexion and bleached blonde hair in a Shirley Temple. She hung up the phone and turned to me.

"Yes, can I help you?"

"I'm here to visit Mr. Shapiro."

Her nametag read GRETA SPALDING and she had a friendly look that made me feel better.

"Are you a member of Mr. Shapiro's family?"

"Oh, yeah, I come and see him all the time."

Betty Bain came up the hall like a hangman.

"I'm sorry, but Mr. Shapiro isn't doing well today," Betty said with that drippy smile. "He isn't strong enough to have visitors."

"Oh, please, I came all the way from Saint Paul and I haven't seen him for over two weeks. I won't stay long."

She pursed her lips and sighed.

"I'm sorry, but we have to put the welfare of our lambs first. Mr. Shapiro isn't up to having visitors today."

"Could I just step into his room for a few seconds, please, so he knows I haven't forgotten him?"

I took a step towards the hallway and she moved in front of me, as if she didn't want me seeing something.

"You'll have to come back another day. Maybe he'll feel stronger tomorrow."

There was something wrong, I could feel it, and I wanted to let Mr. Shapiro know I was trying to see him, but I could tell she wasn't going to let me.

"I'll be back tomorrow," I said and I looked straight into her little pigeon eyes and I slammed the door.

Outside, I had a plan. I hurried down Upton and luckily found a drugstore a few blocks away on 43rd. I bought a tablet and a box of crayons and I scrambled back to the rest home; it was getting dark. I sat on a stone wall along the sidewalk and printed a message for Mr. Shapiro in large letters with a black crayon. I wanted to print "Hope is the thing with feathers that perches in the soul" as I had for Jerry, but I knew Mr. Shapiro had given up on hope. Then I ducked up the alley and sneaked along a hedge until I figured I was right outside his window. I crept across the narrow strip of grass and peered in the window. A scrawny little man was playing a beat-up saxophone, hunched over in a wheelchair. His eyes were closed and he was swaying to his music. His mouth was an ugly scar, part of his lip and jaw was missing, and I couldn't believe he could still make a sound with the saxophone.

I found Mr. Shapiro's room after three tries and I knocked gently on the window. He was dozing in his wheelchair in his overcoat and hat and he looked like a friendless refugee. I knocked again a little louder and he woke up. Sure Betty Bain would show up any second, I could hardly breathe. I drummed my fingers on the glass until he noticed me and he gazed out with his watery magnified eyes like a fish in an aquarium. Quickly I held up the first sheet.

THEY WON'T LET ME SEE YOU

I pointed at it and nodded. He stared for a minute and then nodded back. I held up the second note.

ARE YOU ALL RIGHT?

He studied the printed message. Then he looked into my eyes and slowly shook his bobbing head and his sadness came through the glass and stuck all over me. A chill ran down the back of my legs and suddenly I was afraid, I didn't know of what, but afraid. I quickly printed another message and held it up to the window.

I'LL BE BACK!

Golly, I was starting to sound like General MacArthur, but I forced a big smile on my face and waved. He lifted a bony hand and weakly waved back. I swallowed hard and turned away, hoping that no one in the home would spot me. I sneaked back to the hedge and down the alley.

It was dark when I caught the streetcar for the journey home. There was something terribly wrong going on, I could feel it in my bones, and I couldn't tell my parents or get their help or they'd know what I was up to. If Betty Bain and her gang didn't allow me to see Mr. Shapiro, how could I help him or find out what was going on? Something about the home gave me the willies. That scrawny old man had no one to protect him. But protect him from what? What was it they were doing with Mr. Shapiro that they didn't want me to find out?

Betty Bain, is a pain,
I'd like to push her, under a train.

Chapter 10

That night at dinner I wanted to ask my parents what I should do about Mr. Shapiro but I knew I couldn't. I made it home just in time so my mother didn't ask me where I'd been. My father sat at one end of the table and my mother at the other, with me in the middle. We'd always chatter a lot while we ate but it would always be about little things, weather or school or plumbing and heating, never about big things like, Why were some babies born retarded? or How do you decide what you're going to be in life? or Where do people go when they die? or Did God really know about each one of us or were some of us lost in the shuffle like Mr. Shapiro?

When I'd bring up something that bothered me, like dying or being afraid, my parents would change the subject. That was how we avoided scary or unpleasant topics. I thought of raising the question of my ingrown breasts to see how fast my parents would change the subject, but it might set off a tornado with the rapid upheaval of air currents and sudden change in barometric pressure, destroying half the neighborhood. All in all our dinner conversations were pleasant and cheerful as though my dad and I were conspiring to perk up my mother and make it a happy time for her while avoiding any topic that might rock the boat.

My half-bald father, Howard Meyer, was just shy of six feet, built like an anvil, with muscular shoulders and back and a thick neck. He had forearms like Popeye, powerful hands, and black hair. Sometimes the curly black hair on his iron chest stuck out of his shirt. His soft hazel eyes always ducked away when I looked into them.

He ended up owning the business he'd worked for since he and my mother were married. He was everybody's friend, everybody liked him, and he'd go the second mile to help you. If your furnace quit in the middle of winter at two in the morning, he'd be there, never turn anyone down. But there was something between my father and mother I couldn't explain. Over the years, as I grew up, it was more like a feeling, something unspoken in the air.

My parents had separate bedrooms. I never thought that was strange when I was young because they explained it to me: mother had to get up a lot during the night, to take medicine or when she couldn't sleep, and she'd read and didn't want to keep waking my father because he needed his sleep for all the hard work he did.

But as I got older I'd notice my father would sleep in her room off and on but it didn't seem to have anything to do with when she was sick or not. Sometimes she'd be fine and she'd sleep alone and other times, when she wasn't well, she'd let him sleep with her. It was as if he'd done something wrong, and after she told me about his being in jail, I knew it wasn't that. There was something between them, something I couldn't put my finger on, but it was as if he were always trying to make up for something, always trying to get back into her good graces.

My mother had made her famous meatloaf and I was hungry but I kept seeing Mr. Shapiro looking out at me through that window.

"Mom, when you went and visited your Aunt Tillie did the people at the rest home like it when you came?"

"What do you mean?" my mother said.

"Well, were they nice to you, were they glad you were visiting Aunt Tillie?"

"Yes, of course. Some of those poor souls sat there all day and never had anyone visit them."

She cocked her head and looked at me.

"Why do you ask?"

"Oh, I heard some kids talking about their grandpa and how the people in the rest home are mean to him and don't like people coming to see him."

"That's terrible, they ought to be reported," my dad said.

"I would think rest homes would encourage people to visit as often as they can," my mother said.

"Unless they have something to hide," my dad said.

"Some day I'll be in a rest home," I said.

"Nonsense! Don't talk that way!" my mother said. "You're a young healthy girl, I don't want to hear such foolishness."

I'd rocked the boat and the way she snapped at me I realized I scared her. She was a lot closer to a home for the aged than I was. My dad quickly changed the subject.

"How about those Gophers, beating Iowa 55 to 7 Saturday."

This was the deal: my family didn't have a splendid record when it came to old people, in fact, I didn't have *any* grandparents. My mother explained to me why my father's parents weren't in our life when she told me about his being in jail and his parents disowning him. I wished he'd tell me about that part of his life so I could ask if he knew if his parents were still alive. My mother's father was bitten by a dog and died and my mother's mother was killed in a runaway horse and buggy in Red Wing. They thought a hornet bit the horse and it went racing downhill and my grandmother was thrown out and killed. Up against rabid dogs, angry hornets and runaway horses, my family's longevity wasn't doing too hot. So much for grandparents. But if Mr. Shapiro could help me find my real parents, I had the happy thought that maybe I had living grandparents, too.

I called the home after school on Tuesday and Betty Bain told me Mr. Shapiro wasn't up to having visitors. I told her I was going to call Mr. Shapiro's son in Milwaukee. Over the phone I couldn't tell if that scared her or not, but when I called Wednesday, she said I could come Thursday afternoon. Jean wanted to go with me but I told her it might make things worse so she agreed to ride with me on the streetcar and then read movie magazines in the drugstore on 43rd Street while I was with Mr. Shapiro. We sang a little tune on the way across Minneapolis and laughed.

Betty Bain, is a pain,
I'd like to push her, under a train.

I left Jean at the drug store and strolled along Sheridan. Maybe I always dreaded going to the rest home because I was afraid of dying. Maybe everyone was, or maybe some of the chickenhood was still alive in me. No one else talked about dying, what was wrong with me? Did being afraid have anything to do with being adopted, as if you were scared a lot because you didn't have your mother or father in your corner?

I smuggled some cheer and optimism past Betty Bain when she gave me the third degree and I distracted her by asking her who played the saxophone. She told me his name was Woody, a professional who'd played with Tommy Dorsey.

"What happened to his mouth?" I said.

"Cancer of the mouth and throat and it's in his lungs. Said he'd been a chain smoker since he was fourteen."

"I don't see how he can play at all."

"He can only play so long and then he's exhausted. Says he wants to die playing."

"Does he always play the same song?" I said.

"Mostly . . . for some girl he loved when he was young."

"That's funny 'cause it's my favorite song, too."

I listened for Woody's music on the way to Mr. Shapiro's room but he must have been in his exhausted state. One look at him had convinced me that I'd never smoke. With a mouth like that no boy would *ever* kiss me.

When I got to Mr. Shapiro's room, he was sitting in his overcoat and hat with his suitcase packed like someone who missed a train twenty years ago and was still waiting in the depot for a train that no longer ran. The scary thought hit me that maybe I'd miss my train if Mr. Shapiro died without remembering anything.

He didn't look good but I was so glad to see him I gave him a hug.

"*You* back again?" he grouched.

"Yep," I shouted, "you can't get rid of me."

I rolled the bed table in place and set up the board. We started playing Chinese checkers when Elsie stalked into the room with her camera aimed like a big game hunter.

"Smile," she said and I did and she snapped the photo, blinding me for an instant.

"Nice picture," she said and she moused out into the hall.

"Looney!" Mr. Shapiro said. "This is a stinking looney bin."

Woody started doing scales on the saxophone and I had to laugh. This place was so weird my friends wouldn't believe it. We played Chinese checkers and I had a hard time talking to him because I was sure Betty Bain was lurking outside the door. He bawled me out for making a stupid move, he was always teaching me how to play, and I tried to bring him back to 1933.

He moved his marbles with his shaking hand and passed gas like a plow horse and his breath rattled in his chest and came out smelling like death, but he gave me the biggest thrill so far.

"I might have done an adoption," he said.

"What did you say?" I shouted.

"It seems to me I did an adoption or two."

I just about hit the roof.

"Do you remember Howard and Gladys Meyer? They adopted a baby girl in the spring of 1933."

"My son will be here any minute," he said.

Darn, he'd slipped back into that groove and whenever he did I'd never get anything more out of him. I didn't have the heart to tell him the son who wished he'd die was never coming.

"Do you have other children?" I shouted.

"Yes . . . we had three."

"Where do they live?"

I hoped that maybe they'd be more helpful than Ivan.

"My girl and youngest boy drowned."

"Oh . . ."

"It was July, a wind storm, they were in a canoe on White Bear Lake. It just came up and swallowed them."

I didn't know what to say. The more I learned about his life the worse it got.

"How old were they?" I said.

"What's that?"

"How *old* were your boy and girl?" I shouted.

"The girl was sixteen, the boy just turned fourteen."

I didn't want to know their names, didn't want to know any more of Mr. Shapiro's sorrow, but I could see their faces smiling at me from the photos on his dresser as if they were calling out for another chance at living from the bottom of White Bear Lake.

He had all his marbles home and half of mine were still strung out in the middle of the board. I leaned close to his ear and spoke so Betty Bain couldn't hear me from the hallway.

"Why don't they want me to see you?"

"How's that?"

I almost gagged on his halitosis.

"Why don't they want me to see you?" I said a little louder.

"It's the money."

Like a phantom Betty Bain pigeoned into the room.

"I think Mr. Shapiro has had enough excitement for today," she said. She rubbed the top of his head. "Did you win again, Arny?"

"Go to hell," he said.

"Now, now, we mustn't talk that way in front of your young friend," she said and she winked at me.

While she wheeled the bed table aside I leaned over and hugged him.

"I'll see you soon. One of these days I'll win a game."

I tried to smile and he followed me to the door with his watery puppy-dog eyes. Out in the hall, Betty Bain escorted me to the front door.

"Aren't you afraid he'll just walk away some day when he's got his hat and coat on?" I said.

"Heavens, no. He couldn't make it to the front door. Elsie's the only one we have to keep an eye on around here. We let him pack his suitcase, it occupies him for a while, and then when we have him in bed we put his things back in the dresser. The only way he'll get out of here is in a hearse."

She said it so coldly it made me mad, even though I knew she was right. Mr. Shapiro had run out of hope.

Jean was waiting outside in the dark and I squealed with the news that he remembered he might have done an adoption. I felt I was close, that with a few more games of Chinese checkers I might know the name of my real mother and father. I asked Jean what she thought he meant when he said it was the money. Were they taking money from him? How could they do that, other than some petty cash he seemed to have?

We caught the streetcar and rode home through the rush hour. My feelings were jumbled and confused, but still I couldn't keep my heart from dancing. I was giddy. He had done one or two adoptions and he remembered!

Chapter 11

Dave Neuberg had passed Jean a note on Wednesday that he'd be in the back corner of the Grandview Theater on Friday night. She'd been sweating BBs ever since, afraid her folks would find out, but not wanting to miss the romantic rendezvous. She could see herself at Derham Hall, having the joy squeezed out of her by the nuns, missing all the fun at Central with her friends. But she loved Dave and she asked me to go with her for cover.

We took the streetcar and transferred at Snelling and rather than wait for a streetcar on Grand we walked through Macalester College campus the four blocks to the Grandview. I felt like a spy when I bought the tickets, as though the Communists were following us and would give us away at any moment. Jean had her jacket collar up around her face and a scarf over her head and she looked like an old granny when she caught up with me in the lobby. I gave the tickets to the nifty college-boy usher and we slunk into the already darkened theater like robbers.

We hesitated for a minute to let our eyes become accustomed to the dark and then Jean fumbled her way along the back row. We tripped over another couple and found Dave wearing a stocking cap down over his eyebrows. They pulled off their jackets and stuff and slumped down in their seats and started necking like an atom bomb was already falling through the sky over Saint Paul. I turned slightly with my back to them and watched the movie, *White Heat*, with James Cagney and Virginia Mayo, but the only heat at the Grandview that night was coming from the two seats in the corner of the back row.

Just before the movie ended and James Cagney went up in flames, Dave pulled on his stuff and stumbled across my legs.

"Thanks," he whispered and he hurried down the aisle and out the back door.

Jean and I sat there until the lights came up and at first I thought it was her lipstick that was smeared all over her face. Then I realized the lipstick had long ago been worn away and it was her raw lips and skin that were red.

She checked her face in the rest room mirror and tried to cool it off with cold water but we decided we'd watch the second show for a while and then go home when her parents were in bed. She got off the streetcar at Watson and I rode two and a half blocks farther to Bayard. I'd come home late at night so often that I'd gotten to know the motorman who usually drove that run. His name was Fred and we'd talk some. After ten o'clock there never were many riders and when he'd stop and let me off, I'd walk around in front of the streetcar and up Bayard to my house. He'd wait and watch to see that I got home safely. I had to walk in the street because there was no sidewalk on our side and when I'd turn in at the sixth house up he'd drive away.

"Been to the movies?" he said while I stood up front.

"Yeah, over at the Grandview."

"Any good?"

"Jean loved it."

"What was it about?" he said.

"A Catholic girl and a Jewish boy who love each other but their parents break them up."

I didn't feel bad telling him that because he'd told me he never went to the movies.

"Sounds kind of sad."

"It is."

When I turned in between the two large maple trees in our front yard I noticed the streetcar pull away.

Monday I couldn't go see Mr. Shapiro because I had a *Cehisian* staff meeting after school that I couldn't miss and by Tuesday I was feeling the heebie-jeebies. Then, in D.B. Sandersen's physics class I got in a tight spot and thought I'd end up with seventh period again.

Once before that fall some of the more brazen boys had bamboozled D.B. with his hearing aid but they knew they couldn't do it too often or the teacher would catch on. Tuesday they'd decided to give it another run. The teacher kept his hearing aid in his shirt pocket with a small wire running under his shirt and out the back of his collar and up to both ears. The hearing aid worked on batteries. Well, when D.B. asked the class a question, one of those boys was the first to stick his hand in the air because he knew he didn't have to really know the answer.

After D.B. had covered some stuff in our text book, he chalked some examples on the board. On the wall above the blackboard, printed boldly on a plaque, were these words.

I COMPLAINED BECAUSE I HAD NO SHOES
UNTIL I MET A MAN WHO HAD NO FEET.

The first time I saw it I was touched that he'd hang it in his classroom, as if he were telling us something about himself. When he finished writing out examples, D.B. turned and began asking questions.

"What would be the specific gravity and explain how you arrived at the answer?" the teacher said.

Steve's hand was the first in the air. D.B. nodded.

"Mr. Holland?"

Steve looked right into the teacher's face and started talking.

"To find the specific gravity . . ." Steve said out loud and then started moving his lips as if he were talking but made no sound. D.B. started tapping the hearing aid in his shirt pocket. Steve went on moving his lips and once in a while he'd talk out loud, ". . . and I arrived at the answer . . ." and then go back to mouthing words. D.B. smacked the hearing aid with his fist and Steve said out loud ". . . and that's how I calculated the specific gravity."

Steve looked him right in the eye and D.B. just stared at him for a moment, thoroughly confused, and we tried to keep from having a cow.

The class played a big part in the prank because they had to be perfectly quiet while Steve was mouthing words. But it was always boys giving the silent answers and when D.B. called on girls, he could always hear them, and being the scientist he was, I thought he'd finally figure that out. As if he read my mind, he ignored the boys and called on me.

"Miss Meyer?"

The kids looked at me and though I knew I might end up with seventh period and would miss seeing Mr. Shapiro again I couldn't let them down. I think that no matter how scared I was I wanted to show off for Scott.

"If you take the square root . . ." I said and then I moved my lips but made no sound.

D.B. whacked himself in the chest, twice, and then I started talking out loud again. I went in and out of sound three times and had him rapping his hearing aid like he was trying to restart his heart. The bell rang, and the class let loose with the laughter they'd been heroically restraining for the past fifteen minutes. As I walked past the teacher, who looked quite confused, he had his hearing aid on the counter and was checking the batteries.

"I complained because I had no batteries," Steve said, coming right behind me, "until I met a man who had no ears."

Paul Dietl plowed into the hall and shouted, "I complained because I had no fun, until I met a teacher who had no brain."

I'd escaped without landing in seventh period and several boys applauded my performance. Scott caught up with me and walked me to my next class and for a minute I couldn't remember where I was going.

I sucked in as much fresh air and happiness I could in the four blocks to the home and I found Betty Bain at her desk.

"You're sure you're feeling well today?" she said.

"Yes, I'm fine."

"There's a lot of colds and flu going around and it would be extremely dangerous for Mr. Shapiro to catch something."

"I know," I said and I tried to be pleasant with her and not let on what I really thought of her.

"Very well, but don't overtire him."

When I got to Mr. Shapiro's room he wasn't sitting in his overcoat and hat, he was in his birthday suit, stark naked, and the room smelled like a toilet. I stopped in my tracks but he saw me.

"What are *you* looking at?" he said.

His body was worse than I'd imagined, a plucked starving chicken, no flesh or muscle, just saggy yellowed skin and bones. I turned to leave and bumped into Greta Spalding coming out of the bathroom with a towel. Her wrestler's arms bulged out of her short-sleeved dress and I figured she could throw Mr. Shapiro through a plate glass window.

"Oh, good, you can give me a hand," she said.

Then Elsie moused into the room, aiming her camera.

"No, Elsie, no picture today," Greta said and gently steered her back into the hall. Greta shut the door and then draped the towel over Mr. Shapiro's lap and handed me a pair of clean pants.

"We just had a little accident, didn't we, sweetie," she said as if she were talking to a child.

"Go to hell," he said and I could tell how humiliated and ashamed he felt.

I helped Greta get him dressed, held him when she had him stand so she could pull up what looked like a diaper and his pants. Then she gathered up his soiled clothes and left the room. I tried to act as if nothing unusual had happened. I wheeled the bed table in place and set out the Chinese checkers and we played. After a few minutes he started talking.

"I dreamed about my kids. They were drowning and I was trying to save them but no matter how hard I swam I couldn't."

CHAPTER 11

"It's just a bad dream, Mr. Shapiro, you couldn't have saved them."

"I was with them in the canoe," he said.

"In your dream?"

"No, that day, I was the duffer, sitting in the middle on a life jacket."

"Oh, gosh, I—"

"When the wind came roaring across the lake I shouted to Sarah to put it on. She shouted back, 'No, you take it, Dad, I'm a stronger swimmer.' I was scared, the wind was shrieking and all but picking the canoe up into the air. I put it on," he said and paused.

Then he fixed his magnified eyes on me like headlights.

"If I'd made her wear it like a good father she'd be alive today. We capsized. When the wind finally let up they were gone."

He and I were family, both chickenhearted.

"You couldn't help it, Mr. Shapiro," I said for both of us.

"I was a coward. I was so ashamed I wanted to slip off the life jacket and drown with them, but I couldn't even do that. Seven people died on the lake that day. They had the number wrong. It was eight, I died that day with my kids."

We played without talking for several minutes and my heart ached for Mr. Shapiro. I glanced at his children's faces, framed on the dresser in perpetual smiles. I tried to find hope in the fact that he remembered that terrible accident so clearly, but I realized, in comparison, my adoption was a trivial thing that held no importance in his life.

"Make friends with an angel," he said as though he were alone.

"Pardon me," I shouted.

"Make friends with an angel if you ever get the chance."

"How do you find one?"

"It's hard, they come in many disguises."

I didn't know what he was talking about. I slipped out of the upholstered chair and crept to the door and peeked down the hallway. Betty Bain was at her desk. I rushed back to Mr. Shapiro and sat on the edge of the chair.

"What did you mean last week by The money?"

"How's that?"

"Why don't they want me to come and see you?"

He glanced at the doorway and spoke softly.

"It's the checks."

"What checks?"

He nodded at the dresser. "My checks."

I pulled open the top drawer and in one corner there were several envelopes and a small box. I looked in one of the envelopes and it was a bunch of canceled checks. I pushed the drawer closed and tiptoed to the open door. Betty Bain was still far up the hall at her desk.

"They're robbing me blind," Mr. Shapiro said. "That's the way it is in the world, the strong prey on the weak and helpless."

"Not everyone, Mr. Shapiro, people are good."

"You're young . . . you'll learn."

I opened the drawer and looked closely at the checks. They all had his shaky signature and seemed to be for normal stuff: the newspaper, a few to a drugstore, several to the home for his keep. I couldn't see anything out of the ordinary. I quickly closed the drawer and sat facing him again.

"How do they steal your money?" I shouted.

"It's the numbers."

"What numbers?" I said

"On the checks, on the checks," he said with a growl.

Darn it, I could hear those squeaking crepe-soled shoes of the pigeon woman coming down the hall. I hadn't found out anything about my adoption and somehow Betty Bain and her gang were stealing Mr. Shapiro's money and it seemed I couldn't do a thing about it.

Betty Bain pigeoned into the room.

"Time to be going."

"All right, just a few minutes to say good-bye," I said.

Without asking she abruptly wheeled the bed table aside even though she could see the game wasn't over. Mr. Shapiro tried to hang onto it but had no strength.

"Hey, we're not finished," he said and the owl fixed his eyes on the pigeon and I expected feathers to be flying.

"Haul your ass outta here," he said to her.

Betty Bain glared at him and he stared back with his bird-of-prey eyes and I could see a fierce anger in them that seemed to drive her out of the room.

"Listen," I shouted right in his ear. "I'll be back tomorrow. Try to remember about the adoption and I'll do what I can about the checks."

He broke wind and I hugged him and I caught a whiff of his rotten breath. Flakes of dandruff clung to his thick lenses and his sorrow clung to both of us and I could only think of one thing I could do. I kissed him on the cheek.

Arnold Shapiro, it isn't fair,
They never told you, you'd end up in there.

Chapter 12

I called Sunset Home on Wednesday and Betty Bain informed me that Mr. Shapiro was having a bad day and wasn't strong enough to have visitors. I'd learned to call before riding all the way across Minneapolis for nothing, and sometimes I believed her; he was so weak and frail. But, darn it, now I knew someone was robbing him and I understood why they wouldn't want anyone who was interested in him coming around. They'd picked a helpless old man the world had forgotten and I wanted to find out how they were doing it and have them thrown in jail.

On Thursday I tried to gather a bunch of happiness and cheer around me like a little cloud and drag it into that waiting room of the morgue, as Mr. Shapiro called it, to do battle with the gloom. I found him sitting in his overcoat and hat with his worn leather suitcase packed beside him. Down the hall Woody was playing "Someone To Watch Over Me" so mournfully he seemed to be putting a melody to Mr. Shapiro's prayer, like the background music in a movie. Mr. Shapiro turned his far-sighted lenses toward me.

"Didn't think I'd see *you* again," he said but I could tell he missed me.

Elsie followed me into the room as if she'd been waiting. She handed a photo to Mr. Shapiro and said, "Nice picture."

Mr. Shapiro held it for a second without looking at it and let it flutter to the floor like a dead leaf. Elsie's sweet little face didn't show any disappointment before she scooted out of the room.

"Thanks, Elsie," I called, and I picked up the picture.

"That looney's always giving me snapshots. When you're a walking corpse you don't look in a mirror."

I studied the photo. In it I was playing Chinese checkers with Mr. Shapiro, smiling into the camera in my dickey and short-sleeved yellow sweater, as flat-chested as a barn. I was letting my hair grow longer and I liked it but I always wanted to be blonde and my hair was somewhere between dark brown and black. I stuck the picture in my coat pocket and rolled the bed table in place.

After we played awhile I asked him again about the money and the checks.

"Look at the numbers," he said with his wheezing voice.

I took one of the envelopes of canceled checks from the drawer and laid it in my lap. While we played I thumbed through the numbers on the checks and they seemed helter-skelter at first. But after I started putting them in order I realized there were some numbers missing. Either the bank didn't return all of his canceled checks or someone had destroyed them.

"Who's doing this?" I shouted

"Don't know, maybe while I sleep."

"Have you told anyone?"

"Who's to tell, you're the only one who pays any mind. I warn the other relics in here, but half of them don't even know where they are."

"How about visitors?"

"Tell some of them, when I can," he said and coughed.

"Don't they do something?"

"Naw . . . they plaster a simpleton's smile on their kissers and back away like I'm a Jehovah's Witness."

"Someone's forging your checks and cashing them?"

He moved a marble with his trembling hand.

"Look in the box," he said.

I took the box of unused checks from the drawer and sat down, ready to duck it under my skirt if anyone showed up. I moved a marble and opened the box. It had several books of new checks with Mr. Shapiro's name and address printed on them. They were from First National Bank. I didn't know what he wanted me to look at.

"The numbers," he said out of his owllike eyes.

I took the first book and started reading the numbers. 1150, 1151, 1152, 1153, 1155, 1156. Wait, 1154 was missing. Someone was taking blank checks. I found three more missing out of two books. I slipped the canceled checks and the box back in the top drawer and resumed playing checkers. What could I do? I was angry and scared. I could tell the police, show them the missing checks. The bank must have a record of cashed checks and the amounts.

"I had an adoption around 1930," Mr. Shapiro said out of the blue and he just about knocked my socks off.

He was remembering.

"It was a baby boy . . . some folks from Afton adopted him. I think I got $35 for that job. I think their name was Robinson."

"That's peachy, Mr. Shapiro, that you remember," I shouted. "Can you remember anything about Howard and Gladys Meyer. My dad is about five eleven with a stocky build and black hair. My mother—"

"I had a divorce, too," he said but I didn't want to let him slide into another rut.

"My mother is slight and dainty and she had long brown hair and she's about five foot three. They gave $970 for the adoption, to pay for the mother's medical bills. Do you remember, Mr. Shapiro, do you?"

"My wife left me," he said.

"Oh . . . I'm sorry."

"Just up and walked out on me after thirty-one years, said she couldn't stand to live with me another day."

"Gee-whiz, that's tough."

"I know it was the life jacket."

"The life jacket?" I said.

"She'd never say, but even after ten years I knew she blamed me, no longer respected me. I let my kids drown when I had the only life jacket. She just couldn't get over that. I don't blame her."

Did we all excrete an aroma that either attracted people or drove them away, like bees to flowers or the way a skunk drives off enemies? Did Mr. Shapiro's agony and shame cause the stench that hung around him like a little cloud, that drove away his family and friends? Did I drive away the boys I liked with some smothering emotional scent, did I repel my real mother and father?

I hadn't noticed Betty Bain in the doorway but Mr. Shapiro had. She stepped into the room.

"Don't you realize by now that he can't remember the kind of details you want from him? Why don't you leave the poor man alone?"

She sounded like she was on Mr. Shapiro's side and I was the person hurting him and she really ticked me off. I stood back as she rolled the bed table out of the way with our game unfinished again.

"But he *did* remember, an adoption in 1930, and he remembered it was a baby boy and he remembered their name and he even remembered how much he charged them and if he can remember details like that he can remember my adoption."

"You don't have to shout with me," she said. "I'm not hard of hearing."

I hadn't realized I was shouting and I blushed slightly as she left the room.

I went down on one knee beside his wheelchair. Every time I hugged him good-bye I had the impression we were thinking the same thing: Would we ever see each other again?

On the trip home I felt numb, sitting on the bench seat near the front of the streetcar, really bushed and awfully blue. How could anyone be so mean that they'd rob a helpless man like Mr. Shapiro? I didn't know people could be so cruel. I'd seen the horror from the war on the newsreels but that seemed unreal, so far away and on a movie screen. My stomach knotted and I didn't know what I should do. If I told the police they'd investigate and my parents would find out what I was doing and Mr. Shapiro might die from all the excitement and trouble.

If I could find a way to get his canceled checks from the bank before they mailed them I could take out the forged checks and show them to the police. Whoever it was, they'd have to endorse the back of the check and I'd bet my bippy on Betty Bain's name. I wondered how much they'd take each time. Too much and it might arouse suspicion. Twenty dollars, fifty?

I forgot to get a transfer when I got off the Harriet car and I had to spend another token to get on the Selby-Lake at Hennepin. Really down in the dumps, I thought maybe I ought to give up, maybe I wasn't meant to know who my mother and father were. I could just quit looking and sic the police on whoever was robbing Mr. Shapiro and be done with it.

When I was finally on the Randolph streetcar I remembered that Jean was having a huge slumber party Saturday night. That would be fun and I hoped Scott would show up. Then it hit me like a ton of bricks. Scott's dad was a big wheel at *First National Bank!* the very bank where Mr. Shapiro had a checking account.

Saturday night Jean Daley's house was busting at the seams. There must have been fifty kids listening to records or dancing or just trying to talk over the noise in the basement rec room. A few guys were competing with their yo-yos, Around the World, Rock the Cradle, Walking the Dog, trying to outdo one another with an audience cheering. I kept an eye out for Scott, couldn't wait to see him, but now it wasn't just because of how much I liked him. I wanted to talk to him about his father and the bank.

I'd come early to help Jean with the food and stuff. I told her how Mr. Shapiro remembered an adoption back in 1930 and I told her about the checks. We were both excited and we sang as we worked.

Arnold Shapiro, you're my hero,
If you don't remember, I'll be a zero.
Betty Bain, is a pain,
I'd like to push her, under a train.

Jean's mother heard us singing and asked who in Sam Hill was Arnold Shapiro and we laughed and told her it was just a nutty song. You could tell she really liked us kids, always doing stuff for us. Jean's brother Don, who was killed in the war, loved apple pie. One day in the fall, three years later, Jean came home and found her mother baking pies. There were pies cooling all over the kitchen and dining room. She'd baked eleven apple pies from scratch and was still going strong, as if something had snapped and she thought if she baked enough apple pies she could pull her son out of the English Channel and bring him back to life. Jean got her to stop by suggesting that they deliver pies to all their neighbors, that Don would have liked that.

Scott and Jerry showed up when it was almost nine o'clock and I had to catch my breath I was so excited. But when I tried to get Scott alone, right off a lot of the boys started razzing Jerry, teasing him and laughing and rough-housing, and I couldn't get to Scott. The boys were always punching each other on the shoulder, I don't know why, it must have hurt, but they were always doing it. What they were razzing Jerry about, that made him blush and pull his jacket over his head, was what happened in school Friday.

In speech our desks were arranged in three rows of a semi-circle. Jerry sat in the second row next to Myra Malone, a cute junior girl who must have lived on chocolate malts from the day she was three years old because she filled her sweater as well as anyone in the school. Myra probably enjoyed talking with Jerry, one of the nicest-looking boys at

Central and a jock as well. Somehow Jerry had soft-soaped Myra into scratching his back as he slumped over his desk top. Miss Lornberg traipsed back and forth from the prop room and left the class to polish the two-minute speeches they were about to give.

Myra lightly scratched Jerry's back and no one paid much attention. After five minutes Miss Lornberg settled at her desk at the side of the room and called on Bill Overby.

Jerry sat up and Bill stood at the front of the class and gave his speech. When he finished Miss Lornberg ran her pencil down the grade book.

"Jerry," she said.

Jerry just sat there with a queer look on his face.

"Jerry, let's hear your speech," the teacher said.

Jerry didn't move and the kids were wondering what was going on.

"I haven't got one," Jerry finally said.

"Of course you do, I have it right here on my desk."

Jerry loved to give speeches and he was good at it. He'd always do something funny and make everyone laugh, but now he just sat there with a hangdog face.

"Jerry Douglas, get up here, you're wasting our time."

"I can't," Jerry said.

"Are you ill?" the teacher said.

"No."

"Well then, get up here," she said.

"I forgot it," Jerry said.

Then some of the boys in the back started quietly laughing and some of the girls whispered behind their hands and Jerry squirmed in his seat. Myra was blushing and Miss Lornberg was getting steamed.

"Jerry, if you don't get up here this instant I'll have to give you a failure for the assignment."

"Thanks, Miss Lornberg, but I'll take the 'E'."

"If you don't feel well, just say so and—"

"No, I'll take the 'E'."

Miss Lornberg made the mark in the grade book and some of the boys in the back row began a low muffled chant that only the kids close to them could understand.

"Jerry's got a hard-on, Jerry's got a hard-on . . ."

Miss Lornberg shook her head as if she were baffled why one of her best students wouldn't get up and give that simple speech, something he did better than any of them and who always handled even impromptu speeches with ease. It would be one of those mysteries that teachers have to live with when they suspect that they were the only one in the room who didn't know what was going on. Some kids caught on, some were in the dark with Miss Lornberg, and some had it explained to them in the hall after class, but Jerry Douglas didn't leave the safety of his desk until he was the last one in the room.

When things calmed down after Jerry's arrival at Jean's slumber party, I brought a tray of Cokes down to the rec room and caught Scott.

"Hi, want a Coke?" I said.

"Yeah, thank you," he said with his polite manner.

He took a bottle and I handed the tray to Steve and pulled Scott over beside the piano where Jean was playing and kids were singing and I almost had to shout.

"Does your father work in the part of the bank that handles checking accounts?" I said.

"No, he works mostly with businesses who need loans."

"Could he find out about a checking account?"

"Gosh, I don't know," he said, "why?"

"Oh, there's an old man, a long-time friend of my family, who's having trouble with his checking account and it's at your father's bank. He does work at First National doesn't he?"

"Yeah . . . I guess I could ask him."

"Oh, would you, that would be swell," I said and it felt so good just to be standing so close to him and talking with him.

"What's the problem?"

"I think someone is forging his checks, stealing his money," I said.

"Jeez, that sounds bad."

"Will you ask your dad about it?"

"Sure."

Steve grabbed Scott and dragged him over to the piano where Jean was playing the Central fight song and everyone was singing. The boys had been challenging each other over which team would do the best, basketball or hockey or swimming, and in the middle of all the hubbub I felt like I was going to explode with hope or joy. Mr. Shapiro was getting close to remembering, I just knew it, and Scott was going to talk to his father about the checks, and I was sure that Scott really liked me.

Jean's mother shagged the boys at midnight and we girls gabbed and laughed and carried on until almost three. We slept on the rec room floor in sleeping bags and all kinds of bedding and when it was dark and finally quiet, I felt terribly sad and I didn't know why, as if my heart knew something I didn't and it was warning me.

Chapter 13

On the Wednesday night before Thanksgiving, while I was getting ready to go to the Turkey Trot with Scott, I started brushing my teeth with Ben-Gay. Gosh, I was flat out giddy because I could tell he really liked me. We bumped and bounced to the dance in a panel truck from Finley's Market where Cal worked on Saturdays. Cal's father didn't own a car and Mr. Finley let Cal use the truck. It was nifty because there were no seats in the back and Jerry and Sally and Steve and Jean slid around on the back deck, with blankets for a little cushioning. I perched on Scott's lap in the front seat with Cal and Lola and we were so crammed together that Lola had to move the stick shift when Cal used the clutch.

We laughed and hooted and I was in heaven, sitting there in Scott's lap with his arm around my waist, and I didn't care that the inside of the truck smelled like onions and ripe bananas and that we probably would too.

We finally got to the dance at the Columbia Chalet after Cal had zoomed around town for a while. The Societtes and Sphinx were putting on the dance and Gary Berg's band was playing and I finally figured out how to get Scott out on the floor. I'd ask him if he wanted to dance and he was too polite to turn me down. The basketball team had scrimmaged Washburn that afternoon and Scott said he shouldn't get too close to me because he was coming down with a cold. I told him I didn't care and I made the poor boy dance most of the night.

Scott had called me Sunday evening to ask me to the dance and I was so excited I almost forgot to ask him if he'd talked to his father about Mr. Shapiro's checking account. Scott said he was waiting to catch his dad in the right mood and I knew what he meant.

I got to see Mr. Shapiro on Tuesday after passing Betty Bain's usual inspection but he'd slipped back into his old ruts, talking about his son coming to get him and how he was going to live in Milwaukee. He did remember to ask if I brought any of my mother's sleeping pills and I didn't understand how he could remember some things and totally forget others. I took a peek at his checks in the top drawer and they appeared to be exactly the way I left them. When we'd finished a game of Chinese checkers and I knew it was time to go, I knelt in front of his wheelchair.

"I'm going to adopt you," I shouted.

"What are you talking about?" he grouched.

"I don't have a grandpa and I'm adopting you."

I smiled and laughed but he didn't change his hollow-cheeked grump.

"That's poppycock, you can't adopt a grandpa."

"Well, I just did and you're my grandpa," I shouted and I gave him a hug.

I noticed he wasn't such a cold fish and how he leaned into the hug a little.

"Good-bye, Grandpa Shapiro, I'll see you soon."

"I'm not your dad-blamed grandpa!"

I felt hopeless when I left and I started to believe Betty Bain, that he'd never remember my adoption. But I was mad, too, at the way they were treating him, and I decided he was my grandpa Shapiro and I'd keep visiting him no matter what he remembered and maybe they'd treat him better, knowing I was coming around. And maybe, with Scott's father's help, we'd put one of them behind bars.

After the dance we ate at the drive-in over by Minnehaha Falls and Scott and I were so squashed together we had to feed each other. I'd dip a French fry in catsup and stick it in his mouth and then he'd feed me one. We shared a chocolate malt and it seemed I could feel my breasts growing right there in the grocery truck. Scott surprised me when he told me I had some malt on my lip and kissed me, the way it happens in the movies. It was heavenly, and he tasted like chocolate. Then he quickly turned his head and sneezed and just about blew me off his lap except we were wedged in the truck so tightly there was nowhere to be blown.

On the way home I was praying that Cal would get up the nerve to park. I figured he wouldn't, being so new with Lola, but at least he drove around for another half hour before dropping us off. I kept wishing Scott would find more malt on my lips.

When Cal walked Lola to her door in the Highland Village apartments, I stayed on Scott's lap, though there was room on the truck seat, and he held on to me as if he didn't want me to move. He kept blowing his nose and sneezing but I wasn't about to let that keep me from such bliss. At my door I reminded him about talking to his father and he said he would for sure over our four-day holiday. Then he blew his nose and said good-night and quickly retreated to the truck.

Thanksgiving Day we went to the worship service at House of Hope and I was giving thanks like crazy and I came home stuffed like a turkey with hope. When we sat down to our Thanksgiving dinner my mom said a special prayer for Amelia Earhart and all the people who were being held captive in dungeons that day. My mom talked about her so often that I started believing Amelia *was* still alive.

Friday I started feeling lousy, my head felt fuzzy, and I told Jean I couldn't go to the movies with her and I went to bed early. By Saturday I had a full-blown head cold and I laid around all weekend, terribly disappointed that I couldn't see Scott. He was laying low also and he apologized for giving me his cold when we talked on the phone. I told him it was worth it and then blushed at what I'd said and was glad he couldn't see my face.

I was worried about Mr. Shapiro, and I did everything I could to get rid of my cold. I slept a lot, drank lots of tea

and ate buckets of chicken soup and took aspirin and stuck
Vicks VapoRub up my nose and on my chest. I did homework and felt lousy and couldn't wait for my life to begin
again.

On Monday I told my mother I felt fine and forced myself
to go to school because I figured my cold was about over
and I knew if I stayed home I wouldn't be able to see Mr.
Shapiro. I hadn't seen him for almost a week and I dreaded
thinking about what might have happened. By afternoon I
was really bushed but somehow I sensed my only chance at
finding out who I was could be slipping through my fingers
and I was getting close enough to taste it.

I called the home and Betty Bain said I could see him,
probably relieved that I hadn't been around for so long. The
streetcar trip seemed longer than usual and I caught myself
biting my fingernails twice and it always made me so mad
and my fingers looked terrible. All of a sudden I got the
chills and I started coughing and I could tell the cold had
settled in my chest.

When I transferred at Hennepin I dashed in the drugstore
and got a box of Smith Brothers cough drops. When I
walked the four blocks to the home I sucked two cough
drops as fast as I could and I was afraid Betty Bain would
send me home without seeing Mr. Shapiro. I rounded the
corner and saw a long black car parked in front of the home,
a hearse! The fear I slept with every night had followed me
into the daylight; Mr. Shapiro had died. I started to cry and
when I reached the home a bored-looking man in a long
black topcoat was leaning against the hearse.

"Who died," I said, wiping away tears with my soaked
hanky.

"You got someone in there?" He nodded at the home.

"Yes, my grandpa."

"It was a guy named Woodrow Gamble."

"Oh . . . thank you, that's not him."

Inside another man in black was going over some papers with Betty Bain at her desk. She paused and looked up at me.

"I thought it was Mr. Shapiro," I said and I blew my nose. It was a perfect cover.

"No, you can save your tears." She moved her head like a cooing pigeon. "Mr. Shapiro is still with us."

"Who did die?" I said and I edged down the hall.

"Woody," she said and she turned back to the undertaker.

Woody had gotten me by her and I hoped he was already happy in heaven making music for his long-lost love.

I felt a sneeze coming on and halfway to Mr. Shapiro's room I sneezed into my scarf, almost gagging myself in an effort to stifle it.

Mr. Shapiro was sitting hunched over in his wheelchair and when he turned his large magnified eyes on me it was like a big owl perched in a tree, a mad owl.

"Didn't think *you'd* be back."

He was hurt and I could imagine him sitting there all those days watching for me and I didn't show.

"Oh . . . I'm sorry, grandpa, the days just got away from me. Don't you know I'll always be back?"

"No skin off my hide if you come or not," he said with his gravelly voice, "and I'm not your grandpa."

I knelt beside his wheelchair and hugged him and his stomach sounded like a flushing toilet and I thought I felt a sob shutter through his scrawny body. In his trembling hands he held an old photo of his three children and with his large watery eyes I couldn't tell if he'd been crying but the front of his shirt had several damp spots.

"You bring the pills?" he said quietly.

I shook my head and wheeled the bed table between us.

"Have you been having bad dreams again?" I shouted.

He didn't answer as he set the photo on his dresser with a trembling hand.

We played Chinese checkers and I told him I had a very important man at First National Bank looking into his missing checks.

"Don't care about the money," he said.

He broke wind and I realized I didn't much notice anymore, that his gas and his rotten breath and his ornery disposition didn't matter. I'd caught a glimpse of the man hiding behind those thick lenses and I knew he was terribly lonely and scared and I knew he'd never admit it. He hated himself for being a coward, refused to forgive himself, and I knew how brave he was to carry on when he was so unloved and his life had turned out so badly and I realized I liked him.

"You don't care that they're robbing you?"

I'd kept my scarf around my neck and I coughed into it as quietly as I could.

"No . . . I don't care about the money. Everything I did was for money, my whole life was a mistake."

I could feel him giving up, like he didn't care about anything anymore.

He moved a marble several spaces and then turned those large red-ringed eyes on me.

"I think I remembered the spring of 1933 last night."

My heart just about popped out of my chest.

"Oh, Mr. Shapiro, try to *remember.*"

"Had my first grandchild in May of '33, a little girl, or was it '34?"

"What else do you remember?" I shouted and I sneezed into my scarf and hoped Betty Bain was still busy with the undertakers.

"Or was I dreaming?" he said as his head bobbed gently, "can't tell the difference anymore."

"Try, Mr. Shapiro, try to remember."

"I remember it was a rainy spring . . . and I think I did the legal work on an adoption. It was a girl, but she was almost a year old and I remember thinking my little granddaughter would be that big some day."

"Oh, Mr. Shapiro, that was *me!* Do you remember the name of the man who brought me to you?"

"No . . . no . . . but it's funny, I don't think I liked the man."

"Try to remember, please, what was his name?"

I was breathing hard and I started to cough and I couldn't stop. I sprang out of the chair and gulped a drink of water from the glass on Mr. Shapiro's night table and the coughing stopped. I popped in another Smith Brothers and sat back at the checkerboard.

"Can you remember his *name?* he wanted $970," I said.

"It'll come to me . . . it'll come to me."

Betty Bain slipped into the room like a bad mood.

"Well, who's winning today, as if I didn't know?"

"He's remembering 1933, please, can I stay a little longer?"

I didn't dare look at her. My chest ached and my head was so plugged I thought it was going to explode but I was so close. Mr. Shapiro broke wind, a cannon shot, and that distracted her.

"Still tooting along, aren't we, Arny." She looked at me. "I'm sorry, but you'll have to go now—"

"Please, just this once—"

"I'm sorry, but our patients' welfare must take precedence over all other matters."

She rolled the bed table away and I crouched in front of Mr. Shapiro.

"Try to remember the man's name, and if you remember, please write it down, please."

"Come, now, let's let Arny rest," she said and she stood there like a jailer.

He looked at Betty Bain. "Haul your ass outta here!"

I hugged him and picked up my coat and went into the hall with her.

"Will you please write down the name if he remembers?" I said.

"Certainly, I'd be glad to help," she said and I didn't believe a word of it.

"You sound like you have a cold," she said as we walked towards the front door.

"I was crying," I said and then I used the family ploy. "Did Woody die while he was playing?"

"We don't know. When we found him he was deader than a doornail. His saxophone was on the floor in front of him."

"I hope he was," I said.

I buttoned my coat and wrapped my scarf around my head and tried not to cough until I escaped into the fresh air. Along Sheridan I caught a glimpse of a crow in the coming darkness, gliding silently into a huge spruce, roosting for the night. I hadn't been to my cave in a long time and I longed to curl up in the arms of the St. Peter sandstone.

All the way to the streetcar I prayed that Mr. Shapiro would remember, prayed that I could get back before he lost the name again in the cluttered attic of his memory. The ride back to Saint Paul took forever and by the time I got home I was chilled to the bone and I went straight to bed. My mother brought me chicken soup, and though I felt terrible and I was sad about Woody, I was dizzy with joy. I wanted to tell my mother that Mr. Shapiro remembered a little one-year-old girl and that little girl was *me!*

Chapter 14

Darn it, I was sick in bed Tuesday and Wednesday and ready to send for a strait jacket, about to start peeling wallpaper off my bedroom wall. I agonized over Mr. Shapiro and how close he was to remembering my adoption. My mother hovered over me like a brooding hen so I couldn't call the home to see if he was all right. Scott called Wednesday night and told me he'd talked to his dad about the checking account and his dad gave him the name of a man I could see at the bank, a Mr. Dale.

Thursday I was well enough to go to school and I planned on calling the home after school but gad, some of the boys in Miss Mauleke's trig class started fooling around and I was afraid I'd get trapped in another seventh period. One of the boys, I think Bill Bosshardt, brought a small corked bottle from chemistry lab filled with hydrogen sulfide and hid it in his desk. Once class started and Miss Mauleke was explaining problems on the blackboard, the boys started passing the bottle around like a time bomb, knowing that before long the gas would build enough pressure to pop the cork. The trick was not to have it in your possession when it did.

It wasn't long before the cork popped with a quiet sucking sound and the stink of hydrogen sulfide, which smells like a truckload of rotten eggs, spread quickly from Ken Kirchoff's desk. Everyone around him held their nose and groaned and Miss Mauleke stopped explaining the problem on the board and asked what was going on. She was plenty strict and usually no one tried anything in her class. She sauntered back between rows to where the commotion was but by then the boys had the bottle re-corked and moving.

Everything calmed down and the hydrogen sulfide passed from hand to hand like borrowed money, slowly at first, with kids mentally counting the seconds, and then, when they knew time was about up, the bottle was zipping from kid to kid, under desks and across aisles and finally that light little pop warned you to plug your nose.

Everyone tried to look innocent and the game of nerve went on. Miss Mauleke marched around the room, she had to smell that terrible stuff, and tried to figure out what was going on right under her nose.

"Is someone ill back here?" she said, gazing around the room, and we couldn't prevent a short burst of laughter.

I knew that volatile gas would only stay corked so long and she would eventually catch someone and that someone could be me and I could be sitting in seventh period after school and I raised my hand.

"Miss Meyers," she said.

"May I go to the lavatory," I said.

Some boy whispered loudly, "Sandy's doing it," and an undercurrent of laughter spread and I was really embarrassed.

"Very well," Miss Mauleke said.

I scooted out the door and I heard the cork pop behind me. I waited in the girl's lavatory as long as I dared and then went back to the classroom. The bottle sat on Miss Mauleke's desk without a cork, the room smelled like a sewer, and Bob MacGregor, who had been caught red handed and didn't rat on anyone, had seventh period.

After school I hurried to the drugstore on Dunlap and called the home. Greta Spalding told me Mr. Shapiro was doing poorly and he couldn't have visitors. She was the kindest worker at the home and I believed her.

Finally over my cold on Friday, I felt like a yo-yo and someone was doing Around the World with me. I planned to go see Mr. Shapiro after school but I had a bad feeling in the pit of my stomach.

In study hall Patty Hogan passed me the "Bull Sheeter," a hand printed gossip sheet that Mike Birt made up whenever he had time. Mike had a great sense of humor and he was up on everything going on at Central. He hand-lettered it in narrow columns like newspaper print and he was really a good printer but it must have taken him hours.

I was reading and laughing to myself about D.B. Sandersen's trouble with stuck windows and faulty hearing aids, and a newly found poet laureate at Central, Jerry "Feathers" Douglas, but what really cracked me up was the mystery of the month: Why couldn't "Feathers" Douglas stand up in speech class? Then, jeepers, my heart jumped for joy when the paper included Sandy Meyer and Scott McFarland on a list of new couples walking the hallowed halls of Central.

I called the home right after school from the drugstore on Dunlap and Betty Bain told me Mr. Shapiro was sick and he couldn't have visitors. I asked if I could come Saturday and she told me it would probably be a week or more before I could see him. Like a slap in the face, I knew what I'd suspected all week; I'd given him my cold! I slammed down the phone and kicked the side of the phone booth. I wanted to scream. How could I be so stupid? And what was I doing to that poor man?

Friday night Scott and I went to *House Of Strangers* with Jerry and Sally and I thought it would be the story of my family. I loved movies. It was at the Highland where I'd seen every Saturday matinee since I was old enough to go by myself. I'd look forward all week to the serial and couldn't wait to see what would happen next and I loved the cartoons. I'd daydream about the time I'd come with a boyfriend and sit in the double seats and neck during the movie and there I was, with a boyfriend, as if my dreams were coming true, although we didn't sit in one of the double seats yet.

Jerry parked along the River Boulevard after we ate at the Flat Top and Scott and I had the backseat to ourselves.

There I was, having my perfect date, and I couldn't quit worrying about Mr. Shapiro. While Scott worked up the nerve to
cross that scary no man's land and kiss me, I kept thinking
Mr. Shapiro could be taking his last breath at that very
moment and I'd be the one who killed him.

Even though it was a little early, I didn't want to take any
chances. I asked Scott if he'd like to go to the Deb-Soko
Dinner Dance on December 27th, one of the biggest dances
of the year. He stammered for a minute, and I about died,
but then he said he would and he thanked me for asking
him. After only about two or three newsworthy topics at my
door step, he kissed me, but no matter how heavenly that
was, I tossed and turned most of the night in my sleepless
bedding.

Sunday afternoon I couldn't stand it any longer and I asked
my father if I could use the car. That in itself took a ton of
nerve but I was desperate. I never wanted to lie to my
parents but I couldn't tell him where I was going. It was as
much an excuse to be gone for the afternoon as it was to use
the car.

We had a 1941 Ford station wagon with wood siding on
the doors and back that my father treated like another member of the family. He'd found every excuse imaginable to put
off my getting a driver's license but the past summer I finally
got mine a year or two after my friends. He'd let me take the
station wagon on solo flights a few times but he was always
a nervous wreck by the time I got home with the car
unmangled and the engine still intact. He'd go out and fuss
around it as though he expected a door ripped off or the
grill missing.

He always said as long as we had the streetcars there was
no need to drive, that the streetcars were much cheaper and
safer, and the way he talked you'd think the war was still on
and you needed gas rationing coupons. He kept the station

wagon clean, polished and in the garage, and he usually took the streetcar to work. I didn't really mind that much. I never wanted to drive to sorority meetings or games or other school events because I always hoped to be offered a ride home by some neat boy.

After I helped my mother zip through the dinner dishes, I found my father in the living room, camped in his favorite green upholstered chair, reading the Sunday paper. I stood beside the matching chair like I was pleading my case in court. He'd gone on and on at the table about how terrible it was that the Communists had taken over China, as if they'd be coming down Highland Parkway any day now, and I knew he probably wasn't in the best mood, but I couldn't go another day without seeing Mr. Shapiro.

"It's my turn to drive," I said while my father's face filled with storm clouds. "A bunch of us girls are going to a movie downtown and it's no fun just meeting there when we all come from different directions on the streetcar and we'll probably get something to eat afterwards. Please, Dad."

"You want to drive *downtown?*" he said as if I'd asked to drive to Toledo.

He lowered the paper to his lap.

"Yeah, I'll be careful, the girls drive downtown all the time."

"Are you sure you're well enough to be going out?"

"Gee-whiz, yeah, I've been back at school since Thursday."

He frowned and cleared his throat.

"I don't think there's much gas in it."

"That's okay, the girls always chip in and put a dollar's worth in, maybe even more," I said and bounced a little on the balls of my feet.

"It's awful sloppy out right now with that recent snow," he said as he looked out the window to check weather conditions.

"I'll take it easy so it doesn't splash much."

"I really need to change the oil before we drive around much more."

My dad always changed the oil himself as if he didn't trust anyone else to do it right.

"I won't drive far, Dad, just a few miles."

I noticed my mother standing in the doorway with a slight smile on her face. My father glanced over at her and she nodded.

"Well . . . okay . . . but you be careful and get home before dark," he said as if he were resigning himself to never seeing his precious station wagon again, not to mention his daughter.

"Oh, thanks, Dad, I'll be super careful and we'll put gas in it and—"

"You needn't do that," he said and he laid his paper aside and pushed himself out of the chair. "I'll back it out of the garage for you."

After I picked up Jean I crossed the Ford Bridge and headed out Minnehaha Parkway and 50th. I drove pretty fast even though I was not yet well acquainted with the workings of the clutch. This was the deal: you had to take your left foot off the clutch and take your right foot off the brake and put your right foot on the gas pedal all in about one second and do it smoothly as my dad would say. When I didn't get the sequence just right the station wagon would either buck down the street like a horse or the engine would stop dead.

What scared me most was when I had to stop on a hill. By the time I'd take my foot off the brake and let out the clutch and give it some gas I was always rolling backwards and I really hated it when the car behind me would pull right up tight and not allow any leeway for back rolling. I roared the engine a few times and about snapped Jean's head off starting up at stop signs but I pulled up in front of the home safe and sound without a scratch on the station wagon if maybe a little wear on the gears.

Jean and I waited in the car until a couple about my parent's age headed into the home. I got out and followed them, but kept my distance. I waited about two minutes after they'd gone in and then slipped through the front door as quietly as I could. The couple and a nurse were half-way down the hall and I tiptoed behind them as quickly as I could. They turned in a room on the right and I hurried past.

I made it to Mr. Shapiro's room undetected and when I swooped in it was like getting kicked in the stomach. The room was all tidied up, the bed neatly made, but Mr. Shapiro wasn't there. What really scared me was that his wheelchair *was* there, which meant he was nowhere in the home. Had he died?

I stumbled and almost fell running up the hall. I found a young lady I'd never seen before, sitting at the desk in a light-green dress, sorting through old magazines.

"Hi, can you tell me where Mr. Shapiro is?" I shouted.

"Mr. Shapiro?" she said as if she'd never heard the name.

She had a cute friendly face, curled black hair and tiny little mouse ears.

"Yes, Mr. Shapiro, he's not in his room and it doesn't look like he's been there today and golly, I'm really worried."

"Are you part of Mr. Shapiro's family?"

"Yes, I'm his granddaughter."

"Have you had in the past two weeks or do you now have a cold or flu or other sickness?" she said as though she'd memorized it.

"Yes, I mean no, please, can you tell me where he's gone?"

"I haven't worked here very long," she said, "I just work weekends, but let me look."

She thumbed through a drawer of file folders and pulled one out. She opened it and scanned down the page.

"It says here that Mr. Shapiro went to the hospital on ah . . . Thursday, no, on Friday, December 2nd."

"But I called . . . does it say what time he went?"

"Looks like first thing in the morning, ambulance pickup at eight o'clock."

I'd talked to Betty Bain Friday afternoon and she hadn't told me a thing about it.

"What hospital?"

"Ah . . . here it is. Miller Hospital in Saint Paul."

"Thanks," I shouted and I dashed for the car.

Chapter 15

All the way across 50th and Minnehaha Parkway, Jean kept shouting things like Holy cow! and Watch out! and I knew I was driving too fast and I knew if I got a ticket I wouldn't be driving the station wagon until I was aged and friendless but I didn't care, I had to reach Mr. Shapiro while he was still breathing. I killed the engine twice and unintentionally peeled rubber several times in a way that would've made Steve proud.

We raced across the Ford bridge and I wheeled down Snelling to Grand and took Grand all the way downtown. I'd been to the Miller Hospital a lot to visit my mother and I didn't like it that it sat on the side of the steep hill not far from the Cathedral. I hated trying to parallel park but I found a level space on a side street and Jean shouted at me to run.

Inside I charged up to the reception desk where a stern-looking woman about my mother's age hung up a phone and looked up at me.

"I'm here to see Mr. Arnold Shapiro."

She thumbed through index cards in a box and pulled one above the others.

"Mr. Shapiro is in critical condition. Are you family?"

"Yes . . . I'm his granddaughter, I have to see him."

"Take the elevator to the third floor and check with the head nurse up there."

She pointed at the elevators and I hurried over and pushed the button. Several people were already waiting and the elevator didn't come and I saw a doorway marked STAIRWAY and I pushed through the door and ran the two flights to the third floor, sure that every second counted.

A nurse was drinking coffee at the counter in the center of the hallway.

"Hello, I'm Sandy Shapiro," I said, catching my breath, "and I just heard about my grandfather, Arnold Shapiro, and I have to see him."

The thin young nurse had a kind face and she sort of winced when I told her I was his granddaughter.

"He's not doing well . . . I don't know if he's even conscious, Sandy, let me check."

She whisked up the hall a few doors and into a room. I was praying as fast as I could and scolding myself. I'd come so close and then I'd blown it, given poor Mr. Shapiro my cold. How could I be so stupid!

The nurse came out of the room and I could tell by her expression that Mr. Shapiro was a goner. She took my hand in both of hers and I thought she was going to cry.

"He's in a coma, he's very weak," she said. "You're the only one who has come. Seems he keeps hanging on for someone, keeps saying She'll come, she'll come. The last time he was conscious he told me to take the life jacket, to put it on."

"He lost two of his kids in a drowning accident," I said.

"You can go in, talk to him, but he may not hear you, he's awfully weak."

She squeezed my hand and let go.

"Okay," I said and I hurried to the room.

Arnold Shapiro looked as if a vampire had sucked all the blood out of him, so pale and small in the high hospital bed. He lay in an oxygen tent and through the plastic he looked like a corpse on display in its coffin. I leaned over the bed and put my face right up to the tent so he could see me.

"Hello, Mr. Shapiro, it's Sandy."

He didn't move and his breathing sounded like the bathtub drain.

"Mr. Shapiro, it's Sandy, your granddaughter," I shouted. "I'm so sorry I gave you my cold, it's my fault you're in here, I feel horrible and I pray that you'll get well."

He didn't move, didn't blink, I was too late.

"Can you ever forgive me, Mr. Shapiro?" I shouted louder, "I'm so sorry, I didn't mean—"

His eyelids flickered and he opened his eyes. He turned his head slightly on the pillow so he could look straight at me. He didn't have his thick glasses on and I could see his normal-sized brown eyes floating in their salty sea. His lips moved but I couldn't hear anything.

"I'm so sorry I made you sick, I feel terrible," I shouted.

He strained to lift his head off the pillow and brought his lips up to the tent and I put my ear close to his mouth.

"Thank you," he said with a faltering voice, "you helped me get out of here."

"But I gave you my cold and—"

"Best gift I ever had."

It was like the movies and I had Lionel Barrymore dying in my arms and I couldn't bring myself to ask him. I couldn't take up his last minutes of life with the same old questions I'd pestered him with for months, questions he couldn't answer because he couldn't remember, and I let my search for my mother go.

"I figured you'd come," he said with a wheeze.

"They didn't tell me you were here or I would've been here sooner." I started to choke up. "You're going to get better and be back at the home in no time and we'll play Chinese checkers."

"Don't want to."

He embraced me with his eyes and I was trying not to cry. I'd never been with a dying person before and I didn't know what to say. He was tired of his life and I knew that going back to that home was worse than death for him.

"Listen carefully," he said as he struggled to breathe in violent, stabbing gasps.

I bent close to his face, pressing against the oxygen tent with my ear. With all his might he lifted his bobbing head off the pillow.

"The man who sold you to your parents was Myron Wilbershy." He gagged and tried to catch his breath. "He was a big clumsy man who kept wiping perspiration from his face with a hanky."

His head dropped back onto the pillow and he closed his eyes, but I could tell he was struggling, fighting to gather the strength to tell me more. He opened his eyes and strained to lift his head again.

"I think he was a jeweler . . . had one of those jeweler lenses on his glasses . . . small needlenose pliers and screw-drivers in a vest pocket."

He was blurring in the bed because I couldn't stop the tears in my eyes. His head fell back onto the pillow.

"You *remembered all along,*" I shouted, wiping my eyes on my jacket sleeve. "You remembered all along!"

He hurled the words from his dying throat.

"Was afraid . . . you wouldn't come . . . see me anymore if I told you . . . I'm sorry."

"It's okay, Mr. Shapiro, but you're my grandpa, I'll always come to see you."

I gently squeezed his arm under the blanket.

"Myron Wilbershy," he said, "W-i-l-b-e-r-s-h-y. Was about thirty-five . . . think he worked downtown . . . wouldn't tell me anything about himself."

"Oh, thank you, Mr. Shapiro, thank you, thank you."

He strained to lift his head off the pillow, fought for every inch with his scrawny neck and unshaven face.

"I hope you can find him," he said, gagging on his own death, the words raspy and broken, a voice out of a drowning heart.

I wanted to throw him some kind of a life jacket but I didn't know how. His head plopped back onto the pillow like a heavy stone, his eyes closed, as if he'd burned his last candle. I couldn't leave him like that, believing he was unwanted, a piece of rubbish on the human dung heap with no family or loved ones to wave good-bye. I leaned close to the oxygen tent and shouted as loudly as I could.

"I love you, Mr. Shapiro! you're my hero! you'll always be my hero!"

He didn't open his eyes, gave no sign he heard me. I pulled a chair up beside the bed and sat for most of an hour. The breath rattling through his chest sounded like a rusty porch swing, back and forth, in and out. The nurse came in and checked him and told me he might be like that for days.

I wandered around the hospital trying to find my way out, going up the stairs instead of down, but I gathered my senses enough to get a piece of notepaper from the nice nurse and write down the gift Mr. Shapiro hung on long enough to give me. MYRON WILBERSHY. I'd used one miracle to find Mr. Shapiro. Now I'd need another to find Myron Wilbershy, a man who might be my father. But that would have to wait. I couldn't look for anyone for a while.

Jean was reading magazines in the waiting room when I found the front door.

"How is he?" she said as she dropped a *Ladies Home Journal* and stood up.

"He's unconscious, in a coma."

"Will he live," she said as we pushed through the door and walked for the car.

"No," I said.

"Oh, gosh, that's too bad."

"No, it's what he wants, he wants to see his kids."

Arnold Shapiro died that night. But even though he wanted to die, he held on like a bulldog until he could tell me what I needed to know. That was when I really started to believe that through all the heartache and mysteries of life I was meant to find my mother and discover why she didn't keep me.

Arnold Shapiro, hang on to your hat,
You never should've ended up like that.

Chapter 16

The next week was the hardest of my life. I ached to tell my parents and friends what had happened, how bad I felt and only Jean knew and she was really swell. She even cried with me once on the way home from school. I didn't try to find out about Mr. Shapiro's funeral because I didn't want to see if his son Ivan showed up or if cows flew. I knew Mr. Shapiro would understand and I tried to believe that now he was happy with his boy and girl and they would forgive him for taking the only life jacket.

I still didn't know what Mr. Shapiro meant when he told me to make friends with an angel if I had the chance, that angels came in many disguises. Was Mr. Shapiro an angel? I didn't know but when my candle of hope was flickering out, he relit it. I wrote down every word he said before he died, I didn't want to forget a thing, and I kept it in my school note-book so my mother wouldn't accidentally come across it when she was tidying up my room.

When I got home Sunday it was dark and my dad was out pacing in our driveway, sure he'd never see the old station wagon again. He inspected the car with great relief and I wanted to tell him that cars and things don't matter much, but I didn't.

I called Miller Hospital Monday morning and they told me Mr. Shapiro never came out of the coma, that he died at eleven o'clock Sunday night. After school on Tuesday I went downtown to First National Bank and told Mr. Dale every-thing I knew about the checking account. It made me feel close to Mr. Shapiro, as though he were still around. Mr. Dale looked like an undertaker and he kept raising his bushy eyebrows the more I told him and on the way home I started to understand what Mr. Shapiro meant when he said the money didn't matter.

Scott invited me to the dance Saturday night and I almost turned him down, as if it would be a dishonor to Mr. Shapiro's memory to be going out and having fun and laughing when he was lying cold in the ground. But another part of me wanted to go out and have fun and live every minute with all the sizzle and feeling I could muster before my life was over and I'd be sitting in the waiting room like Mr. Shapiro, old and helpless with nothing to do but stink up the place and nowhere to go except into the grave. I told Scott I'd love to go. I talked Steve into asking Jean so she could live every minute too and not waste her precious life waiting for the time she could be with Dave.

Scott had his father's brand-new Kaiser, and we were eight with Cal and Lola. We girls acted kind of crazy and all but deserted the boys for a while. We danced the lindy together because the boys didn't know how, and we giggled and had more fun acting like grade schoolers. In the middle of the dance the girls put one shoe in a big pile on the dance floor and backed against the wall. Then the boys, who were waiting outside, dashed in and grabbed a shoe and that was the girl they danced with. Scott got Katie Mills' saddle shoe, a darling junior girl, and Dick Hermanson, a nifty senior, grabbed my loafer and danced with me. I kept track of Scott and Katie like a private eye, wishing I wasn't so jealous.

Towards the end of the night Scott and I danced and I think I scared him the way I was clinging to him and pressing my head against his cheek. I wanted to tell him about Mr. Shapiro and that every day is a gift and we shouldn't waste one minute of our years at Central.

Afterwards we ate at the drive-in and then Scott drove around for a while. I knew he wouldn't get up the nerve to park, especially with that slapstick combination of couples, but I didn't want to go home and I tried to think of something wild we could do because we were alive and we were young.

"Let's go knock on that crazy guy's door over on Summit," I said.

"The Runner? naw, it's too late, he'd be sound asleep, not tonight," they chimed in.

Steve looked at Lola. "You ever pull a trolley?"

"N-o-o-o, that sounds super," Lola said, "let's do it."

"Does it hurt anything?" I said.

"Naw," Jerry said, "they just hook it up and drive away."

"Let's do it," I said and everyone went for it.

Scott turned up Grand and found a Grand-Mississippi streetcar headed downtown.

"Oh no you don't," Cal said. "If we're going to pull a trolley, go over to Selby or Snelling. This is my dad's line."

Cal's dad was a streetcar motorman and Cal was pretty protective of his dad's line. Scott headed for Selby and I felt my throat go dry. Had I really overcome my chickenheart?

"I don't see why pulling that rope makes the streetcar stop," Jean said.

"It pulls the trolley off the cable," Steve said.

"There's a grooved wheel that runs along the electric cable," Cal said, "and that's where the streetcar gets its power. It's like unplugging your toaster."

"You really know all about them, don't you," Lola said.

"I ought to," Cal said, "I've heard it eleven million times."

"Gee, it sounds kind of scary," Jean said.

"That's what makes it fun," Lola said, snapping her gum.

"Some guys won't chase you," Jerry said, "but others will come like gangbusters."

"My dad chases every kid who pulls his trolley like they were Nazis or something," Cal said. "One night he chased a boy four blocks, leaving his empty streetcar dead on the tracks. The dumb kid was so scared he ran straight home. My dad marched up to the door and told the kid's father what he'd done, said he wanted to see the kid punished. The father found the kid hiding in his room and whaled the daylights out of him to my dad's satisfaction. When my dad got back to his streetcar, a stumblebum drunk was staggering around inside trying to find a light switch."

A streetcar came up Selby from downtown and Scott hurried ahead to the stop sign at Fairview and parked. We slipped out the right side of the car and ducked behind a parked truck, waiting for the streetcar to come to a full stop.

"Who's going to be first?" Cal said.

"We will," I said and I grabbed Scott's hand, not giving my sissyskin a chance to whisper in my ear.

Before the streetcar started to move, Scott and I came blazing out from behind the truck. I was laughing and Scott was yelling, "Grab the rope, grab the rope!"

As the streetcar turned onto Fairview I got hold of the rope and pulled but around the corner the streetcar picked up speed and I couldn't keep up.

"Aw, phooey, I almost had it," I said and we scrambled back into the car like a jail break.

But I'd done it, jumped off the high board, and I wanted to tell my dad.

Scott passed the streetcar when it turned onto Marshall and we raced down to the stop sign at Cleveland and parked. We crouched behind the car and watched Lola and Cal run for it, but she couldn't pull the rope hard enough and the streetcar took off. We all cheered her good try as we piled back into the Kaiser.

"What's really fun is to hit the same streetcar twice," Steve said. "A couple summers ago Cal and I stopped one three times on St. Clair and boy was that guy ever mad. The third time he came running bloody murder and we had to bomb all the way to Jefferson before he quit chasing us."

We had to chase the streetcar several blocks into Minneapolis, but Jean pulled the trolley and stopped the streetcar and I was so proud of her, the shortest one of us. When she jumped and got a hold of the rope, she was hanging there with all her weight off the ground and the trolley popped off the cable and the streetcar stopped dead and went dark.

"Run," Steve shouted, "run!"

Steve beat it across the street, but golly, Jean just stood there for a second, not knowing which way to run. The motorman came out the front door and Jean took off across someone's lawn, shrieking like a plucked chicken. The man stood there as though he couldn't believe a girl pulled his trolley and then the party-pooper took some of the fun out of it when he didn't chase her.

"I'll bet he'll never tell the other conductors that a girl nailed his streetcar," Cal said.

I didn't want to go home, I wanted to act crazy all night, to do something exciting and to laugh and play with my young friends who would one day sit in the waiting room of the morgue, though they never suspected. When I ended up there I wanted to remember that I ran while I could run and danced while the music played and sang my song while I had my voice.

"Someone To Watch Over Me" was playing on the radio and I could see Woody playing his saxophone with half his face eaten away with cancer and I didn't understand how he could be so brave. I didn't understand how we were all so brave. We wake from a dream and find ourselves on a journey in the forest to some unknown destination that beckons like home, and along the way we lose legs and arms, are eaten alive by disease, but we go on. We get old and are deserted and forget who we are, but we go on. Those we love are ripped from our arms, mothers and children and brothers, still we go on. We are so sick and nauseous and in pain we can't eat, but we go on. We find ourselves abandoned, betrayed, lost and bewildered, but we go on, we *do* go on. Why don't we just lie down beside the road and give up, lie down in the ditch and die? What is this magnificent thing within us that makes us go on?

Bravery!

Right then I felt really close to my friends and I wanted to hug them and thank them for being so brave and tell them to squeeze every drop out of every day they were alive.

Scott took Lola and Jean home first and he found the nerve to kiss me good-night, but no matter how swell that was, when the boys drove away I felt awfully mixed up and I didn't know what was going on inside of me. But I knew it was time to start looking for my father, Myron Wilbershy, and I was scared. I think I was afraid to find out who my father was and what kind of a person he might be to have sold me for $970.

Chapter 17

The next week of school was our last until after New Year's and every day I caught myself hurrying to my locker after sixth period to get my coat and catch the streetcar for Minneapolis. Then I'd remember Mr. Shapiro was dead. My friends kept asking what was wrong with me, said I didn't seem myself. I'd smile and fake it and say I was fine as my mother always did. I even caught myself thinking What would Amelia do? Only Jean knew, and sometimes I didn't know myself what was going on inside of me. Miraculously I had the name of my father on my tongue and all I needed to do was find him. I'd find myself short of breath and forgetting where I was going.

Tuesday afternoon Jean and I began the search in earnest at her house. Her mother was working at the Red Cross and we had the place to ourselves.

"And you checked with Minneapolis information?" Jean said as we sat cross-legged on her big bed.

"Twice. There's no listing for Myron Wilbershy in Saint Paul or Minneapolis. I couldn't even find another Wilbershy, some relative who might know what happened to him."

"He could be dead," Jean said and bit her lip, as if she didn't want to hurt me.

"I know, or he could have moved away, he could be living in Borneo."

"What else did Mr. Shapiro tell you?"

I pulled my notebook out from under the books I'd lugged home.

"I wrote it all down that night, every word," I said.

I flipped to the page I was looking for.

"Mr. Shapiro said he thought he was a jeweler, that he had one of those jeweler's lenses on his glasses," I said, "and he had a small needlenose pliers in his vest, whatever that is, and several tiny screwdrivers."

"A jeweler?"

"That's what Mr. Shapiro thought, and for some reason he thought he worked downtown."

"Maybe he still does," Jean said.

"Oh, and here, he said he was a big clumsy man who kept wiping sweat off his face with a hanky."

"That could be anyone in North America," Jean said and then raised her eyebrows and shrugged. "Sorry."

"He thought Myron Wilbershy was about thirty-five years old."

"That's it?" Jean said.

"That's all he could tell me before he died."

"So Wilbershy would be around fifty-two," Jean said.

"I figured between fifty and fifty-five, give or take a few years."

We sat there facing each other for a minute and then I remembered.

"One more thing. A few weeks ago, when Mr. Shapiro pretended he was remembering little scraps to string me along, he said he didn't like the man. I remembered that. I thought it was funny that if he couldn't remember anything about the adoption that he'd remember he didn't like the man."

"That doesn't help much," Jean said. "We look for a big, clumsy, fifty-year-old jeweler we don't like much."

We laughed.

Jean bounced off the bed and ran downstairs and I could feel the sadness coming back. She ran up the stairs and plunked down on the bed with the telephone book.

"We'll check every jewelry store in town," she said. "Maybe he still works for one of them."

She started flipping through the book, and gosh, I suddenly felt a chill and my hands got clammy and I didn't know what I was afraid of but I was scared.

"What if we get him on the phone?" I said. "What do I say?"

"I don't know, tell him who you are."

"Oh, keen. Hello, Mr. Wilbershy, I'm the daughter you got rid of in 1933 and like a pet skunk I've come back, how are you?"

"Well, what do you want to do?" Jean said, looking up from the phone book.

"I want to see him first."

"*See* him!"

"Yeah, see him, see what he looks like, see how I feel about him."

"Gad, that sounds kind of crazy," Jean said.

"Well you wouldn't know, you've *always had* your father!"

She shut the phone book and turned her face and I felt terrible for snapping her head off. I didn't know what had gotten into me but Jean and I fought sometimes and we always got over it.

"I'm sorry," I said, "I'm scared. What if he turns out to be an ice-pick murderer or a rhinoceros?"

Jean looked at me for a moment and then broke out laughing.

"I can see where it would be scary," she said. "But did you ever think that maybe their circumstances changed and they regretted losing you and they've been looking for you?"

"No . . . I figured if they got rid of me they sure didn't want me back. But I daydreamed that a lot, that they made a mistake and they loved me and they were looking for me. That would be nice."

"You never know, at the time they thought it was best for you to have a good mother and father, but maybe they've been lonesome for you ever since."

She opened the phone book again and started flipping through the pages.

"We'll make a list of all the jewelry stores in Saint Paul and we'll walk into every one of them until we find him. And

if he turns out to be a Nazi or an orangutan you can forget
the whole thing."

"You'll go with me?" I said.

"Jeepers, yeah, I might sell tickets."

I pushed her over backwards on the bed and I wanted to
tell her what a good friend she was. I told her my latest
rhyme and we chanted it over and over together.

Myron Wilbershy, I'm so high,
If you're not my father, I'll just die.

Jean and I didn't get downtown that week with school still
going. We each belonged to several clubs that volunteered to
decorate the large Christmas tree in front hall after school
and we did that Wednesday. That night my father was really
upset at dinner because the paper said the company was getting rid of the streetcars and replacing them with buses. My
dad went on and on about the crooks who were ruining the
finest streetcar system in the world and he was plenty mad.
He said he'd start driving to work and I thought it must be
pretty serious for him to go that far. I couldn't imagine what
the city would be like without streetcars.

I was worried about my mother; she didn't look well and I
was afraid she'd be sick again. When I'd ask her what she
wanted for Christmas she'd say Just a smile and a few kind
words. She'd do that every Christmas and it didn't help
much with my shopping list. My folks let me cash a ten
dollar war bond when I told them I needed money to shop
even though my dad always gave me money to buy gifts.
I always felt it wasn't fair for him to give me money to buy
him a present.

It was a tradition that after assembly on the Thursday
before Christmas vacation, students gathered in front hall to
sing carols around the Christmas tree. We filled the front hall
and then some, up both stairways, and it was fun singing the
Christmas songs and right in the middle of it all I started

choking up. Suddenly I realized that my high school days were almost over and all of us would go our separate ways and my throat filled and I couldn't sing. Tears ran down my face and I felt so close to the kids who were singing, they were my family, and I never wanted to leave them, and I wished I could stay there, singing around the beautiful tree, forever.

In the school cafeteria I usually sat at the table where all the Debs ate and Scott sat with his friends at a table in the lunchroom balcony and sometimes, like on Friday, I'd catch him looking at me and I'd get so excited I couldn't eat. We played Wilson in our first conference basketball game on Friday night at Hamline field house and the boys won a heart-stopping game, 54 to 52, and they were really happy because Wilson had the tallest team in the city.

Jerry had the car and after the game we went downtown to Mickey's Diner, a replica of a railroad dining car. Someone had written "Kilroy was here" on the side of the diner, the slogan American GIs left all over Europe and the South Pacific, and I thought of Jean's brother. Had he written "Kilroy was here" on the bottom of the English Channel?

We sat on the red swivel stools at the long counter and played the jukebox and ate grilled cheese sandwiches and I had a chocolate malt, though it wasn't doing any good. A wino slumped on a stool at the end of the counter, a dirty old unshaven man with the shakes. Jerry went into his act, pretended he was having a fit, the way he often did around such men, though he never let on to the winos that they were the cause of his shenanigans. Sally and Scott played along and pretended to hold Jerry down as his face bulged and his body straightened like a board while he muttered, "I'm gonna get that mick."

They were laughing and having fun, but I saw Mr. Shapiro sitting there, struggling to keep his balance and not fall off the stool, trying to get some food down before his stomach would pitch it back onto the floor, fighting to stay alive in his tormenting nightmarish world, and I couldn't play along. Was I becoming a killjoy? Was that what growing up meant, taking everything seriously and missing the joy and laughter of life?

Jerry calmed down as though the seizure had passed and they didn't seem to notice I hadn't taken part in the charade. We ate our grilled cheese sandwiches and played "Red Roses for a Blue Lady" and "I Don't Care If The Sun Don't Shine" on the jukebox and were entertained by the strange variety of night life showing up at the diner.

I hung back and when the other three were out the door I slid down to the end of the counter and hugged the little wino. He smelled like a brewery and I couldn't think of anything to say so I just hugged him real hard. He felt frail and bony like Mr. Shapiro. What heartache and tragedy brought him to that stool in Mickey's Diner that night when once he'd been a bright-eyed little boy?

When I let go he regarded me through bloodshot eyes with an expression of utter confusion.

"Can you spare a dime?" he said.

I reached in my coat pockets with both hands and found a dime in one and a quarter in the other, thanks to my mother's constant admonition to never leave the house without enough to call home. I put the thirty-five cents in his grubby hand.

"God bless ya," he said.

Scott had come back for me and was standing in the doorway with a frown on his face. I turned for the door and had a crazy thought. Could that filthy little man be an angel? He sure had a great disguise.

"What were you *doing?*" Scott said with shock in his voice and I could tell he didn't approve of wino hugging. "Do you know him?"

I took Scott's arm and we joined the Friday-night bustle on 8th Street.

"He might be my father," I said.

Chapter 18

Jean and I didn't launch our search on Monday because she was feeling punk and getting over a cold and I couldn't work up the nerve to go alone. Tuesday was wintry and blustery and we bundled up in scarves and overshoes and winter coats and caught the streetcar for downtown. We planned our strategy on the way.

If a jewelry store had a woman up front we'd simply ask if Myron Wilbershy worked there. If she said No, we'd be out the door. If she said Yes, I'll get him for you, we'd say Oh, no, that isn't necessary. We just wanted to make sure we were in the store a friend recommended, said Myron Wilbershy was a salesman there. And then we'd let the woman show Jean engagement rings because she was going to get engaged when her boyfriend came back from the Army and I'd drift to the door and out. Then Jean would thank the woman and leave, and we'd watch the store until Myron showed his face. I didn't know for sure what I'd do next.

If a salesman was up front, Jean would go in alone and go through the engagement routine and try to get the salesman's name. If we found him that way, she'd come out and tell me we'd hit the jackpot. Jean wasn't very keen on the engagement story, said she was too nervous, but I told her to just pretend she was getting engaged to Dave and she'd do just fine. I had the feeling we'd find him that day and I could hardly stay in my seat as we approached downtown.

We got off at Seven Corners and walked back up 7th Street for several blocks, up one side and back the other. We found one jewelry store. We stood outside and stared through the frosted window like little kids peering into a candy store with no money in their mittens. We could see our reflection in the glass, Mutt and Jeff, bundled against the frigid wind, looking like refugees. Inside a woman behind a glass case showed jewelry to a grey-haired man in an expensive-looking top coat. With the trembles I had when I stepped out onto Steve's running board I pushed through the glass door.

I drifted casually along the glass display counters, gazing at bracelets and necklaces and watches, and Jean stuck to me like lint. The saleslady smiled and nodded as if she would take care of us in turn. I was rehearsing my question when a man appeared from the back, a balding medium-built man with a jeweler's lens attached to his glasses.

"Good morning, girls, may I help you?" he said with a buttery voice.

For the moment I forgot what we were going to do if it was a man. Then I remembered I wasn't going to show my face. I turned my eyes to the floor and nudged Jean, who was almost standing in my overshoes.

"We just stepped in to get warm," I heard her say and I couldn't believe my ears.

"Oh, that's fine," he said, "it's nasty out there today."

A young couple bustled into the store and he pranced over to wait on them.

"What are you *doing?*" I whispered.

"I couldn't remember what to say."

We hurried out of the store into winter's blast. I hunched down in my coat and leaned into the wind as we headed towards downtown.

"That could have been him," I said.

"He wasn't big enough, he was too young, and I liked him."

We crossed at Seven Corners, laughing, and started down Kellogg Boulevard. We covered Kellogg quickly, only finding one jewelry store before we reached the bridge over the railroad yards that separated downtown from the East Side. There was a saleslady up front and we had to wait behind Christmas shoppers but she didn't know any Myron Wilbershy. I realized that if we didn't find him downtown, we'd have to look on the East Side and South Saint Paul and West Saint Paul and I was freezing.

We cut over a block and started back along 4th Street. After a few fumbling tries we were getting our lines down and Jean was warming up to the idea of pricing engagement rings. I got excited on our way back down 4th Street when we'd found a bulky man in a store who wore glasses and who could be in his fifties. Jean went in and I watched her giving him her spiel. He brought out a tray of rings and pointed out things to her. I couldn't see the man very well from the street but my heart was thumping and I allowed myself to believe that he could be my father, right there in Saint Paul all those years.

Then Jean smiled and nodded and turned for the door. I walked down the sidewalk a ways so we couldn't be seen from inside, just in case. Bundled Christmas shoppers were ducking in and out of stores, moving briskly along the frigid streets. Jean looked around and spotted me and hurried over.

"No sale," she said and I felt little flakes of hope flutter to the ground with the lightly falling snow.

We worked our way down 4th Street, foot by foot, store by store, and then battled the north wind over to 5th Street. I looked at my watch and was surprised that it was one forty-five.

"I'm starved," I said, "let's eat."

"I know a place," Jean said and she led me over Wacouta to 7th Street and the Gopher Bar and Grill. It squatted on the corner and I didn't think it looked like much of a place to eat, and certainly no place for two unescorted girls.

"You want to eat in *there?*" I said as we crossed 7th.

"You'll like it."

"Do they have chocolate malts?"

"Something better," Jean said.

Two rough-looking men in winter work clothes barged out the door, laughing and braying as if they'd had a few too many.

Inside, above a long bar, a large picture of a plump nude woman hung and the place was decorated with a hodge-podge of sports pictures and memorabilia, including three deer heads. Plain unvarnished customers jabbered noisily at plain unvarnished tables, a jukebox played "Riders In The Sky," and at the back a grill was smoking like a campfire. It felt warm and cozy and I smelled something good cooking, but I wondered what on earth we were doing there. Out of a couple dozen customers there were only four females that I could see and that included us and the waitress. Jean found an empty table and claimed it. I took off my scarf and settled next to her.

"Have you been here before?" I said.

"Yeah."

She pulled off her coat and tossed it on an empty chair. I slipped out of mine and noticed a little woman sitting in the far corner chain-smoking. She had the face of an old prize-fighter.

"Some kind of art," I said and nodded at the nude.

"Yeah, Miss Bellows, casting her pearls before the swine."

We were both cracking up when a chubby waitress bounced over to our table wearing a cheerful smile and a short skirt.

"What'll you have?" she said while chewing gum lickety-split.

"Two coney dogs and two cokes," Jean said without batting an eye.

"Comin' right up," she said and before I could protest she was gone.

"Coney dogs?" I said.

"You'll love 'em, coney dogs right out of heaven."

"When were you here before?" I said.

"A long time ago."

With her eyes she followed someone behind me.

"Look," she said and nodded.

A large oafish man trudged in the door and covered a stool at the bar. He wore glasses, was at least fifty, and filled a baggy suit and tie. We eyeballed him, he seemed to fit our skimpy description of Myron Wilbershy. He ordered a beer and glanced at us. I instinctively ducked my face and turned to Jean.

"It could be him," she said, "I don't like him."

We both laughed and then we chanted:

Myron Wilbershy, I'm so high,
If you're not my father, I'll just die.

"Here ya go," the waitress said and she plunked down two coney dogs on a paper plate and two bottles of Coke.

Jean picked up her coney dog and looked at me.

"Here's one for Don," she said and she took a big bite.

I was momentarily taken back, that she mentioned her dead brother like that out of the blue. I picked up my Coney Island, bulging with chopped onions and meat sauce and topped with brown mustard, and I nodded at Jean.

"Here's one for Don."

I sunk my teeth in and Jean was right, it was like heaven. The mingled aromas melted in my mouth and I thought I'd never tasted anything so delicious. We ate like lumberjacks.

"They were Don's favorite," she said with her mouth full. "He used to bring me here."

"He brought you *here!*"

"This was our secret place, no one else in our family knew. Ever so often he'd say let's go get a Coney Island. We'd talk about all kinds of stuff and I could tell him everything and he never bawled me out or scolded me but he'd give me good advice about things."

"Do you still miss him?"

"Every day . . . he was my best friend."

The waitress came by and Jean called out to her.

"Two more, please." She looked at me. "Okay?"

"Okay."

Jean didn't talk for a few minutes and I could tell she was thinking about her brother. Out of the corner of my eye I kept track of the large clumsy man at the bar. He was enjoying his beer and smoking a cigar and I hoped he was a regular customer.

"Did you know that Don joined the Army before he had to?" Jean said.

"No, I didn't."

"He told me right here, eating coney dogs, that he was going to join up. He didn't want me to tell anyone, said he'd wait until it was a good time to break it to the folks. He joined four or five months before he'd have been drafted. I begged him to wait but he said he wanted to do his share, he wanted to fight for freedom."

She choked up, and I glanced at the little worn-out woman in the corner necking with her cigarette.

"He died landing at Normandy, he never reached the beach."

"Oh, gosh, Jean, I didn't know, I'm sorry."

"If he'd waited until his number came up, the war would've been about over, he might never have gone overseas . . . I wish he'd waited . . . I wish he was here right now."

Jean banged her fist down on the table, almost knocking over the coke bottles. People glanced our way.

"He never even got to fight. I wish he could have fought, even for a few hours. After all that training and hard work he wanted to help, to fight those filthy Germans. Jeez, Sandy, I hate Germany and all those rotten Germans. I hate them!"

"Here ya go," the jolly waitress said as she delivered two more coney dogs.

"Pardon me," I said, "but do you know that large man over at the bar?"

She glanced over at the row of men bellying up to the bar.

"You mean Ralph? Ya, he's in here every day, works at the paper, why?"

"Oh, I thought it was someone I used to know," I said. "Do you happen to know a man named Myron Wilbershy?"

"Wilbershy? No, don't think so," she said.

"Do you remember Don Daley?" Jean said. "He used to come in here during the war and eat coney dogs, a good-looking high school boy."

"No, I don't remember him, but maybe it was before I worked here," she said.

"He died at Normandy, he was my brother, he never reached the beach."

"Oh . . ." The waitress frowned. "That's really tough, hon."

She scooted away and I picked up the coney dog and I had a crazy thought: Would Mr. Shapiro's life jacket have saved Jean's brother? I looked at the hurt in Jean's face and I changed the subject.

"I wonder if that's the guy who took our picture," I said.

"What picture?"

"Oh, when I was in fifth grade at Ramsey a bunch of us were making pyramids on the lawn after school. We had one four layers high, you know, everyone on their hands and knees, and I was the skinniest so I got to be on top. Gosh, there were ten of us: Cal, Marlene Helland, Les Wade, Pat Rydeen, Georgia Carey, Jim Dudley . . . we were laughing and shaking and ready to come down in a big heap when a man hurried over and told us to hold it. He took our picture and said he was from the paper and it would be in the *Pioneer Press*. We kids watched the paper every day for a month, told our teacher we were going to be in it, and we never were. I'm still mad at the paper."

"Does Ralph over there look like the guy?" Jean said and brightened up some.

"I don't remember."

I picked up the coney dog and paused.

"For Don," I said and I bit off a mouthful.

"That day he told me he was joining the Army he said Every time you come here have one for me and when I come back we'll clean them out of dogs."

"Do you come here a lot?" I said.

"The first time it took me over two years to get up the nerve. I'd plan to bring someone with me because I was so young to be going in a bar, and then I'd think I ought to go alone. I'd bounce back and forth and keep putting it off."

"I'd have come with you," I said.

"I know. It's too hard still. I've come a few times. I always have two, one for me and one for Don."

We worked the street until dark and then caught a cozy streetcar for home. We finished most of 5th Street but found no one who knew Myron Wilbershy. I never realized there were so many jewelry stores. We were bushed and had been chilled to the bone. I thanked Jean for her help and we laughed at some of the crazy stuff that happened. When she hopped off at Watson I watched her bundling down the street through the snow for home. To watch her, out horsing around with her friends, hanging from the back of a moving streetcar, pulling a trolley, who'd ever guess that inside she was bleeding for her lost brother.

Chapter 19

I couldn't believe the excitement cascading through my body, feeling I was close to something, something good and happy and bright. I still found it hard to believe the miracle that happened that night in Miller Hospital, but when Mr. Shapiro remembered my adoption from his deathbed, I secretly believed I'd find my father and mother by Christmas, sort of a Christmas present from God. But though Jean and I had covered most of the jewelry stores down-town, we hadn't found hide nor hair of Myron Wilbershy. It was like trying to find a ghost, a man who existed in 1933 but now was only a shadow from Mr. Shapiro's mind, and that shadow wasn't much to go on, and that mind was old and moth-eaten. But I had a feeling, a good feeling, and I woke up every day with high expectations.

One of the Christmas traditions in my family was picking out a tree. Like clockwork, on the 22nd of December, after we'd eaten our supper, the three of us would go out and find a Christmas tree. As far back as I can remember, we all got to put our two cents in about which tree, and it wasn't about finding one with a perfect shape. We'd pick a tree that needed us, one that undoubtedly wouldn't make it into any-one's home and therefore miss its reason for growing up. It always surprised me because my mother was so fussy about other things, wanting everything to be more or less perfect and lovely. So we'd end up with some real doozies, lop-sided, crooked, skinny runts, and I'd notice the salesman looking at us as if we were the three blind mice. But I could tell that my parents, from something in their past, felt good about doing it this way.

My dad would lay old blankets on the roof of the station wagon, not to scratch the finish, and he'd tie the dog of a tree on as if we were driving to Argentina. Everything went according to tradition Thursday night but the happiness had been sucked out of it. Before we left, my mother had to rush to the kitchen sink where she lost part of her supper. She washed it down and told us she felt fine, but when I looked in the sink a clot of fresh blood stuck in the drain.

When we got home my dad attached the stand to the tree out in the garage while my mother and I moved furniture to make room in the corner of the living room, in front of the big windows where our tree could stand proud and show off as one of the chosen. My dad brought the orphan in and set it up and we gave it water and welcomed it to our home. As the lopsided tree thawed it exhaled its fragrant aroma, as if it were coming alive again after being dead, and its unforgettable pine scent carried memories of all my other Christmases.

I remembered when I was a little girl and my father had brought a tree home after I was asleep. I woke in the morning to the aroma of a pine forest, like smelling the coming of promises and hopes and dreams. I jumped out of bed and raced down the stairs to behold the magical tree I had already seen with my nose. I loved that wild fragrance and Thursday night I left the door to my bedroom open so I wouldn't miss any of it.

But I couldn't fall asleep, worrying about my mother. I'd missed seeing Scott all week and I remembered the Soko-Deb dinner dance just two days after Christmas and I couldn't wait. I was feeling good about Scott and I didn't want to jinx us but we'd been going out for almost three months and that was a record for me.

Lying under the covers in my darkened room, I tried to visualize Myron Wilbershy from Mr. Shapiro's skimpy description. I wanted to believe I would find him. Before I fell asleep I remember smelling the aroma of pine, tiptoeing up the stairs like hope.

Christmas Eve was hard. My dad and I tried to make it a happy time for my mother but we could tell she was struggling against her pain and nausea no matter how hard she tried to hide it. We had our usual candlelight dinner: ham, au gratin potatoes, string beans and pumpkin pie, which was catered by Ramaleys. My dad and I did the serving and clearing while we chattered like squirrels as if my mother's pain would rush in if we allowed one moment of silence. Even though I'd been a bona fide member of the Clean Plate Club all through the war, I was too upset to finish my Christmas dinner and what I did eat settled in my stomach like spoiled fish.

When we were done and the dishes stacked in the kitchen, we hauled out the lights and balls and went to work on our misfit of a tree. My mother had to leave the room several times and my dad and I could hardly look at each other. She directed the decorating from her favorite chair and we all went through the motions as if everything were hunky-dory.

When it was time to go to church, my dad said he was really bushed and that maybe we would skip it and just stay home. We pretended we believed him and we sat around the lit tree with the other lights in the house turned off. My mom put a record on the phonograph with Christmas carols and my eyes were filling with tears as we talked about old times as if this could be our last Christmas together. I thought of Jean's brother and I realized that every Christmas could be our last together.

My dad made a big thing about hanging our stockings over the fireplace, like he always did. Before they went upstairs, my mom gazed at the Christmas lights and wondered out loud what it would be like for Amelia that night, in a dungeon, believing she was forgotten? My dad helped her up the stairs, they'd sleep together. I sat on the carpet by the tree for a while and my head and heart were spinning. I thought of Scott and wished he'd called. He was never out of my thoughts and I knew I was in love with him, hopelessly in love.

I wondered where Myron Wilbershy was spending Christmas, if he was alive, and I remembered Mr. Shapiro and Elsie. Had she taken a snapshot of her Christmas, gathered with the family she couldn't remember? I thought of the wino sitting in Mickey's diner. Was he spending Christmas Eve under some bridge? And then, though the house was silent, I could hear Woody playing his saxophone, far off in the distance, "Someone To Watch Over Me," and I couldn't erase the vision of the blood clot in the kitchen drain.

My mother seemed better in the morning, she had good color in her face and we went downstairs to see if Santa had come. Our socks were full of candy bars and gum and tooth brushes and apples and silver dollars and my dad's was overflowing onto the mantel because we all thought my mother wouldn't be up to filling his sock as usual so all three of us did.

After a big breakfast that my dad cooked, we sat around the tree and opened presents. I got a luscious pink cashmere sweater from my folks and I held it up to the mirror and wished I could fill it with more than radishes. The gift my mother seemed to enjoy the most was a box I'd wrapped filled with cut squares of paper with kind words on them, and one snipped out of a magazine with a big smile. The squares had words like I love you, You're the best mom in the world, You're beautiful. She really laughed, it was no act, and I felt good.

I gave my dad some warm dress gloves and a wool scarf but the gift I enjoyed giving the most was a nifty chrome guffer's knob. Once he told me about driving around when he was a kid and using a guffer's knob on his jalopy. He hooted when he saw it and went right out to the garage and bolted it to the station wagon's steering wheel.

Monday, Jean and I searched the jewelry stores on 7th Street and north towards the Capitol. We didn't find a trace of Myron Wilbershy. What worried me most was I could tell Jean was wearing down and giving up.

"He's probably in Buffalo," she said on the way home, "or in some graveyard."

On Tuesday the Soko-Deb dinner dance was only hours away and I wasn't half ready. Scott had called Monday night and told me we'd be doubling with Cal and Katie Mills, a pretty blonde junior.

I'd had my hair in rollers most of the day and with a few hours before Scott arrived, I got my mother's sun lamp and lay under it on my bed. I wanted my face and bare shoulders to have some color like they did in the summer.

The pain woke me! I'd fallen asleep. I sprang out of bed, my shoulders and face on fire. When I looked in my dresser mirror I was horrified. My face was bright red, my neck and chest down to my slip. I'd fried my face! I grabbed a jar of Noxzema and smeared it over the burn. It hurt to blink, it hurt to move my mouth, I looked like a tomato, a ripe plump tomato. I was afraid if I smiled the tomato would split.

Scott would be at the door before long. I couldn't show up at the dinner dance like this. I had to call and tell him what happened and miss the dance! I started to cry but that hurt too much. I put my hair in a shower cap and stood in a cold shower, letting the water run over my face and it hurt and felt good at the same time. Out of the shower I covered my face with Noxzema again. When I thought my mother would have a cow she was unusually calm, thought I ought to stay home, but I knew she didn't want me getting serious with Scott and I knew this was a big and important date for us.

I fixed my hair and patted the Noxzema off my face. When I stepped into my pale-blue formal and stood in front of the mirror, I thought I'd scream. I wanted to be so pretty for Scott and instead I was a baked eggplant. I had hoped he

might ask me to go steady that night at some romantic
moment, like in the movies, and I remembered to clip my
Deb sorority pin on my formal so we could exchange pins.
But who'd want to go steady with an eggplant? I wanted to
run down to the river and crawl into my cave.

Scott came to the door looking handsome in his double-
breasted suit and blue tie and he was swell about my sun-
burned face. I told him I was sorry and he said I looked fine
and he gave me a white gardenia to go in my hair. When we
got to the car, Cal busted out laughing and said I looked like
a boiled lobster and it helped, they all broke out laughing,
and I tried to but it hurt too much. I felt like a zombie
because I had to talk without moving my lips.

At the dance I managed better than I'd hoped, most kids
just said Hi and tried not to gawk. Except for the pain I was
doing all right. We sat at round tables in the St. Paul Hotel's
main ballroom and ate a delicious prime rib meal. I should
say they ate a delicious prime rib meal; my face hurt too
much to chew and Scott had no problem eating mine. When
they were done eating the band started to play and kids
began to dance. Scott sat there visiting with some of the
boys and I didn't want a repetition of the Homecoming
dance so I told him dancing wouldn't hurt my face and he
got the hint. But he held me like a fragile china vase while
we danced and I was afraid he wasn't having much fun.

Once Cal danced with me and I told him how miserable I
felt and how I'd ruined that lovely romantic night with Scott
and Scott was dancing with Katie and I was so jealous
because he was holding her closer than he'd held me.

Scott's parents were chaperones at the dance and towards
the end of the evening Mr. McFarland came over and asked
me to dance as if he were making up for his son's inatten-
tion. I had blisters on my chin and cheeks and I was oozing
from my face and I'd made several trips to the rest room and
dabbed my sunburn with Kleenex, but what could I do?

He took my hand and led me out onto the dance floor
and swept me into his arms and I tried to follow. He was an
excellent dancer and he held me tightly and my face was up
against his white tux jacket. I tried to hold my head away
but I couldn't. I was oozing onto Mr. McFarland's tuxedo
and it was a fitting end to that night of doom. When he
brought me back to our table I glanced at his white jacket. It
had a wide pinkish smear and I was mortified.

We drove across Minneapolis to the Rainbow Cafe and I
recognized the familiar store fronts and used car lots I
passed going to visit Mr. Shapiro. I watched for jewelry
stores, knowing I'd have to start searching in Minneapolis
soon. I felt like an orphan, as if I didn't belong anywhere or
to anyone. Scott was wonderful and kind and polite and a
million miles away. We laughed and joked and goofed
around and I hoped he was having fun. The dinner dance I'd
looked forward to for so long with such high hopes was a
disaster!

Scott gently kissed me good-night but it was like kissing
your uncle. I limped into the house with my Deb pin still
fastened to my formal and my hope wilting with my
gardenia.

Chapter 20

Tom Bradford was having a New Year's Eve party and I hoped Scott would call. Jean and I covered every last foot of downtown Saint Paul on Wednesday and Thursday but we tried to have fun doing it and we had coney dogs at the Gopher Bar & Grill. Jean didn't turn sad or anything even though we each had one for her brother Don who never reached the beach at Normandy. When I suggested we try the East Side on Friday, Jean said she had other things to do and she couldn't go with me. I didn't blame her. Myron Wilbershy was like a phantom, maybe only a figment of Mr. Shapiro's imagination.

I called Jean late Friday afternoon and asked her if she was going to Tom's party. She was hurting. She was going to try to spend New Year's eve with Dave, but at the last minute his parents insisted he go with them over to Wisconsin to visit relatives. She said she was going to stay home and sulk but I convinced her to go to the party with me instead; there would be plenty of guys without dates.

Tom lived on Summit at Saratoga and the big three-story house was crawling with kids. I was sure Scott would be there and my face had healed and looked nice and brown and I wore my new pink cashmere sweater, though I certainly didn't do it proud.

"If it bothers you so much, use cheaters," Jean said on the streetcar.

"No," I said, "that's false advertising. A boy gets up his nerve to caress you and finds sponge rubber, I'd be mortified."

"Don't worry about it, you're a doll," she said.

"Easy for you to say, you've got breasts."

Tom's parents were home so there was lots of food and pop but no drinking and the house was bouncing. I went from room to room and in each room there were kids doing something crazy: singing, playing charades, dancing, but no sign of Scott. Donny Cunningham shadowed me from room to room and I was in a goofy mood so I convinced him to dance with me. He barely came up to my shoulders and I could tell he felt foolish at first but he was a good dancer and we started doing the boogie-woogie and everyone was laughing and clapping and Donny puffed up like a rooster. He even seemed a little taller.

Around eleven I told Jean that maybe Scott was sick because he'd sure be at Tom's party if he could. Then, like a sledge hammer to the rib cage, Scott and Katie Mills came bouncing into the house, laughing and holding hands like an old married couple. I couldn't make myself breathe. My stomach rolled over and didn't come back up. I watched them for a minute as they shouted to friends, they'd been to a movie, and then I ducked into a bathroom. I was sure I was going to throw up. I knelt by the toilet bowl for a while and then someone was knocking on the door.

I had to get out of there. Jean said she'd come with me but I knew she could get a ride home with some of our friends and I told her to stay. It was cold and I started walking and I didn't know where I'd go, or care. I wanted to go down to the river and crawl into my cave and seal the entrance. I listened for the call of a crow, but they roosted silently at night. Was God sleeping? Then I realized I wasn't far from Cal's apartment and he hadn't been at the party. I hurried down Summit and cars were honking and I figured it was midnight, 1950, and I didn't give a hoot.

I turned at Wheeler and cut down the alley and I could see a light in the kitchen. I tiptoed up the back stairway and quietly knocked, in case his parents were asleep. I waited. The door opened and Cal stood there in stocking feet with his shirt unbuttoned and I realized I'd caught him on the way to bed.

"Hi, Bean, can I talk to you a minute?" I said.

"Yeah, sure."

I slipped into the kitchen and Cal closed the door.

"What's the matter?" he said.

I sagged into a chair at the table.

"You're my best friend, Bean, you've always been, and I feel so bad. I was at Tom's and Scott showed up with *Katie.*"

"Oh, gosh . . . I'm sorry . . . maybe she asked him."

"No, I found out, *he* asked her. It's only been four days since the dinner dance and then . . ."

Cal sat at the table with me and I pulled off a glove and saw my terrible fingernails and I slipped the glove back on.

"Remember how your tongue was stuck to the fence?" I said.

"Oh, golly, yeah, I'll never forget how—"

"That's how it feels, only it's my heart. I need someone to pour bean soup over my heart so it won't be stuck on Scott."

"Boy, I wish I could, Sand."

"I wish you could too, it really hurts, it really hurts."

We sat there for a minute and I tried not to think about Scott and Katie back at the party together.

"Do you think there's something wrong with me?" I said.

"Heck, no, there's nothing wrong with you, what do you mean?"

"Why didn't my real mother or father keep me?"

Cal looked at the worn linoleum floor as if he were trying to find an answer. Then he looked at me and his face brightened.

"I don't know," he said, "maybe they were poor and couldn't feed you and buy you clothes and things and they wanted you to have a good life or something."

"I wouldn't have eaten much, Bean, I didn't need much."

Cal glanced at me and then looked at the clock over the stove.

"I've got to get home," I said and I thanked Cal and hurried down the back stairway.

I walked along Wheeler, all the way to Randolph, and I

caught a streetcar coming from downtown. There were quite a few passengers for that late at night because of New Year's Eve. Fred was driving the graveyard run and I sat right behind him on the bench seat. He asked me what I was doing out so late alone and I told him I'd misplaced my boyfriend.

"The guy must be a dope, a sweet kid like you," he said.

"Thanks," I said.

"You been to Florida?"

"No, I fell asleep under a sun lamp."

I watched couples snuggling up to each other and looking into each other's eyes and I kept imagining Scott and Katie together. It was like having my teeth drilled. When Fred stopped and let me off, I didn't know if I could carry the concrete tumor that had grown in my chest as far as my house, but he waited until I was at my door before he drove away. It was long past midnight when I got to bed.

What had I done wrong? Again. Was I too much of an eager beaver, did I run boys off? I realized by how much it hurt just how much I'd come to love Scott. Was it my horrid sun-burned face? Was it hugging the wino? Was there something basically wrong with me, a hidden flaw only others could see? I hoped I could sleep, but I was afraid that when I woke in the morning it would still be midnight.

Chapter 21

I loved Central High School. The swell kids and my crazy friends and the games and social life and the good teachers and the goofy ones. Usually I couldn't wait to get there, but it was hard for me to show up Monday. I didn't know what I'd do when I saw Scott and, with him in two of my classes, I knew there was no way to avoid him. It would be like having surgery without ether.

On the way to school with Jean I couldn't help but wonder what it was that made Scott give up on me. Katie Mills was a darling girl and she sure didn't need any chocolate malts. Maybe that was it. After agonizing all day Sunday, I still clung to the hope that Scott only wanted a little variety and he'd ask me out for the coming weekend.

January was the hardest month of my life. I tried to concentrate on finding Myron Wilbershy, pouring my time and energy into my search, which was taking me all over the city, and with each cold dark day I was losing hope. I'd go every day after school unless one of my clubs or organizations had a meeting. I didn't want to miss any school activity in case I'd run into Scott.

Scott was always kind and polite when we'd unavoidably end up face to face in the hall or before or after a class. I'd become an expert at small talk, eating supper every night with my parents, and I never found the courage or felt it was a good time to ask Scott why he didn't keep me. But he didn't and the next weekend came and went and the next. Jim Hondray called and asked me to go to a movie and I figured word was out among the boys that Scott had no more interest in me. Still, I told Jim I was busy because I didn't want to be unavailable in case Scott did call. Jim was a nifty quiet boy who played on the hockey team and I scolded myself for turning him down. He was in some of my classes and we talked in the hall some times.

I started going to hockey games and a few swimming meets because it was too hard watching Scott play basketball. The swim team beat everyone, they were really good, and the boys looked nifty in those skimpy little suits they wore. Not many showed up for the swim meets, mostly parents or girlfriends, and at one meet at the Wilder pool, Jim Stubbs must have forgotten there would be spectators because he came flying out of the locker room, bounced once on the diving board, and soared above the water like a cannon ball, bare naked as a baby. You could tell by the expression on his face that he suddenly realized, in midair, what he'd done, sailing above the pool in full view of all the mothers and girlfriends. He stayed under the water so long we thought he'd drowned and when he came up his face was beet red. It was news to me that when there were no spectators the boys swam in the nude.

Jean still hunted for Myron Wilbershy with me now and then but I could tell she figured it was hopeless. I went alone more and more, riding the streetcar until I'd spot a jewelry store and then pulling the cord and getting off. Out Rice Street, over on the East Side, along University all the way to the edge of Minneapolis, down into South Saint Paul and West Saint Paul, all through January and the awful cold and heavy snow, but Myron Wilbershy had become a winter ghost. I wanted to give up, let it go, but something deep inside me wouldn't quit. I tried to listen to Emily Dickinson. "Hope is the thing with feathers, that perches in the soul . . ." To make things worse, I seldom saw a crow anymore, as if they were all hiding from winter's gloom or had migrated to warmer places.

Then I felt terrible when I got Cal hung up in one of Kirschbach's zany seventh periods. Cal was taking Gretchen Luttermann out of school for a day of fun. Gretchen was an odd duck who was always alone and dressed like a zombie, a real misfit. I felt sorry for her but she never responded when I'd say Hi. What Cal was doing was awfully nice and I got blank passes for them when I worked in the office and forged the names of teachers. But the next day Cal got caught when Miss Bellows asked Coach Mulligan why he took Cal out of her class, and when I realized he might've been kicked off the team I about died.

January 16th we were shocked by the murder of a young woman right in our neighborhood. The *St. Paul Pioneer Press* had a huge headline: MANIAC STABS WOMAN TO DEATH. The poor woman, Mary Kabascka, was on her way home from a concert at the university, walking alone, when someone gouged her throat repeatedly and slashed her wrist to the bone. My parents were so upset they couldn't sit down. My mother was having a cow. She wanted my dad to hang a light out by the curb to light up our front yard and my dad said I would have to be more careful going around at night. I knew how infuriated he was when he hinted that I'd have to take the station wagon more after dark. Jean and I eyed men on the streetcar with suspicion and a lot of the girls at school were spooked.

One bitter cold afternoon on the East Side I'd gotten off the streetcar on 7th Street when I spotted a jewelry store and after I found out there was no Myron Wilbershy working there I began walking into the cutting east wind. It seemed there were more breweries on the East Side than jewelry stores and I was really bushed and hungry and bone cold. It was already dark when I realized I wouldn't make it home in time for dinner, and I shuffled into a store that had a lot of junk in the window, antiques and musical instruments and stuff like that. Inside it was more of the same, tools and guns and radios and golf clubs and I realized I was in a pawnshop. A tall thin man in shirt sleeves came down the aisle with a green cellophane visor on his head.

"What can I do for you, little lady?" he said with a syrupy
voice. He had a nose like Pinocchio and buck teeth.

"Do you have a telephone I could use?"

"You got anything to swap?" he said.

"No, but I have money."

"Haw, just kidding," he said. "The phone's right over there,
help yourself."

"Thank you."

I clomped to the back counter where the phone sat beside
stacks of dog-eared catalogs. I pulled off my mittens and it
felt good to be inside. I dialed and waited while it rang. I
knew my mother would worry. The man stepped behind the
counter and into an iron mesh cage that enclosed the back
part of the store. It looked like a jail but I think it was to
protect the most valuable stuff. He sat on a high stool and
started working on something, a watch I think, and he had a
bright light shining on the work bench.

"Hello," my mother said.

"Hi, Mom, I'm late and I won't make it in time for dinner.
Don't worry, I'm on my way."

"All right, dear, I'll keep it in the oven. You be *careful.*"

"I will," I said and I could hear the fear in her voice.

I glanced at the man in the cage and my heart stuttered.
I stood there with the phone to my ear, my mouth hanging
open, holding my breath. He'd put on a pair of glasses
and they had a small lens attached to them that he'd
flipped down over one eye. He wasn't a jeweler; he was a
pawnbroker!

I hung up the phone and walked over to the cage.

"Thanks for the phone," I said. "Why do you have that
thingamajig on your glasses?"

"My lens? All the better to see you with, my sweet." He
laughed, imitating a wolf with his voice.

"No, really, do all pawnbrokers have one?"

"It's a ten-power lens," he said, "for all kinds of things:
gems, inside watches, those blasted little serial numbers you
can't read."

I noticed he had several calipers and a small scale with lots of tiny weights for counter balance and several needlenose pliers.

"Is all this stuff what other pawnbrokers use?"

"Why don't you come around here and give my sore back a nice rub and I'll show you how all this works."

"I've got to get home, but I was wondering if all pawnbrokers used the same instruments?"

"Yeah, I guess so, you writing a book?"

"Have you ever heard of a man named Myron Wilbershy?" I said, knowing the guy was too young to be my father.

"Wilbershy . . . Wilbershy . . . it rings a bell but no one's answering the door. Who is he?"

"Oh, just a man I think might be a pawnbroker. Thanks a million, you don't know how much you've helped."

"Then how about that back rub?"

"I gotta go, thanks, thanks a lot."

Out in the winter wind I jumped up and down and twirled around until I almost went down on the ice. My heart was in my throat. The guy was really creepy with all that back rub stuff but like a fine compass, he'd pointed me in the right direction when I was lost in the woods.

I could've outrun the streetcar on the way home. My heart was racing and I wasn't tired anymore or cold, but I could eat a horse. I'd been looking in the wrong place all that time, probably walked right past Myron Wilbershy's pawnshop. How many pawnshops could there be in Saint Paul? I couldn't wait to tell Jean; I couldn't wait to get back downtown. I wouldn't be able to sleep, and for a while, I'd lost that dull ache in my chest that had Scott McFarland's name on it.

Chapter 22

A *Cehisian* meeting kept me late on Friday and I headed out of school and across the parking lot with one eye out for Scott. It was as cold as a bugger when I trudged up Dunlap, disappointed that I couldn't run down one more pawnshop that afternoon. I had a gut feeling that I was finally on the right track. Jean was a good egg and when I told her about the pawnshop, and that Myron Wilbershy might be a pawn-broker, she jumped back on my bandwagon.

We'd found five pawnshops so far without any luck, but all of them were run by men so Jean had to go in and do all the talking. She pretended she wanted to pawn her watch and could she buy it back next month and then finally, what was the man's name so she could be sure to talk to him when she came back. She was a trooper but it seemed the city was shrouded in snow and cold to make our searching a whole lot harder.

I was almost to the corner where I'd catch the Selby-Lake, feeling blue and reminding myself of what I'd learned from Mr. Shapiro; that I wanted to live every day with gusto. I was trying to work up some gusto when a car coming from behind me along Dunlap honked.

"Hey, Sandy, c'mon, we'll give you a ride."

It was "Feathers" Douglas, shouting from the maroon '41 Oldsmobile and it was crammed with boys from basketball practice. My heart leaped into my throat. Scott! I plowed across the snowy street and slid in the back door. There were three boys in the front and three in the back, and Bill Forbes climbed on Harvey Mackay's lap to make room for me. When I saw that Scott wasn't in the car I started breathing again.

Jerry drove down Dunlap to Summit and it felt swell being with the guys I'd doubled with so many times. The car was full of sunshine, faces beaming with hope, and they didn't even know it. I realized how much I'd missed dating the past month and having fun with all of them.

Jerry turned on Summit and a couple of blocks up a Cretin cadet stood hitchhiking in his military uniform. A private Catholic boy's school, Cretin was one of our biggest rivals and we wanted to beat them almost as much as we wanted to beat Monroe. Jerry slowed down and pulled over.

"What are you doing? Don't stop," the boys shouted. "We don't have room."

The cadet had an instrument case, a trombone or something, plus an armload of books. He trotted through the dusk to the car in his heavy military coat.

Jerry turned to me in the back seat.

"Open the door, Sandy."

I opened the back door and the kid stooped and peered in cautiously, but when he saw me he seemed to relax.

"Climb in," Jerry said, smiling at the cadet.

"Thanks," the kid said and he handed in his instrument case.

I climbed onto Ben Bratter's lap, crunching over to make room and the cadet wormed his way into the car, juggling books and barely able to close the door, making it five of us in the back seat. Jerry looked over his shoulder.

"All set?" he said.

"Yeah, yeah," Cal said, "let's go."

Jerry gave it the gas, and at the next house, turned in the driveway and pulled up to the house and stopped.

"Well, here we are," he said.

He turned off the engine and smiled at the kid.

Everyone froze, bug-eyed at Jerry's gall. No one knew what to say. Dead silence. The puzzled Cretin kid didn't seem to catch on. I was so embarrassed I couldn't look at him. He gathered his books and fumbled open the door and stepped out. We passed him his trombone case.

"Thanks for the ride," he said.

That did it. We all folded up like we'd been hit with machine-gun fire. He walked to the curb and started hitch-hiking while we were laughing so hard we couldn't breathe and everyone looked as if they needed an iron lung. I slid back into the empty space and the boys were roaring.

"He said Thanks for the ride," Cal shouted and we all burst out in another explosion of laughter.

It had grown dark and the Cretin kid had worked his way down the street a half a block when he caught a ride. I was wiping tears from my eyes and my stomach hurt. Jerry started the car, backed out onto Summit, and drove off. All the way home, about every two minutes, just when we'd restored normal breathing and started to believe we'd live, somebody would remind us that the kid said Thanks for the ride.

When I slid out of the car in front of my house, my stomach was so sore I could hardly stand up. Jerry waved and I felt happy again. I'd go to the basketball game with Jean that night and watch all those zany boys play hard for Central. Right in the middle of the game, when the boys were in a timeout, I planned to shout as loudly as I could, The kid said thanks for the ride!

And maybe tomorrow I'd find my father.

Jim Hondray and I were getting to be friends. I'd been to four hockey games and I couldn't believe how fast he could skate. Steve was a good goalie despite his polio leg and you could tell he wanted to get out on the ice and mix it up with the other team. When he got a chance around the goal he'd level someone. I hadn't gone to a basketball game most of January until last Friday when they lost to Murray, but it was still hard for me to see Scott, and Jean and I got out of there fast when it was over.

Wednesday I persuaded Jean to haunt pawnshops with me and I felt guilty, as if I were blackmailing her to go because of our friendship. On the streetcar crossing the Robert Street

Bridge I told myself I wouldn't do it again. I'd discovered four more pawnshops without any luck. When I imagined all the pawnshops and jewelry stores in Minneapolis it was overwhelming. I could see myself when I was forty-five, working my way through the pawnshops in eastern Tennessee.

We rode along Concord into South Saint Paul and watched for the Square Deal Pawnshop I'd found in the phone book. I was glad January was behind me and I'd resigned myself to the fact that boys didn't find me very attractive. I'd given up on the theory that chocolate malts would increase your breast size, only now I was hooked on them.

"There, there it is!" Jean shouted as we passed the Square Deal.

I pulled the cord and we got off at the next corner. Jean had more enthusiasm than I did and she led the way along the icy sidewalk towards the sagging wood building. She'd taken a liking to the pawnshops and always found something tempting to buy. At the front door she nodded and went in like a seasoned scrounger. I loitered in front of the large window that was piled with stuff people had once cherished but had no more use for and I thought of Mr. Shapiro and how the Sunset Home For The Aged And Friendless was like a pawnshop.

I couldn't see through the glare on the glass very well, but Jean was talking to a large man. He hunched over on a stool behind a counter and he wore glasses but he didn't have any magnifying lens attached to them. I could see Jean handing him her watch and he was talking to her. He reminded me of Charles Laughton, only he was bigger and older. I got tired of squinting into the glare and I walked up the sidewalk. I'd noticed an old beat-up saxophone in the window and I was thinking about Woody and I started humming "Someone To Watch Over Me." I knew he was hoping it would be his long-lost girlfriend who would watch over him but maybe now he knew it was God. I thought they should have chiseled it on his tombstone. I scanned the neighborhood for a crow but found none.

When I turned around, Jean had come out of the Square Deal and was looking up the sidewalk for me. I was nearer the corner where we'd catch the streetcar back into Saint Paul so I waved and waited for her. She ran.

"It's him! It's him!" she said, hardly able to breathe.

"Are you sure? How do you know?"

"How many pawnbrokers have the name Myron Wilbershy?"

She squealed and hugged me and we twirled around and around in the dusk of South Saint Paul until we fell into a snow bank. I sat there in the snow and my heart was pounding and I thought it would fly away. We helped each other up.

"What do we do now?" Jean said.

"I want to get a better look," I said and we hurried back.

From a corner of the big window I tried to see him more clearly but he kept shuffling around. A man inspected some golf clubs and two boys were examining a bow and arrows. Then he came almost up to the window. He did look like Charles Laughton, the nose and jowls and those thick lips. He was big but not fat and his shoulders were hunched up around his head so he seemed to have no neck. I felt goose bumps down my legs. Was I looking at my father?

Jean pulled me aside.

"We've found him! Do you believe it, we *found* him!"

Her face was bright with delight and happiness.

I lost my smile and frowned at her. "But . . ."

"But what?" she said.

"That might be my *father.*"

"So . . . wasn't that the idea of all this?"

"He doesn't look like I expected, he looks like an old Charles Laughton."

"Well for Pete's sake, who'd you expect, Cary Grant?"

Like a fist in the stomach Jean made me realize I hadn't prepared myself for the shock of who my mother and father might be, gangsters or Gypsies or Holy Rollers, and suddenly I was afraid to find out.

"What do we do now?" Jean said.

"I want to find out where he lives, that's where I'll talk to him. I don't want to do it while he's waiting on customers."

"How are you going to find out where he lives?"

"I'll get the station wagon some day after school and follow him home. What time does he close?"

"Five o'clock," Jean said, "it's written right on the window."

"That's only ten minutes. Let's wait and see what kind of a car he drives?" I said.

"Maybe we'll luck out and he lives right around here."

I hadn't thought of that. We crossed Concord and watched the shop from there. Promptly at five o'clock he came out the door and locked it, leaving a light on inside. He tried the doorknob and shook the door hard to be sure, and then he walked towards Saint Paul. We followed from the other side of the street and at the corner he crossed over to our side. We turned and looked in the window of a barber shop. A man was having his beard trimmed by a Chinese barber. Myron stood on the corner and looked our way. I cringed for a minute, worrying that he'd already spotted us when I realized he was waiting for a streetcar.

"C'mon," I said and I pulled Jean towards the corner. It was getting dark and the street lights came on and a Rice-South St.Paul streetcar came up Concord. When it stopped and Myron got on, we ran and caught it and climbed in. Myron had moved way to the back and was sitting on the bench seat. Half-way back we found an empty seat. Like spies, I sat with my head turned towards Jean so I could keep track of him out of the corner of my eye.

He got off downtown at 4th and Robert and lumbered up 4th Street. We stayed close in case he jumped on another streetcar. Just when we were thinking he lived downtown, he

shuffled into the St. Paul Public Library. We couldn't decide
if we should follow him in or not and before we could come
to any decision, he was back on the street with several books
underarm. He trudged over to Wabasha and caught a
University streetcar.

Like tax collectors, we were right on his tail. The streetcar
was jammed and we stood, hanging onto a strap, but I could
see the back of his shoulders and hat in the muddle of
riders. Out University the crowd slowly thinned and a bunch
of people got off at Snelling. Jean and I slid into a seat but
Myron continued standing. A few blocks down he pulled the
cord and moved to the back doors. Jean and I hurried to the
front doors and got off when he did.

We stood on the curb until we could tell which way he
was heading. He waited to cross University, which was busy
with traffic, and then he plowed across and started down a
side street. We dashed through the headlights and followed a
half a block behind. At the first intersection we saw by the
street sign that we were on Herschel. He trudged another
block and crossed St. Anthony. Three doors down he turned
in at an imposing three-story stone house. Up onto the large
porch, he unlocked the door and went in. We could see
lights come on in the house through heavy drapes and it
appeared that he lived alone.

"We did it," Jean whispered.

Somewhat overwhelmed, we stood across the street and
gazed at Myron Wilbershy's massive house. There was an
attached stone carport on the side but no car was parked
there. Did he have a car?

"I can't believe it," I said but my excitement and joy were
deflating and I realized how scared I was. We stood there for
a few minutes as if we were dumbfounded by our success
and we wanted to let it sink in. Then we hightailed it for
home.

On the streetcar, with my best friend bubbling about how
wonderful it was that we'd found my father, something

didn't feel right. I'd imagined my father to be this really nifty handsome man who would take me in his arms and hold me tightly and tell me how sorry he was, that it had all been a terrible mistake, that he'd been looking for me for sixteen years. Maybe Myron would do that, but now that I'd finally found him, that I'd seen him, I was already hoping against hope that Myron Wilbershy *wasn't* my father. I didn't dare tell Jean what I was thinking after all she'd been through helping me find him, but to myself I was saying,

Myron Wilbershy, hello, good-bye,
If you're my father, I'll just die.

"When are you going to talk to him?" Jean said.

"Maybe tomorrow."

Chapter 23

After school Thursday I rode the streetcar out Selby to Herschel Street and walked around Myron Wilbershy's neighborhood, promising myself I'd talk to him when he got home. Donny Cunningham got off the streetcar when I did and followed me at a block's distance. It was a free country.

Myron's hulking gray stone house dominated the frame houses in the neighborhood, though some of them were large three-stories. It looked as if it had been there first, the landlord of a large estate, and the others came squatting when land was sold off and the city grew. The spacious yard was a full lot between his house and the house on the north. The walk was neatly shoveled and there was a large stone two-story garage on the alley with living quarters upstairs from the days of servants and horse and buggies. I couldn't tell if anyone else lived in the house; it was awfully big for one person. Most of the windows had drapes or shades drawn and I got the feeling that a lot of the house went unused. I tried to work up the courage to stay until he came home and talk to him, but as it got dark I chickened out and turned for home, promising myself I'd do it tomorrow.

The Minute Men and Sigs were putting on a dance Saturday night, the Jalop-Hop at the Mac Lodge with Gary Berg's band, and Jim Hondray asked me in school Friday if I was going. It was kind of like a date, letting each other know that we'd be there, and Jean went with me, Mutt and Jeff. She forgot her money and I lent her the 75¢ to get in. My stomach had resident butterflies and I knew it was as much about talking to Myron Wilbershy as it was about seeing Scott and Katie dancing cheek to cheek. I wondered if life was always this fouled up.

Dave was at the dance, stag, and he and Jean were dancing and I felt sorry for her because she loved him until it hurt and she was talking about getting married secretly. I did my best to ignore Scott and Katie, and Jean danced with Steve a few times for cover, in case their parents had spies. She wanted to know if Presbyterian was halfway between Catholic and Jewish if she and Dave decided to meet in the middle. I had fun despite the butterflies and Jim rode the streetcar with us until he got off at Fairview. I thought he was swell, but I still loved Scott, and Jean pined for Dave, and we rode the streetcar home like an ambulance from the war of love.

I procrastinated all weekend, trying to gather the nerve to introduce myself to Myron Wilbershy. I promised myself I'd do it before the next week passed and when I confessed to Jean on Monday that I hadn't done it, she lit into me.

"After all the time we slogged around in our overshoes and runny noses!" she said in the sub-basement lunch room as we stood in line for a hot lunch. "Why haven't you gone? My gosh, he might be your father."

"Easy for you to say, you *know* who your father is. I don't know if he'll hug me or kick me off the porch. And don't forget, Miss Know-It-All, he's the guy who sold me for $970."

Jean turned and looked at me with kindness in her eyes.

"You *are* scared, aren't you."

"You're darn tootin' I am," I said and I nodded at the server that I wanted gravy on my mashed potatoes.

"You want me to go with you?"

"No . . . no thanks."

I was afraid to have Jean along, afraid to have anyone know if it turned out badly. Maybe my father would desert me again.

I drove to the hockey game Monday night down at the Saint Paul Auditorium, and I knew I was trying to fill my life so full I didn't have time to knock on the door of that gray stone house over on Herschel Street. My father insisted I take the station wagon with that maniac running loose, and it felt good to know he cared more for me than his beloved Ford. Jim and the Central boys played so well and then, with only two seconds to go, Monroe scored a goal past Steve and won 4 to 3.

I hung around after the game in hopes I could offer Jim a ride but he was going with Bill Hann and other teammates. I gave a bunch of kids a ride home and I knew I couldn't put off knocking on that door much longer or I'd be in the booby hatch. My father always said, Sandra, you're like an overcharged battery, and he'd told me that again at supper.

The next night, after I'd gone to bed, I heard my parents talking about money, something they never did around me. They were in my mother's bedroom and I couldn't catch it all but they were worried about my mother's doctor and hospital bills. It sounded as if she'd have to go back into the hospital for a while. My dad was talking about mortgaging the house or something and how it would all be okay, but I could tell by their voices it wouldn't.

At breakfast the next morning my mother informed me I might have to put off college for a year, get a job and save some money. I told her I didn't mind although I knew that most of my friends would be going to college in the fall and I really wanted to be with them. It was just one more thing to stir into my stomach's churning and I was too busy trying to work up the courage to confront Myron Wilbershy to even think about next fall.

The weather had turned mild, like a good omen, and on Friday I waited beside a large elm tree across the street. A little before six he trudged out of the darkness along Herschel like a wounded gorilla, throwing his legs and arms forward as if he were going against some unseen current. His back was hunched slightly and he gave the impression he was very weary or terribly sad. When he'd gone into the house I waited for about ten minutes, telling myself I had to let him get settled. Finally, I crossed the street, walked up to the house, and balked.

I scampered off the porch and headed around the block, reminding myself that I'd stood out on that running board playing Rotation, promising myself I'd knock when I got back to the house. I wanted to be strong and angry and I remembered that he was the man who sold me! My teeth were chattering and it wasn't cold, in fact it felt more like April than February. I must have circled the block five or six times before I finally forced my legs to carry me up onto the porch again. It felt like the time my friends had me knock on the Runner's door and I wished they were standing there with me. I expected him to come barreling out and chase me or do something horrible. I took a deep breath and knocked.

After a minute the porch light blinked on along with two light posts on either side of the porch steps. I shivered. The door opened and he loomed in the doorway. He was bigger up close.

"Yes?" he said with a deep soft voice.

"Hello, are you Mr. Myron Wilbershy?"

"Yes."

"I think you might be my father."

Golly, that's not the way I rehearsed it but the words just popped out.

"What!" he said and he regarded me as if he were trying to figure out how this harebrained girl landed on his porch.

"I think you might be my father."

My voice quaked and I was shaking like a leaf.

"Why would you think a thing like that . . . a crazy thing like that?" he said and he wasn't loud or harsh as I expected but more like a timid boy.

"I was adopted in 1933 and the lawyer who did the adoption told me you were the man who brought the little girl to him because the mother was real sick and couldn't take care of her," I said without taking a breath.

He stared at me with a blank expression as if he were trying to figure out what I was selling and I felt like a screwball.

"Are you serious, young lady . . . are you serious?"

"Yes," I said but my voice faded and I was melting.

"Oh my, that's the most ridiculous thing I ever heard," he said and giggled, "the most ridiculous thing I ever heard."

"You needed $970," I said, "for your wife's hospital bills."

"I'll bet someone put you up to this," he said with a slight smile, "you're pledging for some sorority or something."

He looked past me out into the dark street.

"No, I'm not . . . you brought a baby to Mr. Shapiro."

"Oh my, I think you've made a mistake."

"The lawyer gave me your name."

"Well, that's impossible. You see I've never been married, never had any children." He knotted his hands like a big bashful kid. "So you've obviously got me mixed up with someone else . . . mixed up with someone else."

"If you'll just listen for a minute I can explain."

"What's your name, young lady?"

"Sandy."

"Well, I'm sorry, Sandy, but I'm afraid my supper will burn," he said shyly, "my supper will burn."

He kept repeating himself, slowly, as if he were thinking about what he just said.

"Please, if you knew how hard I've been looking—"

"I'm sorry I can't help you, but I have to go in now . . . better go in now. Excuse me, good-night."

He closed the door softly and the porch light winked out.

I stood there on the darkened porch with my heart going lickety-split and I couldn't catch my breath and it was turning out all wrong. Just when I thought I'd finally find out who I was I had the door politely shut in my face and my only clue to find my mother was a dead end. The man thought I was pulling a prank or something. He certainly didn't rise to the bait. Nothing I told him seemed to ring a bell, his expression never changed. What a letdown. What could have been, Oh, Sandy, how wonderful, I've been looking for you with a broken heart, turned out to be, My supper is burning, don't bother me with such nonsense.

I drifted out to the sidewalk and turned. I gazed at the forbidding house, muffled in shadows and darkness, and it seemed to breathe, as if it were alive. It whispered its secrets to me but I couldn't quite understand the words. If I'd known then what it would all lead to, I might have smashed down the door or run all the way home. Instead I felt like a big drip and I was terribly disappointed. I wanted to cry. Had Mr. Shapiro been confused, had he gotten it all wrong?

I slogged home with my tail between my legs, doubting that I was ever meant to know who I was or find out anything about my real mother and father. I ran the block from the streetcar to my door, just in case the maniac was out prowling.

Chapter 24

All the following week I wandered around mixed up and defeated, shilly-shallied between hope and utter gloom, kept asking myself Was Mr. Shapiro wrong? Some of the time I'd answer Probably, realizing how moth-eaten his memory was. But then I'd recall how he remembered so many details about his children's drowning and I'd feel a shiver of hope and I'd say No, Mr. Shapiro wasn't wrong or confused. I found a flesh-and-blood man named Myron Wilbershy and Mr. Shapiro couldn't have made him up. He guessed he was a jeweler and his clues led me to a pawnbroker who fit Mr. Shapiro's description, brief as it was.

In my heart I knew I couldn't give up that easily, I had to go back out on the running board, go back and knock on that door.

Tuesday was Valentine's Day and Jim slipped a sweet Valentine into my locker. On it he asked me to go to the dance Saturday and I tried to work up some enthusiasm to tell him I would. He showed up at the Deb meeting Tuesday night at Sue Cross's house and he walked me home. Shy and quiet, he didn't say three words on the way but I could tell he was pleased that I accepted his invitation to the dance. I'd met the complete opposite of Scott. At my doorstep Jim said good-night halfway up our walk and in seconds was gone like a shadow.

While D.B. Sandersen was taking attendance in physics, Steve jumped out of his seat and shouted, "Mouse, a mouse!" and pointed at the floor.

D.B. looked up with a startled expression. He kept several cages of white mice in the lab for demonstrations. They were his pets and he knew them all by name.

"Over here!" Hugh Meier yelled from the other side of the room.

Girls clambered up on their chairs and screamed and D.B. rushed from behind his counter and tried to catch his precious mouse. The physics classroom was built like a theater, with each row of desks a step higher than the row in front, so everyone could see the demonstrations. D.B. flew up the stepped floor as though he'd lost one of his family.

"There he goes," Marjorie Huelster shouted from down in front and D.B. raced back.

Without a rehearsal the kids were doing a great job of keeping D.B. dashing around the room with the latest sighting of the mouse, but no matter how fast he moved he not only couldn't catch the mouse, the frantic teacher couldn't even spot it.

"Up here!" I screamed and I jumped onto my chair and D.B. came flying.

Probably figuring the teacher would catch on sooner or later, or out of simple mercy, Scott sprang out of his seat and shouted, "There it goes," and he slammed the door to the lab.

We all let out a big Whew, doing everything we could to keep from cracking up. D.B. carefully opened the door to the lab and slipped in, closing the door behind him. We waited, keeping it down, while the teacher was counting his mice. When he stepped back into the classroom, we were all sitting there as if we were worried about his little pets. He stood by the lab door and looked at us with a puzzled expression.

"Was it white?" he said.

Everyone burst out laughing, except a few who really thought there had been a mouse. Ignoring the roar, D.B. looked at us as if he were trying to figure out what was so funny about asking if it was white.

When I left the class Scott walked beside me, laughing and reliving the prank as though we were old buddies. Didn't he realize my heart ached when I was around him, knowing he didn't love me?

The Valentine's Dance was at the Mac Lodge and we doubled with Paul Deitl and Mary Weiss. Paul had the car and Jim settled cozy close to me in the back seat but he just sat there like a stranger on the same streetcar. He couldn't dance but neither could Scott, in fact, most of the boys couldn't dance a lick. They all did the one-step.

While Jim and I were doing the one-step and the band was playing "I Don't Stand a Ghost of a Chance With You" I had the notion to go over and tell Scott, who was dancing with Katie, that they were playing our song, but I knew I had to grow up and get over him. It wasn't his fault he didn't love me, and maybe it wasn't my mother's fault that she didn't either. I saw Jim Stubbs at the dance and I wanted to ask him if he performed in the nude at every swimming meet but I knew it would embarrass him. The swimming team won the city title Friday night by a wide margin and they did it with their cute little suits *on*.

We ate at the drive-in after the dance and I didn't have a chocolate malt. I felt a little guilty, still madly in love with Scott and letting other boys spend their hard-earned cash on me. I knew it wasn't fair and I only shared an order of fries with Jim. Once I was home and in bed, I couldn't fall asleep. I kept rehearsing for my second assault on Myron Wilbershy's porch and this time I wasn't going to let him off so easily. In my warm bed and the safety of my bedroom it was easy to be brave.

By Wednesday of the following week my courage had come flooding back, and with it some hope, and I was determined to try again. I told myself Myron Wilbershy could move or die and that would be the end of it forever. When I came out of school I spotted a crow perched on the tennis court fence. It was hunkered down with its feathers all puffed out against the cold but it was a crow and I smiled.

I got to Myron's block and watched from across the street until he plodded down the sidewalk and into the house. I waited about five minutes, wrestling with the chickenheart in me that wanted to run. I was gulping air when I marched up onto the porch and pounded on the door as if it were the Runner's. I could feel his heavy step coming behind the door. The porch light popped on and I noticed a sign he had in the narrow window beside the door. NO SOLICITING. I figured when I got done with him there would be another sign. NO QUESTIONS. When he opened the door I didn't give him a chance.

"I'm sorry to bother you again, Mr. Wilbershy, but a lawyer gave me your name and said you brought a baby girl to him in 1933 for adoption and I'm that baby girl and I want to find out if you're my father and who's my mother and I'm staying on your porch until you tell me."

I felt faint.

"Oh, yes, oh yes," he said meekly, "you were here a couple weeks ago."

He had a dish towel tucked over his belt as an apron.

"Yes, and I'm not leaving until you talk to me."

My nostrils flared and I was determined to make a stand.

"Someone's made a mistake," he said and he pursed his lips. "I'd like to help you . . . ah, Laura, was that it?"

"Sandy."

"Yes, Sandy, I'd like to help you but you have the wrong guy. You better check with the lawyer, Mr . . .?

"Mr. Arnold Shapiro."

"Yes, check with him, he can probably straighten it out . . . straighten the whole thing out."

"I can't, he died."

"Oh my, well . . . did he write the name down?" he said as if he were disappointed.

"Ah . . . no, he couldn't, but he spelled your last name."

"Only the last name?" He wrung his hands. "Only the last name?"

"Yes, he said Myron Wilbershy, and then he spelled out Wilbershy," I said.

"Well, you see, that's probably where the problem lies. You must have heard him wrong: Myron, Byron, Marion, Mervin? You've just made a simple mistake . . . a very simple mistake."

I didn't know what to say. He was right. I just heard Mr. Shapiro *say* the name, whisper it with his dying breath through the oxygen tent window. My legs trembled, I'd come so far, I was so sure, and now it all seemed to be nothing but smoke.

"I heard him clearly," I lied, trying to keep up some kind of front before crumbling into a heap of ashes on his porch.

"I knew of a Byron Wilbershy," he said meekly. "He lived in West Saint Paul with his family."

He took a hanky from his pants pocket and dabbed at sweat on his forehead and I caught my breath. He was lying! He *was* the man who had sold me!

"I've told you, I've never had any children, so you see, I couldn't possibly be the person you're looking for . . . couldn't possibly be."

"Oh . . ." I tried to gather my thoughts. "Maybe you're not my father, but you brought me to Mr. Shapiro for someone else."

"I know you're trying hard to find your parents, but this is exasperating . . . simply exasperating. I never took *any* baby to *any* lawyer and that's that!"

I could tell he was getting steamed under his polite manner and I didn't want to overdo it so he'd never talk to me again.

"Well maybe I can talk to you again some time."

He took a deep breath and puffed his cheeks with a sigh.

"I'm sorry, but please don't bother me with this anymore . . . not anymore." He stuffed his hanky into his pocket. "Good-bye," he said kindly.

He stepped back and slowly closed the door. After a moment the porch light blinked off.

Not Good-bye, Mr. Wilbershy!

Mr. Shapiro said he was a big clumsy man and he wore glasses and he had a jeweler's lens clipped on them and he was always wiping sweat off his face with a hanky, and Mr. Shapiro didn't like the man. Maybe he didn't like him because he was a liar.

I spun off the porch and hotfooted it up St. Anthony for the Snelling streetcar. I didn't know why I felt so excited and happy because Myron Wilbershy sure wasn't going to help me. But I'd tracked him down and I wasn't going to let him get away until I discovered what happened to my mother. I knew I'd found the right man, the man Mr. Shapiro told me about, and he was lying.

As I rode down Snelling my mind was whirling. I couldn't wait to talk to Jean. Why would he lie about it? What was he hiding? The fact that he sold a baby for $970? And where did he get the baby girl if it wasn't his? I started to believe I was delving into a mystery that was much bigger than I'd ever imagined, that I'd find much more than I'd bargained for.

Chapter 25

Winter was passing and my senior year at Central was slipping away with it, and I wanted to enjoy it before it was gone. Mr. Shapiro taught me to grab each day and live it before all I had left was my muddled memories and a dreary little room to wait in. I wanted to make memories that would zing, I wanted to do things I'd never forget, I wanted to stand up for the Mr. Shapiros of the world. I wanted to love someone who'd never give up on me.

But I was stymied. I lay awake at night, unable to sleep, sensing deep inside that there had to be someone else, somewhere, who knew the truth about Myron Wilbershy and the adoption. But who, and where did I find him or her? I went over it and over it until I was dizzy, racked my brain until it ached. I'd drift downstairs at three in the morning and drink a glass of warm milk to try to get to sleep and my stomach felt like a cement mixer. And despite it all, I had no way to prove that Myron Wilbershy was lying.

Jean put her thinking cap on but couldn't come up with anything. In fact, she thought maybe Mr. Shapiro was confused and that his information probably wasn't that reliable. Scott didn't look at me from the lunchroom balcony anymore, I know, because I sat so I could see him while I ate.

My mother was getting worse and on the first day of March she told me she would probably be going back into the hospital for a while. I was helping with the dinner and I told my mom I didn't know how she could do it, being sick so much with the pain and nausea. She straightened slightly at the stove and said, "I just ask myself what Amelia would do and then I can go another hour, another day."

"Can't the doctors do more?" I said.

"They don't seem to know what's wrong with me."

I helped dish up, pork chops, fried potatoes and corn, and my mother was having a small bowl of Jello. I was pretty discouraged and blue when we sat down and recited our table prayer together.

Heavenly Father, we thank you for this food. May it nourish us to be a blessing to others and good neighbors to all. Amen.

Holy moly, it hit me like a ton of bricks!

"Good neighbors," I said, "it's the neighbors!"

"What on earth are you talking about," my mother said.

"Oh . . . something we're working on in school, kind of a puzzle, and I just got it."

My dad rolled his eyes. I wanted to get up and run all the way to Herschel. I'd have to wait until after school the next day, but surely there'd be one or two neighbors who were living next to him in 1933, there had to be. It would only take one.

"They're going to eliminate the streetcars," my dad said.

"If it isn't one thing it's another," my mother said.

"How will we get around?" I said, trying to sort out my feelings; the sadness for my mother and my happy expectations for talking with Myron's neighbors.

"Buses, stinking buses," my dad said.

"Your nails look a little better," my mother said.

"Yeah, I'm trying." I put my left hand in my lap.

"How are you and that McFarland boy getting along?" my dad said.

"Oh, we see each other now and then in school. I've been going out with Jim Hondray, you know, the hockey player."

"Hondray . . . Hondray . . . I don't think I know that family," my dad said.

"Is he a nice boy?" my mother said.

"Yes, he's swell," I said and I realized from the ache in my chest that I still loved Scott McFarland and I didn't want to talk about it because it hurt too much.

Thursday after school I got to Myron's neighborhood before four, plenty of time. I started with the large two-story house south of his. It was white with green trim, well-kept, and it had a porch. I knocked and waited. After a minute a stocky young man with black hair and a five-o'clock shadow opened the door.

"Hi, I'm trying to find some information about my family that used to live next door," I said and I nodded at Myron's house. "Where you living here in 1933?"

"No, we moved here in '46 when I got out of the Army," he said, and then added with pride, "our first house."

"That's swell, thanks anyway, sorry to bother you."

"Good luck," he said and I headed for the street, thinking he was one of the lucky ones who made it to the beach.

I went directly across the street and rang the bell on a smaller house, two-story, dull yellow with no porch. A lady in a bathrobe answered the door with her hair in curlers.

"We've lived here since 1940, don't pay much attention to neighbors, husband works for the Great Northern, our kids are all grown up."

I thanked her and tried the house directly across the street from Myron's. I kept my fingers crossed, hoping against hope. No one answered. There was a Dodge parked in front but after I rang and knocked several times I realized I'd have to go back some other time.

Next door my heart skipped when the young mother, with one baby in arms and another crawling around behind her on the floor, told me they'd just been there a few months, that the old woman who had been living there for forty years had just died. I crossed the street with an ache in my chest. Maybe I'd just missed, maybe that old woman was the last neighbor with a link to my past.

I bounced up onto the porch of the three-story house next to Myron's on the north. It had a veranda that ran across the front and halfway around the side, overlooking Myron's sprawling yard. I knocked on the heavy wood door and just about jumped out of my skin when I suddenly noticed an old woman in a rocking chair at the corner of the porch, watching me. Rocking slightly, she was decked out like a man, canvas work pants, suspenders, a plaid lumberjack shirt, and smoking a stub of a cigar.

"Oh, excuse me," I said, "I didn't see you."

"Scared ya, huh?"

"Golly, yes."

A beat-up man's felt hat was pulled down over her ears and long white hair streamed from under the hat. High leather logger boots were laced snugly up her legs. I figured she was as old as Mr. Shapiro but a lot livelier.

"What you sellin', girlie?"

"Nothing, I'm just trying to get some information."

"I've been watchin' you, thought you was sellin' Girl Scout cookies or somethin'."

I walked over to the corner of the veranda.

"Pull up a chair," she said.

I sat on a wobbly wooden chair that had no back.

"You a spy?" she said.

"A spy?"

"Lots of Commie spies around these days."

"No, I'm a student at Central High School."

She tipped her head back and blew a lazy smoke ring.

"What kind of information you after?" she said.

"I'm trying to find my parents and I think they lived in that house next door. In fact, I think Myron Wilbershy, the man who lives there now, might be my father."

"Well, ain't that a bowl of fish. How'd you come by all that?"

"The lawyer who did my adoption said he got me from Myron Wilbershy. Myron told him his wife was terribly sick and they wanted to find a good home for the baby girl and they needed $970 for medical bills."

She sat there, rocking gently in the chair and squinting through the cigar smoke at Myron's house as if she was thinking real hard. I waited quietly for what seemed like ten minutes and then, still gazing at the house, she spoke.

"Always wondered about that."

"Do you remember his wife, and his little baby?"

"Like it was yesterday," she said and I wanted to leap off the chair and hug her.

I had a hard time sitting still and I wanted to shout and tell her I believed in angels, that I believed she was one, disguised in those rough logger's clothes.

"Never blamed her for runnin' off, took the child with her. He was older, not a cheerful man, they didn't seem a likely match, like she was just needin' someone to take care of her and the baby for a spell."

"Wasn't it his baby?" I said.

"The first time I saw her in the yard right there," she nodded at Myron's big yard, "she had the baby in arms. Seemed to me he married a woman who already had a child. I'd talk to Myron now and then in passin'. Said he'd gotten married, happiest I'd ever seen him, which meant he'd say hello once in a blue moon and he didn't have his usual gloominess."

"I think she was my mother, I think I was that baby."

"Well I'll be a monkey's uncle, let me look at you, girl."

She studied my face from under her sweat-stained felt hat as if she was trying to imagine me as that baby she'd watched in her neighbor's yard seventeen years ago.

"Heavens to Betsy, would you believe it! You're all growed up."

"Gosh, I'm so glad he's not my father. Ever since I found him I've been hoping he wasn't, something just didn't feel right about him."

"You look more like your mother," she said.

"Did my mother die?"

"Wasn't sick a day of her life while she lived with him, was here the better part of a year. Then one day she left him, ran off with the baby."

The old woman shook her head. I wanted to take notes.

"I don't figure it, he couldn't have adopted the baby out. He showed me the note she left when she run off, said she was takin' the baby back to her rightful father, that she'd made a terrible mistake, somethin' along those lines."

"You saw the note?" I said.

"Yep, remember it because he wasn't in the habit of comin' over to talk to me or my man. Come over like a kid runnin' to his mama with a bloody nose, showed me the note, never saw a man in so much pain. He fought back the tears but I could see he was howlin' just under the skin. Felt real sorry for the man, knew he probably wouldn't have a woman like that again."

She paused and puffed on her stubby cigar.

"Thought for a while he might have a notion to take his own life. Then, over the months and years he's withdrawn from the human race, seldom says hello, just buries himself in that old house, lives alone and goes to work every day like clockwork. Reads a lot, always haulin' books back and forth."

She spit over the railing and dropped the cigar butt in a red coffee can on the floor.

"What did my mother look like?" I said.

"Pretty . . . like a country gal, slim, tall, big eyes that could knock you over. I could understand why Myron was so brokenhearted when she left. Gossiped over the fence with her now and then, don't remember what about."

"Did she . . . like me?"

"Adored you, almost wore you out with love. You were a sweet little thing, healthy as an apple."

I started to cry. I had to stand up and walk down the porch for a minute. My mother *adored me*. I knew she'd never give me up, but now I'd heard it from someone else, it wasn't just wishful thinking. I wiped my eyes and perched on the backless chair.

"What was my name?" I said.

She looked over into the yard again as if she was trying to hear my name on the March breeze. She frowned.

"Don't remember," she said. "Lots of things I can't remember these days, mind's turnin' to ashes."

"Do you remember my mother's name?" I said.

"Hmmm . . . not sure . . . think it was something like Geraldine, no . . . Genevieve, think it was Genevieve, but don't go bettin' your house on that."

I was bursting with joy, she told me what I always knew: my mother loved me. And now I had proof that Myron was lying and I could tell him so. He couldn't worm out of it any longer and I wanted to kiss the old woman.

"Did he ever get married?" I said.

"No . . . never did, not the marryin' kind I suspect, but over the years I think he had a lady friend or two."

She brushed her long white hair from her face and gazed at Myron's house.

"On a warm summer night I'd catch a glimpse of a woman in an upstairs window or hear them talkin'. It was rare though."

"What else do you remember?"

I perched on the edge of the wobbly chair, hardly daring to breathe.

"We battled for a while back in '33 over our dogs. He had a huge slobbering Saint Bernard, friendly as a puppy, kept him tied most of the time. Myron was always complainin', said my dog Buster, a lovable mutt, would come over and eat his dog's food, take his bones. One time Myron even stomped over in our yard and retrieved a bone Buster had dragged home. Imagine, a bone. Talk about a strange outfit. He'd yell at me, throw things at Buster, I'd yell back, dogs got along fine."

She paused, twisting a strand of her long white hair in her crooked fingers.

"One night I let Buster out like always and he never come back. I called him all night, all the next day, still miss that dog. I suspected Myron did him in, but he brought me flowers 'cause he knew I was feelin' bad and he'd bring me fresh vegetables from his garden and I figured it wasn't him after all. Buster was probably hit by a car or stolen."

She gazed over into the yard as if she expected to see her dog.

"Every fall he brings me apples from his tree there, Haralsons, and I bake him a pie, which he is very thankful for. Then, at Christmas, I take over some cookies I bake and that's about it between us."

"What's your name?" I said.

"Clara . . . Clara Singleton. Lived in this house since '17."

"Can you remember anything else about my mother?"

She sat quietly for a minute, thinking.

"A man stopped by the summer she run off, said he was lookin' for his wife and daughter, that he'd had a drinkin' problem but now he'd straightened out. Said she'd sent him a letter, told him she was comin' home, wanted to try again, make their marriage work. She asked him to send some money but under no circumstances come to Saint Paul. She would be home soon."

"Then my mother didn't go back to him, maybe she couldn't find him," I said and I felt a weight in my chest.

"I believe he said he sent eighty dollars right off with a note that he was done drinkin' and how much he loved her and missed her, but she never come home. Weeks went by and he tried to abide by her wish that he not come to Saint Paul, but finally, after six weeks, he'd come lookin'. And that address," she nodded at Myron's house, "358 Herschel, was where he sent the money."

"Maybe she left before the note and money came," I said, "but why didn't she go home?"

"Can't answer that one, wish I knew," she said, rocking in the chair and gazing across at Myron's house.

"What was his name?"

"Told me his name, something different . . . made me think of Bugs Bunny or Peter Rabbit or something like that. It'll come to me, one of these days, it'll come to me."

I stood and I was so excited I thought I'd fly off the porch.

"Can I come back and talk with you again?" I said.

"Why, it'd be a pleasure," she said and smiled.

She had several teeth missing.

"Any of those teachers at Central Commies?"

I thought of D.B. Sandersen and Mr. Kirschbach and Miss Bellows and laughed.

"No, they're an ongoing riot but they're not Commies."

"Have to be careful, infiltratin' our schools, sneakin' in wherever they can. They're destroyin' our streetcars, you know."

"No, I didn't know that."

"Well, they are, and that's only the beginnin'."

"I'll be back, maybe you'll remember more about my mother."

"Land sakes," she said as she slowly shook her head. "It's just plumb amazin' that that little girl turned out to be you."

She pointed towards the back of Myron's yard.

"Used to be a little chair swing there, on the clothes pole, rotted away long ago, but your mother used to swing you in it. I can still hear your sweet little voice screamin' with delight. Ain't that amazin'."

My feet never touched the ground on the way home. I had a living witness who saw me with my mother, Genevieve, and she loved me, and we were in Myron Wilbershy's yard in 1933. I couldn't wait to hear how that big bashful man was going to explain that.

Chapter 26

Myron Wilbershy had become a crafty hibernating bear. He refused to answer the door.

I spent the next week, every chance I got, knocking on his door and ringing the doorbell but he wouldn't come out. My mother was getting suspicious of why I was late for supper so often and I'd chatter about my clubs and boys and try not to lie.

"I know you're in there!" I'd shout. It finally dawned on me he was taking a different route home, probably walking over Pierce or Aldine and coming down the alley and in the back door. But it wouldn't work. It only made me madder and more determined. He'd lied, and now I had the proof. He knew what happened to my mother and I'd get it out of him if I had to pitch a tent on his porch.

On Friday I loitered at the corner of University and Snelling, playing a hunch, and it paid off. Myron got off the University streetcar and lumbered up Snelling to Roblyn. Then he trudged down Roblyn and cut up the alley to his house. I ran to catch up to him. The alley hadn't been plowed after the blizzard we had on Wednesday and it was rutted with tire tracks and the snow was wet and slippery. He turned his large head when he heard me behind him and when he saw who it was he just kept on slogging down the alley.

"I know you didn't tell the truth, Mr. Wilbershy," I said as I kept pace about ten feet behind him. "I talked to your neighbor and she told me she remembers my mother living with you, and the baby girl, too, and I want to know what happened to my mother and I'm going to follow you until you tell me or you're in your grave, whichever comes first."

He didn't hurry, throwing one large arm and then a leg as if he were pressing into a hurricane. He turned into his yard without looking back and escaped through the back door. The large two-story garage had two doors for cars. One looked used, the other hadn't been opened this century. I peered in the side window and saw a big car, but in the dark I couldn't make out much of it.

I walked down the alley and circled around to the front of his house. It was the night of the Mid-Commencement Dance and Jim was picking me up at eight and it was already past six but I didn't want to give up. I had evidence now, and a witness, and I wasn't going to let Myron Wilbershy lie to me any more.

I marched up his shoveled walk and squatted on the top step of his porch. I figured I'd have to run for home by seven. My hair would be a mess but at least I wasn't under the sun lamp. It was cold and dark sitting there with not much light leaking from the house. I tried to remember being on that porch when I was a one year old, tried to conjure up any recognition.

What would it be like for a little girl to lose her mother? Would it be like playing peek-a-boo, and then one time, when you pull your hands from over your eyes, your mother's gone? Do you look around and keep expecting her to pop out and say Boo, the next hour, the next week, the next year? When does the little girl quit expecting her mother to show up, how long does it take for the little girl to forget her? Does she ever?

He scared the gumdrops out of me when he snapped on the porch light and opened the door. I jumped up and backed down the stairs. He could call the police and have me kicked off his property, but he hadn't, and that convinced me he had something to hide.

"Would you like to come in?" he said meekly with his deep voice.

"Oh . . . I don't need to come in. You can talk to me out here."

"Come in out of the cold . . . out of the cold," he said and he backed into the house, leaving the door open.

Was he planning to murder me? I crept up the steps and peered in the door like a mouse approaching the trap. Past the entryway I could see the somber living room, crammed with old stuffed furniture and frilly shaded lamps. He was perched on the edge of an ugly green wing chair in front of a coffee table that had two cups and saucers, a pitcher of something, and a plate of cookies. When he observed me edging in, he nodded.

"Please close the door . . . close the door."

I was shaking but I closed the door and kicked off my overshoes.

"Come in, come in, have some hot cocoa if you'd like."

I settled on the love seat across from him and left my coat and scarf on. He nodded at the food.

"No thanks," I said and I stayed as vigilant as a bird in case I had to run for my life.

"My, aren't you a persistent young lady, as tenacious as a mosquito."

He poured cocoa into both cups and took one in his hands.

"I didn't tell you the truth because I was hoping you'd give up and go away. I was praying I wouldn't have to bring it all up again. It was the most devastating time of my life . . . the most devastating."

He took a sip of cocoa and cradled the cup in his hands. He glanced at me shyly and it felt as if we were little kids playing tea time.

"Can you imagine what it's like to be left behind by some-one you dearly love?" he said.

"Yes . . . I was."

"Yes, well, your mother came to me when I worked in a pawnshop on 7th Street in downtown Saint Paul. She was an angel . . . an angel, and I fell in love with her immediately, the moment I set eyes on her, before she ever spoke a word . . . before she ever spoke a word."

He stared down at the cup and I was all ears. He spoke
slowly and echoed everything he said as if he liked the
sound of his own voice.

"She'd run away from her husband, he was a drinker and
he'd hurt her at times, and she was afraid for her baby . . .
afraid for her baby. She wanted to pawn her wedding ring, it
wasn't worth much. I didn't have the heart to tell her . . .
didn't have the heart. I don't think she had two dollars to
her name. I told her I'd lend her thirty on the ring, way
more than I could have ever sold it for."

His voice grew thick and I thought he was going to cry.

"I helped her find a boarding house for women, and I'd
stop by every morning and evening to see how she was
doing. She was having trouble with the baby at the rooming
house . . . trouble with the baby, people complaining about
crying at night and such."

He bent over the coffee table and nodded.

"You sure you wouldn't like some cocoa to warm the
bones?"

I figured if he was drinking it it must be all right and I
picked up a cup and drank. It was hot and sweet and the
cup warmed my hands.

"Thanks," I said, not wanting to interrupt his story.

"The money ran out . . . the money ran out, and I
convinced her to come and live with me. I told her about
the large house where she could have several rooms and a
bath to herself. She was leery, but she consented . . . she
consented. She really didn't have anywhere else to go. She
insisted on cleaning and cooking and doing the laundry to
earn her keep, she was an excellent cook. It was a wonderful
arrangement . . . simply wonderful. I had that angel living
with me in my own home . . . right in my own home."

He took out his hanky and dabbed at the sweat on his
large Charles Laughton face.

"Little by little I let her know how much I loved her . . .
how much I loved her, and almost every day I brought her

little gifts, a flower, a candy bar, a magazine. She'd never tell me her last name. I think she was afraid her husband would find her. One night, while we were eating and the baby slept, I asked her to marry me. She told me she'd think about it . . . said she'd think about it."

He got up and slowly paced as he talked.

"I didn't rush her, but after a few weeks we went to see a lawyer about her divorce. It would be hard to get . . . hard to get. Her husband lived in Iowa somewhere, she wouldn't tell me where, and he most likely wouldn't consent. She had to show he had a drinking problem and had hurt her. I gave the lawyer twenty-five dollars to work on it. She made me leave the office before she gave the lawyer her last name and where her husband lived in Iowa. I agreed that until she got the divorce, the lawyer would only talk to her . . . only talk to her."

He stopped by the old mahogany dining table and timidly looked into my eyes.

"That lawyer was Arnold Shapiro . . . Mr. Arnold Shapiro."

I almost swallowed my tongue. I set the cup down and nearly broke the saucer. Mr. Shapiro hadn't said anything about a divorce. If Myron Wilbershy had dealings with Mr. Shapiro before the adoption, maybe that was what Mr. Shapiro was remembering, and his description of Myron could be from *that* meeting!

I was crushed and it must have shown because Myron sat down and didn't speak for several minutes.

"What happened to my mother?" I said.

My voice and hands were trembling.

"She consented to marry me and we became lovers. I couldn't believe what good fortune had come to me . . . what good fortune. She was an angel, gorgeous, sweet, kind. I told her that when we were married I'd adopt her baby. I was in paradise, the garden of Eden, and then I fell into hell . . . fell straight into hell."

He picked up a ginger snap, held it for a moment absent-mindedly, and gently set it back on the plate.

"I came home from work one night in early June and she was gone . . . she was *gone*, she and the baby. As suddenly as she'd come into my life, as suddenly she was gone, just flew away . . . flew away. She left a note, said she was going back to her husband. I still have the note . . . still have the note."

He pried himself out of the chair and lumbered over to an antique roll-top desk in a small den. He opened a drawer and pulled out a folded piece of paper. He gazed at it as if it were alive while he shuffled back and then handed it to me and slumped into his chair.

> *Dear Myron,*
> *I'll be gone when you find this. I'm going back to my husband. You and I just weren't meant to be together. I was looking for security for me and my baby but I know it wasn't fair to you and I could never love you the way you want me to. My daughter needs her father. I'm taking nothing but our clothes. I can never thank you enough for all you've done for us. Please forgive me for hurting you.*
>
> *Genevieve*

The piece of white paper was finger-soiled and marked with water spots. I read it again, and then I set it on the coffee table. I felt goose bumps, seeing my mother's handwriting, as if it verified that she had really existed once and was no longer only a figment of my hopes and dreams.

"I read that note a thousand times that night . . . a thousand times, didn't sleep a wink. The following day was a Saturday and I spent that day and the next searching both cities for her, bus depots, train stations, rooming houses. I was beside myself with shock and grief . . . beside myself. Twice I stood on the roof outside the third-story window and tried to jump. I searched for most of five years . . . most of five years, hoping against hope that I would find her."

His head had slumped, his chin on his chest.

"She was an angel and I was sure I'd die without her . . . simply die without her. I've never known such joy and happiness since and I know I never will . . . know I never will. I'll have it carved on my headstone: DIED June 4, 1933."

My mouth was dry and I was breathing as though I'd run from Stillwater. We sat there without speaking and my heart was breaking for Myron and how much he loved my mother. Then he rallied himself and straightened up onto the edge of the chair.

"And *that's* why I lied to you, I couldn't bear to bring it all up again . . . bring it all up again. And now I know no more than you . . . no more than you."

I looked at him and I wanted to hug him. I was happy deep inside because he wasn't my father. If he did sell me to Mr. Shapiro, it wasn't *my father* selling me.

"I'm sorry I can't be of more help, little mosquito."

He sighed.

"Did my mother love me?"

"She cherished you, thought the sun rose and set on you."

I felt warm and happy.

"Did she go back to my father?" I said.

"I don't know if she ever found him . . . just don't know. I tried to get her last name from the lawyer but he said that was privileged information and he couldn't give it to me. I offered him fifty dollars and he took it but he said it was a waste of money . . . just a waste of money. When I asked him why, he told me he could tell she made up the name in his office . . . made up the name, still too afraid of being found. When I asked him what name she gave him he said Jones. He felt so cheap about it he gave me twenty-five dollars back."

A clock somewhere in the house chimed seven o'clock.

"I have to go, Mr. Wilbershy. Thanks for telling me about my mother, I'm really sorry I made you go through it all again. Would it be all right if I stop again some time, in case you think of something more?"

179

"I've told you everything . . . everything, so you needn't stop again. It would just stir up all the pain."

I went to the foyer and pulled on my overshoes. He waited until I had them on and stood up.

"I find it hard to believe that you're that sweet little girl who crawled around these floors . . . hard to believe."

"I can't remember," I said and I smiled at him.

"Would you mind if I hug you?" he said bashfully. "It would be a little like hugging your mother again . . . hugging your mother again."

"It's okay."

He hugged me to his powerful bear of a body and I felt like a little girl in his arms. He had a manly scent, like oiled wood, and for an instant I panicked, helpless in his crushing grip. Then just as suddenly, he set me free and pulled open the heavy door.

"Thank you, little mosquito," he said and I hurried out into the brisk winter night.

On the way home I had to remember where I was going. He said my mother cherished me. *Cherished me!* I wanted to tell everyone on the streetcar and I was trying to absorb all that I'd heard. But all that stuff about Mr. Shapiro muddied the water. Maybe it wasn't Myron who sold me to Mr. Shapiro after all, and if not him, could it have been my mother?

I felt queasy and I kept getting up and changing seats. It was seven twenty and I had to beat Jim to my house. I knew I'd look frazzled but I didn't care. My mother cherished me and I was close on her trail . . . close on her trail, as Myron would say. I laughed out loud when I imagined Miss Bellows trying to get Myron Wilbershy to read a page of Shakespeare.

Chapter 27

I was haunted by that imposing house and yard, drawn back to that neighborhood again and again, trying to resolve the puzzle. I wrote everything Myron Wilbershy told me in my notebook. If he sold me to Mr. Shapiro then he was lying and he knew what happened to my mother. If Mr. Shapiro got it mixed up, and he remembered Myron from the divorce and not the adoption, then Myron didn't know what happened to my mother anymore than I did. In a web of truth and lies how could I decide which of them to believe?

I'd stand on Herschel Street and stare into the yard, straining to recall the swing on the now-teetering iron clothesline 'T', trying to call up some sound or smell or remembrance of that first year of my life. I'd always leave before Myron came home, but I visited Clara Singleton a lot because each time she seemed to remember a little more.

I got home the night of our Mid-Commencement Dance in time to pull on my dress and fuss with my hair before Jim showed up with a carload of kids. The dance was at the Fort Snelling Officer's Club and I was in a dither, bursting to tell someone about my mother. It wasn't until I met Jean in the ladies' room that I could spill the beans and she hugged me and squealed. It was a swell dance and I tried to have fun. Jim and I did a lot of one-stepping and after the dance we went to Mickey's Diner to eat. I kept an eye out for the little wino but he didn't appear and I figured he died in some alley. I started noticing women my mother's age again to see if they looked like me. Did my mother stay in Saint Paul or Minneapolis when she left Myron?

After we ate it was almost one o'clock and I tried to talk the other girls into running through the Selby streetcar tunnel. I'd never heard of a girl doing it and they all said I was crazy, but Steve said he'd do it with me. We had Jim drop us off at the top of the hill by the Cathedral and they'd meet us at the bottom in the getaway car.

This was the deal: the tunnel ran downhill for about two blocks but it was against the law to be in it on foot. It didn't have a smooth surface like the street but railroad ties so you had to watch what you were doing or you'd go down. It had lights but they were pretty dim. The trick was to get through it before a streetcar came along in one direction or the other and if the cops caught you it would be a call to your parents from the police station at least.

Steve and I walked to the entrance and looked back up Selby. No streetcar coming. We looked into the tunnel and listened. We could hear none of those familiar streetcar sounds.

"Ready?" Steve said.

"Let's go," I said and we took off running.

I had an easier time with the ties than Steve with his bad leg and I got out ahead. It was darker in there than I expected and it was hard to see the ties in the shadows. Jeepers, we were flying, hitting those ties, and I was really scared and happy and I started shouting at the top of my lungs as I ran.

"For Mr. Shapiro! For Elsie! For Woody! For Don! For Genevieve! We want to live!"

About halfway through we were huffing and puffing and I heard that familiar sound; a streetcar coming up from downtown. What should we do? There was no place to hide.

"Just keep running!" Steve shouted and I was taking ties three at a time. The streetcar came at us on the left with its one yellowish headlight and we kept blazing down the tracks on the right. The motorman spotted us and slowed down as we went flying by. He shouted out the window, "I'm calling the cops, you lunatics!"

One of my loafers popped off and I had to stop and find it and Steve was ahead of me and really wheeling. I found my loafer in the gravel and pulled it on and took off after Steve. I missed a tie and tripped and fell face first. I was stunned for a minute, the wind knocked out of me, and I took the skin off my right hand and my left knee. Steve heard me and came hobbling back. He helped me up and we heard another streetcar coming from behind us. We hop-scotched down the ties until we came stumbling out at the bottom like cripples from the trenches. The kids were wait-ing and they cheered as we dashed to the car and jumped in.

"Floor it!" Steve said, "the guy in the streetcar is calling the cops!"

We drove up Grand and escaped into our familiar neighborhoods and I was still catching my breath. My heart was racing, I had a bloody knee and a torn dress, my hands were covered with creosote, but I felt happy. I'd promised myself I'd do it and I did, and some day, when I was old and stuck in a wheelchair, I'd remember how good it felt. And besides all that, my mother adored me.

"Back again?" Clara Singleton called from her rocking chair.

I was standing on the boulevard, gazing at the house and yard, the last place my mother was seen, imagining her standing by the back door, watching me crawl across the grass, or swinging me into the sky and laughing. I tried to catch her voice in the air and sometimes, if I'd shut my eyes and concentrate real hard, I thought I *could* hear her, and I could hear my little-girl squeal.

"Yes," I called to Clara and I wandered over and joined her on her porch.

"Still tryin' to figure it all out?" she said, flicking ashes off her cigar.

"Yeah, but I'm not getting very far."

She was the only woman I knew who dressed in men's clothes and smoked cigars but with her it seemed natural. She told me her husband smoked them and when he croaked she missed that aroma and started smoking them herself, made her feel he was still hanging around the house. She wore his clothes for the same reason.

"Do your folks know that our police department has been infiltrated by Commies?"

"No, I don't think they do," I said.

I sometimes wondered how I could sort out what Clara told me.

"Well, you tell 'em, and tell 'em one of our senators is a card-carrying Commie as well."

"I'll tell them," I said.

"I have a surprise for you." She smiled with her yellowed teeth, those that were left.

"Did you remember something?"

I settled on the backless chair.

"It came to me last night, the fella that came around lookin' for your mother. Peter Buggs, that was his name, Peter Buggs."

I scrunched up my face. "Bugs? Like an insect?"

"No, no . . . I think it's B-u-g-g-s, with two g's."

"Oh, that's swell, that means my name was *Buggs*."

"Not the kind of name you'd write home about," she said as she blew a cloud of smoke.

"Oh, but it was *my* name," I said. "Did the man ever talk to Myron?"

"He asked when Myron'd be home and I told him around six, as regular as rain. He had a LaSalle convertible coupe, bright yellow, one of the fanciest cars I ever saw. He was proud as punch of that car, said he'd gone through some hard times but now he had a good job and hadn't had a drop of alcohol since the day his wife left him."

"What did he look like?"

"Strong face, black hair, tall and trim, I'd have followed him after school."

She giggled and spit over the rail.

"Did he seem to be, you know, smart?"

"As I remember, I'd say he was a glamour boy, but he was nice and polite, well mannered as I recall. Said he'd be back after six to talk to Myron."

"Did he come back?"

"I don't know . . . I don't recall seeing that fancy car again."

"Myron would have probably hidden from him," I said, "so he wouldn't have to bring it all up again. He didn't tell me he'd talked to my father. It hurts Myron to talk about my mother."

"Holy Nellie, I thought the man had gone loony the day after she'd run off. It was a Saturday and he never went to work, a whirlin' dervish around that house, like he was tryin' to work himself into exhaustion, sweat pourin' off him, poundin', haulin', fixin' things, in and out the door."

With a finger she took a speck of tobacco off her tongue and flipped it on the floor.

"Same the next day, can still hear that screen door bangin', can still see the clotheslines saggin', dishtowels, sheets, diapers, billowin' in the sunshine, rugs, drapes, you name it. I called over and asked him if he wanted some cold lemonade but he only waved me off, a man possessed, kept it up until dark, and then I could still hear that screen door banging."

"I think he really loved her," I said.

"He was crazy about her," she said, gently rocking and chewing on the cigar that had gone out. "I thought he'd go nuts."

She paused and examined her gnarled hands.

"He's a strange cookie, that one, showed up at my husband's funeral with an armload of flowers, figure that. Didn't say ten words to him while he was alive and shows up at his funeral. Surprised the corn flour outta me."

"I don't think Myron ever talked to my father. When he told me about what happened he still didn't know my mother's last name."

"O-o-o-h . . ."

A frown settled on her weathered face.

"Did you ever tell Myron the name, Peter Buggs?" I said.

"I don't recall . . . never talked about it after he come over and told me what happened, showed me the note. I suppose

I figured the fella would tell him his name when they talked."

"Did you ever see my mother again?"

"Nope . . . when she skedaddled she was gone for good."

"Did he ever tell you he heard from her?" I said.

She tucked the cigar stub into her lumberjack pocket.

"Yeah, come to think of it, he did. That winter I took my usual Christmas cookies over to him and he showed me a card he got from her. He was kind of bashful about it and I think it gave him a smidgen of hope. She wished him well and said she was sorry about leavin' and all. Didn't have any return address on it. Far as I know that was the last he ever heard from her."

I glanced at my watch, five twenty-five. I didn't want to be late for supper again, I had run out of excuses.

"I have to get home, Clara, thanks for remembering my name."

"Funniest thing, it just come to me layin' in bed."

"I wonder if my father ever found her?" I said.

"We may never know that, but they was sure lookin' for each other."

When I was almost a block down Herschel I glanced back and saw a long black four-door car pull into Myron's drive. I think it was a Buick limousine. I paused and watched for a minute from behind an elm tree. He parked in the carport alongside the house and lugged grocery bags inside. He'd driven to work and bought groceries on the way home. I made a mental note and turned for home.

I rode the streetcar with new hope. I was a Buggs. I prayed that my mother and father found each other, but if they did, why did they sell me for $970? I decided I'd talk to Myron again and ask him if Peter Buggs, with a shiny yellow LaSalle convertible, ever came knocking on his door?

Chapter 28

The days were rushing by, spring was coming, and I felt the excitement of a nameless anticipation. I sensed I was close to solving the mystery of my mother's disappearance, as if it were there right in front of my nose, in something I knew, but I hadn't seen it yet.

I tried to keep up with school life but I caught myself going through the motions, even with Jim, who I was spending more time with around school and on dates. I think he thought I was scatterbrained the way he'd be talking and I'd be staring at him with a glazed-over look, my mind back in the spring of 1933 in that yard, not having heard a thing he'd said. We were going to the Fool's Frolic Saturday at the Midway Club and tripling with Cal and Lola and Jerry and Sally.

Friday I got back to the haunting house; that's what I started calling it because I couldn't quit thinking about it. Knowing my mother was there, in that neighborhood, walking on that sidewalk, tormented me. I'd decided to talk to Myron again and ask him about my father. I hated to knock on that door, knowing he resented it and wished I'd quit bothering him, knowing I'd stir up his sorrow.

After he'd been home a few minutes I crept up into that forbidding porch as if into the jaws of a beast. I held my breath and knocked on that ominous door. The days were lengthening, it was light now when he got home, and the weather was mild.

He opened the door with the dishtowel tucked in his pants and when he saw me his huge frame sighed with an Oh, no, she's back.

"Hi, sorry to bother you," I said sheepishly.

"The little mosquito, still buzzing around."

"Can I ask you a couple of quick questions?" I said.

"I'm making supper."

He wiped his hands on the towel.

"It won't take long, please."

I sensed he was struggling to keep his anger from surfacing and he pursed his lips and smiled shyly.

"I've told you how I feel about this . . . how I feel."

"I wouldn't ask if it wasn't super important," I said and I tried to beg with puppy-dog eyes.

"Well, just a minute then . . . one minute."

He didn't move, didn't invite me in.

"The summer my mother left, my father came looking for her. He stopped and talked to Clara Singleton and other neighbors." I lied about the other neighbors because I didn't want to give him the chance to pooh-pooh Clara's story as that of an old fool. "He said he'd come back when you got home from work that day. Did you ever talk to him?"

"No-o-o . . . I didn't talk to anyone about her," he said, slowly shaking his head. "No one came around . . . no one."

"He had a fancy car, a yellow convertible, and he said he'd gotten a letter from my mother and she gave him your address."

I watched his face closely to catch the slightest tick, the tiniest wince or hesitation. Nothing.

"Maybe he found her," he said, "and he didn't have to come back . . . didn't have to."

He wrung his hands.

"Yeah, I thought of that, but then why would they give me up for adoption?"

"Who knows why people do things?"

"I'm sorry to bring this all up again, I know it hurts."

He took a hanky from his back pocket and dabbed at the sweat on his forehead.

"His name was Buggs," I said.

He didn't bat an eye.

"Buggs?" he said, almost in a whisper.

"Yes, he told Clara Singleton, at least that's the name she remembered. My mother was Genevieve Buggs."

"She'd never tell me her last name, I don't know why, she was very guarded about it . . . very guarded."

"Did you ever call the police?"

His head jerked up and he regarded me with piercing eyes. "Why would I call the police? She left of her own free will."

"I mean for a missing person."

"She was only missing to me. For all I know she went back to her family and is living happily ever after . . . happily ever after."

He pulled a pocket watch from his vest and glanced at it.

"Just a minute more," I said. "Do you think the police would help me now if I asked them?"

I wanted to use "police" again to see his reaction.

He giggled slightly and shook his head.

"That was seventeen years ago, there was no crime, only a broken heart . . . only a broken heart. The police don't investigate broken hearts. There's some woman walking out on a man this very minute, down the street," he waved a hand down Hershel, "in Minneapolis, in Duluth. That's the way they are, no loyalty . . . no loyalty. They become unsatisfied, want something more, and they run off. The police can't do anything about it . . . can't do a thing about it."

The sadness was filling his paunchy face, his jowls sagged, and I knew I was twisting the blade in him.

"I'm sorry," I said.

"Sandy, that's your name isn't it?"

"Yes."

"Why don't you just let it go now . . . just let it go. You've done everything humanly possible and your tenacity and resolve are admirable, if somewhat quixotic. Genevieve and Peter could be living in Minnesota or Wisconsin or across the street and they are of no interest to the authorities, they haven't broken any law . . . haven't broken any law."

"Yes they *have*," I said and I felt my face flush, "they sold their baby!"

"Young lady, did you ever consider that your mother put you up for adoption because she loved you and she just couldn't provide for you . . . just couldn't provide? When she left she didn't have a cent and I've always admired her for not taking any money . . . always admired her. I wish she had. Maybe she found your father and he was still drinking, or maybe he had another woman. Maybe she felt hopeless, and she gave you up for adoption so you could have a good life . . . a very good life."

His words shocked me. They could be true. I couldn't think of a response for a moment, my mind blank. Finally I came up with something out of my stunned brain.

"One more thing. Did you get a Christmas card from her after she left?"

"Ah . . . yes, she wished me well . . . wished me well. How did—"

"Clara Singleton mentioned it. Where was it from?"

"There was no return address . . . no return."

"Thanks, Mr. Wilbershy, I'm sorry, but I can't let it go."

He shook his head slowly and said, "Sometimes mosquitoes get swatted. Good-bye."

With a polite little smile he nodded and retreated into his stone fortress. On the way home, thoroughly confused about it all, I hadn't missed his guarded threat.

My mother had rallied again and she seemed her old self and I hoped she wouldn't be going back to the hospital after all. I worked around the house Saturday, and with my mother's help I was done early in the afternoon. I tied up the newspapers and got them out on the curb for the paper drive and then took off for the river. The day was mild and sunny and little signs of spring were poking out of the ground like hope. The sandstone cliff was warmed in the sun and no snow remained in my cave. I sat in the sun with my feet hanging over the edge and watched the river go by far below. I wasn't there long before I heard a crow calling.

I mulled over what Myron said the day before. Maybe he was right, maybe I couldn't follow my mother's trail any further and I should let it go and enjoy my remaining weeks at Central. But there was something there I couldn't put my finger on, I could feel it, like a whisper in the night you hear but can't understand. Maybe I was barking up the wrong tree but it was the only tree I had. There in my secret place I tried to be honest with myself and I admitted I had strong premonitions that my mother was dead, a doom in my heart that had roosted there since I found Myron Wilbershy. I fought against it, I tried to deny it, but it was there, like a cancer in my chest.

But something didn't add up. I'd left my notebook in my locker at school and I wanted to go over every word again until I found what it was that festered in the back of my mind like a thorn, that whispered to me in my sleep. I curled up in the sandstone cave as if I were in my mother's belly. I fell asleep and dreamed I was in the sinking canoe with Mr. Shapiro. I was going down in the violent wind and waves and Mr. Shapiro gave me his life jacket. When I woke up I knew that Mr. Shapiro was all right wherever he was.

Cal was sick and couldn't go to the Fool's Frolic that night and I missed having him along. Jerry and Sally were with us and Jim found the courage to park along the River Boulevard. We listened to the radio while Jerry and Sally were necking in the backseat and Jim held my hand. I was starting to wonder what there was about me that attracted shy boys. Frank Sinatra was singing "Time After Time" and I caught myself wondering where Scott was right then and then I switched to wondering where my mother was right then, Genevieve Buggs. Like Myron said, they could be right across the street and I'd never know it.

While Jim leaned over and shyly kissed me, it hit me like a ton of bricks. I could put an ad in the paper, looking for

Genevieve Buggs, and if anyone knew of her whereabouts, they could call a number. What number? Couldn't be ours. Jean's, she'd do that for me.

Monday I went downtown after school with Jean and we put an ad in the personals in the *Pioneer Press*. Between the two of us we only had enough money to run it for a week and the clerk assured us that the Sunday edition was our best bet.

If you know the whereabouts
of GENEVIEVE BUGGS,
who lived in St. Paul in
1932–33, please call MI-4972

Jean was good about letting me use their number and on the way home she confessed she'd told her mother about my search for my real parents. She assured Jean that it would go no further, that the last thing she'd want to do was see my parents brokenhearted. I trusted Jean's mother, she was a good person, and she knew all about broken hearts.

In school Wednesday I got one of the shocks of my life. A rumor was zinging around the halls that Cal Gant, one of my best friends, was in jail! I didn't believe it until I worked my hour in the office and then I heard it from Miss Hass, the office secretary. Not only was Cal in jail for robbery, but he'd been kicked out of school. Cal was one of the kindest, most considerate boys I'd ever known, and if he was in jail for robbery, either I was dreaming or the world had flipped its lid. With every fiber of my heart and soul I knew Cal was innocent.

I didn't know what to think about the ad in the paper. It was a long shot and I came close to talking myself out of doing it as a waste of time and money. It was so long ago. But who knows, maybe there would be someone who'd see it and point me down another path in the forest. The path I was on had come to a dead end at the solid stone wall of Myron Wilbershy's house.

Chapter 29

Just before the bell in wood shop, some of the football players grabbed Donny Cunningham and stuck his little body upside down in an upper locker. The boys did this quickly because they knew that Mr. Wabley always stepped into the room promptly at the bell. The football players didn't do it to be mean, they liked Donny, everybody did, and Donny was laughing when they shut the locker door on him, standing on his head. The only problem was the locker could pop open accidentally and Donny could be hurt. So the boys wedged a piece of wood between the locker door and the nearest work bench and Donny started thumping on the locker like Rocky Marciano.

The bell rang, Mr. Wabley stepped into the room, and everyone in the class started pounding on their bench, hammers and mallets and rulers banging away so loudly it sounded like a boiler factory. Mr. Wabley cringed from the noise as he walked to the front of the shop and began shouting.

"Knock it off! Stop the racket! Pipe down!"

He held up his hands and waved them forward several times as if he were backing up a locomotive. Finally, everyone stopped banging. Everyone except Donny.

We were all cracking up but trying not to let it show. Mr. Wabley squinted at the lockers with a puzzled expression and just stood there with his hands on his hips, as though he didn't believe his ears. All that racket from lockers that no one was touching. Donny was pounding away like a drummer in the marching band and I figured the blood must have been filling his head like a pumpkin.

Mr. Wabley stomped over to the locker, saw the wood jammed against the door, and yanked the brace away. Out came Donny Cunningham, tricks or treats, right into Mr.

Wabley's arms. Only Donny was upside down and his face was in the teacher's crotch and Mr. Wabley held on to keep Donny from dropping onto the concrete floor head first. Off balance, Mr. Wabley danced a few steps with Donny until Roger Lundbeck and Chuck Brown grabbed Donny and turned him right side up.

Mr. Wabley stomped to the front of the shop and straightened his tie and glasses and glared at the class.

"All right, wise guys, I want to know who put Mr. Cunningham in the locker."

Nobody blinked. Mr. Wabley was smart enough to know that Donny wouldn't rat on them, being as small as he was, and the teacher didn't even look at Donny, who was smiling and having more fun than anyone.

"Those responsible step forward right now or the whole class will have seventh period for the entire week."

That's when it hit me; I wouldn't be able to visit Clara or get down to the newspaper office. A sinking dread wiped the smile off my face and threw a cold blanket on the fun. The class stood there, nobody moved. Then Bill Beardsley raised his hand and I could have kissed him.

"I confess, Mr. Wabley . . . Sandy did it."

The class roared, I started to blush, and I couldn't help but laugh. We all got seventh period for a week.

I was really disgusted about the week of detention. The ad in the *Pioneer Press* hadn't stirred up one phone call but when I renewed the ad the lady told me I ought to look through the obituaries in the old newspapers. I'd spent one afternoon doing that, starting with June 1933, and I'd worked up to September. Now I'd have to give that up for a while. I kept asking Jean if there had been any calls until she barked at me that I'd be the first to know. I apologized for hounding her. I knew she missed Dave a lot and she was talking about getting blood tests and driving to Iowa to get married. We sang "Someone To Watch Over Me" a lot and we'd try to laugh.

One night I was checking the paper to see if my ad was in place. I always did this in my bedroom after my father had finished looking through the paper. By pure chance I spotted a small item in the back pages that took my breath away. Rest Home Employee Arrested for Bilking Patients. The short article told how Greta Spalding had been arrested and pleaded guilty to forging checks of several residents of the Sunset Home For The Aged And Friendless. She was given five years in the Shakopee prison for women. Katzenjammers! it wasn't Betty Bain after all. Greta Spalding, the nicest person in the place, who would have guessed? I was so happy I wanted to run downstairs and tell my parents, but I couldn't. I wanted to tell Mr. Shapiro, and I remembered he said the money didn't matter. I called Jean, and we celebrated over the phone.

Sitting in Kirschbach's seventh period had its advantages. I had my notebook with me and I was finally taking the time to rewrite every word, copying it in good clear handwriting from the scribbled notes I'd scratched down. I looked at the picture of me and Mr. Shapiro and I remembered what he'd told me. Make friends with an angel if you ever have the chance. I'd written it down. Was Mr. Shapiro an angel? He said they come in all kinds of disguises. Was Elsie an angel?

I rewrote Mr. Shapiro's every word and then I got to the things Clara had told me, then Myron's story. The class was pretty quiet, everyone seemed to be doing something constructive for a change, and Mr. Kirschbach was sound asleep in his swivel chair, leaning back and snoring.

Then, as I copied, something jumped out at me, something I'd overlooked all this time. When Clara Singleton told me about that first day after my mother ran off, she said Myron was working around the house like a madman, in and out, like a whirling dervish, as if he were trying to work himself into exhaustion. But Myron said he'd been out looking for her all that next day, and the next, searching bus depots and train stations and rooming houses. How could that be? One story wasn't true. Why would Clara make up such a story? Could it be that over time she remembered it wrong, that he started working around the house the following weekend?

While I was comparing their stories another word leaped out at me that I couldn't believe I'd missed. Clara said the clothesline was sagging with dishtowels, sheets, and *diapers,* billowing in the sunshine. Diapers? My mother had left and taken me with her. Why was he washing diapers? It could be she left a bunch of dirty diapers behind. It could be he was just washing them out for rags. It could be I was still in the house wetting them!

But the discrepancy I discovered Monday afternoon in Mr. Kirschbach's seventh period that sent goose bumps down my arms was what Myron said about my father. He denied he ever met my father and he didn't know his name was Buggs until I told him. He said Genevieve would never tell him her last name. I remember distinctly that I'd never mentioned my father's *first name.* And Myron had said Genevieve and *Peter* could be living in Minnesota or Wisconsin or across the street. He was lying through his teeth. He'd met my father. Or could it be that my mother, who was afraid to tell Myron anything about her past life, would tell him her husband's first name? I didn't think so.

It was a muddle, but putting the three together gave me a strong feeling that Myron was lying, that Mr. Shapiro was right all along, that Myron Wilbershy had brought me to him for adoption and therefore Myron knew what happened to my mother. But what about the Christmas card? Did my mother send it? This was the deal: I'd have to see the card and compare the handwriting with the note she left behind when she ran off. There was only one way I could do that, get into his house. Did he keep the card? I'd bet he did. I looked at my notes and tried to listen to what they were telling me and I was scared.

Suddenly, Mr. Kirschbach tipped over in his chair and hit the floor like a sack of oats. He sprang up, a shocked look on his olive face, dusted himself off, and picked up his magical chair. Before he could speak, his big alarm clock went off, seventh period was over right on schedule, and we all filed out as if nothing unusual happened.

I walked down the deserted halls to my locker and an awful sadness caught up with me. It was as if my heart knew what my mind didn't want to accept. Myron Wilbershy had done something horrible to my mother.

Chapter 30

I served my sentence in Kirschbach's seventh period, going over and over my notes, and the more I studied the discrepancies the more I believed Mr. Shapiro and Clara and the less I believed Myron Wilbershy. Kirschbach let us out early on Wednesday and I took off for downtown. I got through the September and October obituaries for 1933 and still made it home for supper on time. But I didn't get back to the house all week and that didn't feel right.

At lunch on Thursday I told Jean about the riot we had in D.B. Sandersen's physics class. The Dagwood Bumstead of Central's teaching staff probably thought he was going crazy. Steve slipped into the physics lab before class and exchanged fine black dirt for the iron filings in D.B.'s demonstration on magnetic fields. At the big moment, when all theory went into practice and with the whole class standing around watching, D.B. threw the switch and pointed out how all the iron filings lined up perfectly while, instead, they just lay there like dead fish.

D.B. spent the rest of the hour checking every electrical connection, every wire, telling us that he'd have it in a minute, never once suspecting that the iron filings weren't iron filings at all. The kids who knew what Steve had done were hemorrhaging and those who didn't didn't care. They knew that D.B. ran the entertainment hour of the day and never realized he was the star. When the class filed out, unconvinced about magnetic fields, he stood muttering to himself as if he were quietly admitting that he was losing his mind.

Usually jealous of all the fun we had in physics, Jean had her own story about her English class that morning. While the class was supposed to be working quietly on a short story, Joe Dudovitz unconsciously began humming. Mrs. Amanda Johnson glanced up from her desk.

"Joe, would you like to sing for the class?" she said kindly.

"Oh, I'm sorry, Mrs. Johnson, I didn't realize—"

"Why don't you sing for us, Joe," she said and the class cheered. Joe had a good voice.

"Come up here," Mrs. Johnson said and Joe walked to the front of the class.

He sang "When You're Young At Heart" without missing a word and the class cheered again. Then he led the class in singing "Auld Lang Syne" and Jean had tears running down her face and she realized we were almost through with our high school years and she said it was the best hour she'd ever had at Central.

We ate our bag lunches and I didn't look for Scott in the balcony once and I told Jean I was going to pound on Myron's door and see if he could explain why his story didn't add up with the others. Jean didn't think it was a good idea, that he might get mad and then he wouldn't help me anymore, or worse. I told her I had the gut feeling that he'd done something terrible to my mother.

"What do you mean?" she said, about to take a bite of her egg salad sandwich.

"I think he killed her."

It was the first time I'd dared to say it out loud and I scared myself.

"No-o-o-o." Jean leaned close. "Really, murdered her?"

"Yes, and I think she's buried somewhere in his yard."

"Gosh, Sand, maybe you ought to tell the police."

"I can't, yet. I don't have a bit of evidence. Mr. Shapiro is the only witness who saw him with the baby after he murdered my mother and Mr. Shapiro is dead."

"You don't know he murdered her," she said.

"Well, where was she then when he sold me to Mr. Shapiro?"

"What are you going to do?" she said and she sucked at the straw in her chocolate milk.

"I don't know, but the more I look through the obituaries the more I feel it's stupid. If Myron killed her there'd be no record of it in the newspaper."

"Golly, I hope you're wrong, Sand. I hope you'll find your mother alive and well."

Jean was a good friend, trying to cheer me up, but it didn't work. A voice in me told me to let it go, to give it up, to cherish the time I had left of my high school days. But like D.B.'s magnetic fields, another voice drew me towards something I couldn't name, the mystery of what happened to my mother, and I had to go on. But I had to admit to Jean I was plenty scared.

Friday night Jim and I went to the Bunny Bounce at the Midway Y and we doubled with Jerry and Sally. Jim and I did a lot of one-stepping and he kissed me once when we were sitting having a 7UP. It surprised me so much I almost knocked over the bottles and he went back to bashful soon afterwards. We parked beside the Highland Tower and two minutes after Jim managed to tiptoe his arm around me a cop car showed up. They shined their spotlight on us and told us we couldn't be there. Romantically I was doomed.

Sunday I went out to the workhouse near Como Park to see Cal Gant. A sleepy-looking guard led me into the visitor's room where other women were chattering with their husbands or boyfriends or fathers and I felt really strange. Cal seemed embarrassed to see me and we sat on a bench along one wall. I noticed the men who were locked up: all sizes and ages and some appeared to be right at home. I looked for the little wino. Cal tried to act cheerful but I could tell he was really miserable.

"I know you didn't do it, Bean, I just know you wouldn't."

"Thanks."

I tried to fill him in on school stuff, D.B.'s class and Joe Dudovitz singing in Mrs. Johnson's and Donny Cunningham in a wood-shop locker and how I ended up with seventh period.

"Have you seen Lola?" he said when I finally shut up.

"Yes . . . she's . . ."

"I figured she'd be back with Tom," he said and I could see the hurt in his eyes.

I used the proven Meyer tactic and changed the subject.

"I talked to Gretchen the other day."

"How is she?" he said.

"She came up to me in the hall and asked about you. When I told her you wouldn't be back to school, that you were in jail, she looked like she was going to be sick. She just said Oh, no, oh, no, and walked away like I wasn't even standing there."

"Would you do me a big favor, Sand?" he said and he leaned towards me on the bench.

"Sure, anything."

"Get a Nut Goodie and give it to Gretchen and tell her it's from Cal."

"A *Nut Goodie!*"

"Yeah, but don't tell anyone else about it. Will you do it?"

"Sure, Bean, but why a Nut Goodie?"

"Just say it's from Cal; she'll understand."

We talked a few minutes more and when I left, Scott and Jerry were waiting in the outer room to see Cal. A guard ushered them by me and I was glad they didn't have time to talk. When I got outside my heart was racing and I couldn't catch my breath. When would I ever get over him?

Monday I caught up with Gretchen in the hall before third period. I handed her the Nut Goodie and told her it was from Cal and you'd think I threw her a life jacket when she was going down at sea. She lit up like I'd never seen her and thanked me over and over until I zipped down the hall.

Cal's father died Tuesday, and Thursday I went to the funeral with Jean and Sally. It was a gray rainy day and my dad let me take the station wagon so I could get to the funeral and not miss many classes. My heart ached for Cal; he'd lost his father, and I hoped he knew his father loved him and was proud of him. He'd lost Lola it seemed, and I knew how that hurt. And now he'd been kicked out of school. I wanted to go back to Cal's apartment afterwards, everyone was invited, but I knew Scott would be there so Jean and I went back to school.

Saturday night there was nothing going on and Jean and I went over to the Grandview to see *Pinky* with Jeanne Crain. I don't know how he did it, but Donny Cunningham was there and he moved over and sat right behind us. I loved the movies, they could always make me forget for an hour or so and let me fly away to some other world. We had chocolate malts at Lacher's Drugstore, though I no longer believed in their magical ability to increase the size of your breasts. Donny had one with us.

We decided to walk up to Snelling to catch the streetcar and Donny insisted on escorting us so we'd be safe from the maniac lurking on Saint Paul streets. Donny was so small a murderer would step on him without even seeing him. It was a balmy night, spring was here, although it had been raining a lot, and we thanked Donny for his protection when we boarded the Snelling car.

When Jean popped off at Watson, I went up front and talked with Fred.

"How are you?" I said while hanging onto the pole right behind his seat.

"Very sad, very sad."

"Why?"

"I'm losing my streetcar, we all are," he said.

"What'll you do?"

"Drive a bus, maybe, I don't know. It'll never be the same."

He opened the front doors.

"That's what my dad says," I said as I hopped down the steps.

I scampered the block to my house, thinking about Fred and how sad it was that the city didn't want to keep the streetcars.

When I turned in between our two big maple trees he grabbed me from behind. For a second I thought it was one of my friends goofing around, but he was too big and strong. Before I could react he clamped a cloth over my face. I tried to scream but it was muffled. The cloth smelled like a hospital and I tried to suck air through it. A voice shouted from a long way off. My knees buckled and I started to faint.

He hoisted me over his shoulder like a sack of potatoes and started running. My head was bouncing up and down and I was groggy, like dreaming, and I was watching myself being carried away. I heard shouting, closer, and I was limp, floating in air, and Mr. Shapiro was trying to get a life jacket on me and the waves were washing over us and Scott was standing on the shore calling my name. Then suddenly, I hit the ground hard and I saw stars. Nothing seemed to hurt. I was flat on my back and dazed. Someone was standing over me and shouting.

"We'll get you, you filthy bastard!"

He knelt beside me and took my hand.

"Are you hurt, girl?" he said and his voice was familiar.

He helped me sit up and the world was spinning but I could tell by the streetlights I was in the middle of the Horace Mann playground across from our house. How did I get *there?*

"Did he hurt you, are you bleeding anywhere?"

It was Fred, the streetcar motorman. He'd watched me walk home and seen the man grab me.

"I feel kind of woozy," I said, "he made me breathe something."

All of a sudden I shuddered. If Fred had driven on, if in his sadness he hadn't watched for me that one time, I would be dead, gone, and no one would ever know what happened to me.

"Can you walk?" he said and he helped me stand.

He steered me on wobbly legs to my house and rousted my parents. My mother had a cow and called the police. My dad shook Fred's hand like a pump handle and kept slapping him on the back and thanking him until Fred had to run back to the streetcar he'd left sitting in the middle of Cleveland Avenue.

They made me lie down on the sofa and my mother was frantically going on about all the horrible things that could have happened. My father went to the garage and found a two-foot length of lead pipe and immediately started prowling the neighborhood as he did when he was an air raid warden. I'd never seen him so furious and I knew he'd kill the man if he got the chance.

I had to think fast; I knew who tried to kill me but I couldn't tell the police, not yet. I didn't have a shred of real evidence that he'd harmed my mother, though now I knew my hunch had been right, I'd smoked him out. If I identified him as the man who attacked me, he might have an alibi. I hadn't seen or felt a thing that could identify him and that would only put him on alert. Before I told the police I had to first find out what happened to my mother. But I was incensed that he tried to kill me. He had me feeling sorry for him with his that phony polite sorrow. How many nights had he been lurking for a chance at me? How did he find out where I lived?

A police car pulled up in front with its lights flashing and suddenly I felt weak. I had the chills and my body started to shake uncontrollably, my teeth chattered. My mother brought me a blanket. It was sinking in; in a twinkling I could've been dead, my life over, and they would've been looking for me the way I'd been looking for my mother.

I thought how funny it was; Myron would be quaking in his boots, hiding out, thinking the police would be knocking on his big door any minute. How could he know that I'd protect him, what would he make of it? Maybe he'd think I was so simpleminded I couldn't put two and two together. Maybe I'd at least have him confused, rattled enough to make a mistake.

The police were at the door and I figured they'd think it had been the man who'd murdered the woman in January. I'd have to let them believe that for the time being. I couldn't tell them that bashful Myron Wilbershy, at 358 Herschel Street, was a magician: he made people vanish.

Chapter 31

The police went over the area with a fine-tooth comb, trying to find anyone who saw the man or his car. A bunch of policemen on their hands and knees crisscrossed the play-ground, looking for any clue. They found nothing. A detective named Powers, Captain Powers, looked as hard as nails and reminded me of Broderick Crawford. He asked me a zillion questions and sometimes, the way he cocked an eye at me, I thought he suspected I knew who attacked me. Once he came right out with it.

"Sandy, have you ever seen this man before?"

"Gosh, I never saw anything."

They thought it was the man who'd killed Mary Kabascka and several other women in Saint Paul in the past few years, all unsolved murders, but he used a knife, never chloroform.

Jean never made the connection, never suspected it was Myron Wilbershy who attacked me and even I had moments of doubt. It all happened so fast. My dad wanted to drive me to school and pick me up every day but the police assured him that it was a random kind of crime, that the attacker would most likely never cross my path again, that he'd probably never be in our neighborhood again. Boy, were they whistling Dixie.

It was on the front page of the *Pioneer Press*, MANIAC STRIKES AGAIN, and when the kids at school heard about it they were swell. I never realized so many kids knew who I was. The girls were scared when they came up and talked about it and the boys were fighting mad and wanted to help catch the guy and beat his brains out. Even Scott told me he wished he'd been there that night but I know he only meant to protect me, nothing romantic. Steve said he would drive past my house more often and Jerry told me to call him any-time I needed a ride. I'd try not to but I'd get choked up when the kids were so good to me. Fred was praised as a real American hero and the city and police department gave him medals to recognize his bravery.

I wanted to go back to Myron's house after school, but even though I knew he worked until five and couldn't make it home until around six, that first week I was satisfied to come home with Jean on the streetcar and go nowhere alone, especially after dark. It was a gloomy, spooky week, with lots of big gray clouds and rain, and at the strangest times I'd come down with the chills and break out in a cold sweat, knowing I'd been only a minute or two from death. Once I woke myself around four in the morning, jumping out of bed as if someone were grabbing me, and I was covered with sweat.

One night that week I heard my parents arguing downstairs. I was doing homework in my room and trying to concentrate on living a normal life when I heard them. Usually they'd protect me from their arguing or fighting, but that night they weren't trying to hide it. I tiptoed out into the hallway where I could hear them better; they were in the living room.

"If you'd put a light out there when I asked this would never have happened!" my mother shouted.

"You can't run a wire underground when the ground is frozen," my dad said.

"It's not frozen now!"

"Well, it just thawed out and I didn't have—"

"You always have an excuse, just like you did when Bobby died!" my mother shouted in a cruel voice.

"You couldn't wait to bring that up again, could you?"

"Well, whose fault was it?"

"It was no one's fault, he could have died while you were washing clothes or peeling potatoes!"

"You just forgot about him, you let him die."

"You'll hold that against me the rest of my life, all of it!" my father shouted and the front door slammed.

I held my breath. The house went silent and I heard my mother walk into the kitchen.

It wasn't my father's fault, it was mine. Myron Wilbershy wouldn't be trying to kill me if I hadn't dug up the past, if I'd been satisfied with the parents I had. I couldn't bear to have my father feeling guilty about it. I went downstairs quietly and slipped out the front door. My father was furiously polishing the Ford station wagon. He always seemed to be able to talk about things better when he was working on that station wagon.

"Hi, Dad," I said as I stepped into the garage.

"Oh . . . hello . . . sorry you had to hear that."

He stopped polishing in the neat-as-a-pin garage and averted his eyes.

"I want you to know it wasn't your fault that I was attacked," I said.

"I know, Sandra, but your mother's right, if I'd put a light out there where she wanted—"

"I still would have been attacked," I said, "the light wouldn't have stopped him."

"I wish I could have caught the bastard."

He started polishing the hood.

"Who was Bobby?" I said and I leaned against the station wagon.

"He was your brother."

Holy Toledo! I had a *brother?*

"When you were a little over two we went to an adoption agency and told them we'd take one of those kids that no one wants, a kid who wasn't perfect. We got Bobby when he was four weeks old. They said he had a bad foot that turned in and a bad hip. They thought the foot could be corrected in a year or so with a brace. We took him home and named him Robert Howard Meyer."

My dad picked up the can and smeared more wax over the hood.

"Is that why we pick a Christmas tree no one wants?" I said.

"Yeah, I guess so. He was a cute little bugger. One afternoon, when he was about three months old, your mother went grocery shopping and left me to play with you and watch Bobby. We were playing in the living room, Bobby was upstairs asleep in his crib. I was supposed to check on him every few minutes. When your mother came home she asked how he was and I realized we'd been having so much fun that I hadn't looked for ten or fifteen minutes. I told her he was fine and she took the groceries into the kitchen. I hightailed it up to his crib and he was dead. He'd rolled on his face and suffocated."

He walked around to the other side of the Ford and started polishing the roof.

"Your mother never let me forget. That's why we moved from the house on Lincoln, too many bad memories. I wanted to have a big family, as many as we could afford, but after that your mother said we had all we could handle. It was her way of punishing me, reminding me that I wasn't capable of being a good father."

I walked around the station wagon and made him stop polishing. I hugged him and struggled to find the right words.

"You're a swell father, Dad, any kid would be lucky to have you, any kid in the world."

I held him tightly and I could tell he was doing his best not to cry. He didn't speak. I turned quickly and hurried out of the garage.

In the darkness out on the lawn I gazed through the large windows into the living room. It appeared to be such a warm, kind home, and I knew it was a lie. I hated my mother for blaming him, I hated her for not adopting more children, for not taking a chance again, for not living her life!

The following Monday on the way home from school, I caught myself taking a wide berth around our big maple trees where he'd come out of nowhere and grabbed me. I wasn't home ten minutes when the phone rang. It was Jean, there had been a call, someone in Iowa remembered Genevieve Buggs. I grabbed my jacket and sprinted all the way to Jean's house.

Paul Williams from Mason City, Iowa, had left a number. Jean said it was all right, her mother knew about it and I could make the call from there and forget about the money. The operator dialed the number for me and my hands were shaking.

"Hello, Gambles Hardware," a man's voice said.

For an instant I thought she'd dialed wrong.

"Is Paul Williams there?"

"Just a minute."

He put down the phone. I waited, biting a fingernail.

"This is Paul."

"Hi, this is Sandy, I'm calling from Saint Paul about Genevieve Buggs."

"Oh, yeah, I hadn't heard Genevieve's name in ten years."

"Did you know her?" I said.

"Ginny? Heck yes, we were in high school together, you know. I used to be best friends with Peter, you know, it was real strange. My wife's sister sent her a piece of china from Rochester and it was padded with lots of newspaper, you know. I was picking it off the floor and I saw the want ads from the Saint Paul paper, you know, and I looked them over because I've been looking for a used shotgun, you know, and there was your ad."

"Do you know where Peter is now?" I said.

"No, that's why I called. He just disappeared, you know, the craziest thing I've ever seen. He left one weekend, wouldn't tell me where he was going, said it was a big surprise, you know. I always thought he was going to get Ginny, they'd been separated for a while, you know, and I figured she'd let him know she was ready to come back."

"When was this?" I said as my throat went dry.

"Ah, it was in August of 1933. The man just disappeared, you know, left his good job, his house, all his belongings. The police tried to locate him for almost a year. He wasn't in debt like so many of us were then, you know, wasn't wanted by the law. It was so strange. I was sure that one day he'd call me from Timbuktu but I never heard from him. He had some distant relatives in Oklahoma but they didn't show much interest. The house and his stuff were finally auctioned off to pay taxes, you know, it was really sad."

I was trying to keep my voice from melting and my heart was trying to beat its way out of my chest.

"They got married and settled down and after a couple years they had a baby girl."

"I'm that girl," I said and I started to cry.

"No foolin', you're Pete and Ginny's kid?"

"Yes."

"What happened to your mother?"

"I don't know, I was adopted when I was one and I don't remember either of my parents."

"Oh, gosh, that's tough," he said. "Your dad loved your mom a whole lot but he got to drinking, you know, and he got mean a couple times. Ginny left him a few months after you were born. I've never seen a man so broken, you know, he never thought she'd really go. I don't think it was a week after your mother left that he quit drinking, you know. He loved your mom and he tried to find her, you know, but he didn't have a clue. He kept thinking she went to Texas for some reason."

"What work did my father do?" I said with my throat filling.

"He was a car salesman, selling fancy cars to the people around here who still had lots of money, you know. He was a real nice, likable guy when he wasn't drinking."

"Mr. Williams, if you remember anything else would you call me at this number?"

My eyes were so blurry I couldn't see and Jean handed me a Kleenex.

"Why, sure, I'll think about it, but you know, I'd bet my bottom dollar that neither of 'em would've ever given *you* up, you know. I always figured they must've been killed in a car accident or something, you know. He always drove that fancy LaSalle too fast."

"Thanks for your help, Mr. Williams."

I hung up and started crying so loud that Jean's mom came in the kitchen to see if I was all right. She sat on a chair beside me and hugged me and bawled right along with me.

Instead of going home after talking to Paul Williams, I hiked down to the river. The sun fought its way through the clouds and the world was turning green. I felt jittery being alone and I didn't like anyone walking behind me. I ran part of the way and it felt good. I clambered down the face of the cliff and nestled into my sheltering cave. The sandstone smelled sweet and fresh from the recent rain and I curled up in the security of the rock. I could hear God talking to me through the caw-caw-caw of the crows.

I was safe at the center of the earth and everything seemed right when I was curled up in there. I thought every-one ought to have a cave. I was amazed that I'd had a brother, if only for a few weeks, and I started to wonder if I was jinxed. My mother and father, and now a brother, were all dead, and I never got to know him or eat coney dogs with him at the Gopher Bar & Grill. But at least he'd never have to storm the beach at Normandy and drown in the English Channel without Mr. Shapiro's life jacket.

I breathed with the sigh of the bedrock and quickly dozed off. When I awoke the sunlight slanted to the back of the cave. I lay there awake and I knew my only hope was to get into Myron's house. I had to find some clue, some incriminating evidence that he'd killed my mother, and probably my father, too, or see the Christmas card and compare the handwriting with the note she left. I knew the house would be empty all day but I didn't know how I'd get in without him knowing I was there.

I tried to store up strength from the earth and hope from the crows because I knew I had to do it soon. If Myron had kept any evidence of my mother or father, he might destroy it now that he feared the police were looking for him. I hated to leave the cave, to go back into that world where old people were forgotten and babies suffocated in their cribs and people disappeared without a trace. But I vowed to my mother's memory that I'd go to that stone house tomorrow and find a way to get in.

Chapter 32

I procrastinated three days, although I had a legitimate excuse with choir practice every day after school. We were putting on the musical "Joan of the Nancy Lee" the following weekend and were practicing hard. But Friday I hurried out of school and stayed on the Selby streetcar until Herschel. Jean tried to talk me out of it and wait until she could go with me but she had to work on the sets. I walked the five blocks to the haunting house and I felt spooky, as if someone were following me. But every time I turned around there were just the usual neighborhood people going about their business.

I walked up the alley and stood beside the gray stone two-story garage. I hadn't thought of it before, but maybe the garage would be a place to search. I rubbed a circle on the filthy flyspecked side window and peered into the darkness. I could vaguely make out the car he seldom used, the car that had almost been my hearse. My body could've been rotting in its trunk that very moment. I think it was about a '40 Buick, a four-door limousine. As my eyes became accustomed to the dark I could see that the garage was divided into two stalls by a solid center partition. There was a door leading to the other side but it was padlocked.

I jumped back from the window, sure I saw a faint reflection in the dirty glass, sensing someone behind me. My heart was pounding and I kept telling myself that Myron was in his pawnshop on the other side of the city. I scanned the neighborhood and tried to look nonchalant, moving back to the two large doors that opened onto the alley. The door to the right hadn't been opened in years and grass and weeds had grown up along the groove at its bottom.

The second-story living quarters had dormer windows with curtains that appeared to be falling apart on the rods.

On the other side there was a narrow strip of ground between the big garage and Clara Singleton's one-car shed. Two large trees that had never been pruned grew there, towering over both buildings like weeds. The ground-level window on that side of Myron's garage was boarded over.

I startled again. There was a presence in the alley, I could feel it, someone watching me. I peeked around the corner and gazed down the alley and I just about swallowed my tongue. Little Donny Cunningham, smiling at me like a choir boy.

"Donny, what are *you* doing here?"

"Hi, Sandy, I live just a few blocks from here."

With his hands in his pockets and a sheepish grin he shuffled over to me.

"You were following me, weren't you?"

He started to blush.

"What are you looking for?" he said and I thought he could hold his own at our dinner table, changing the subject.

"It's hard to explain, Donny, but I'm trying to find something that's awfully important to me."

"Is it in that garage?" he said.

"I don't know, but it could be."

"Is the garage locked?" he said.

"Yes, and I need to get in without the owner knowing, I can't break anything."

"I can get in," he said and beamed.

"You can!"

He looked up at the stone horse-and-buggy building.

"Sure, nothing to it," he said.

"How?"

"Like Santa Claus."

"Santa Claus?"

"That looks like a big wide chimney to me."

"Donny, you can't go down the *chimney*." I laughed.

"I'll bet I can, you got any rope?"

He was serious.

"Donny, this isn't a prank at school, you could get into a lot of trouble."

He circled the garage, searching for something. I kept an eye peeled for any neighbor who might be watching and thinking about calling the cops. Donny sneaked to the back porch of the house. He stooped under the wooden steps and came out with a coil of garden hose.

"This'll work," he said as he hustled back to the garage.

He took off his jacket and shoved a garbage can up against one of the trees between the garages. I was vacillating between egging him on and telling him to stop.

With one end of the hose in hand he climbed onto the garbage can and up the tangle of branches like a monkey.

"C'mon!" he shouted and he scrambled onto the roof.

At the back of my neck I could feel Myron coming down the alley. Luckily I'd climbed a lot of trees when I was younger and I followed Donny up onto the garage. The wood-shingled roof was steep and I had to turn my feet sideways to make it up to the chimney. Donny was perched on the edge with his legs hanging into the hole.

"It looks okay," he said, "I can see light at the bottom, it only goes to the second story."

"Are you sure?" I said.

"Yeah, I can do it. Hold the hose tight over the edge of the chimney and the friction will let me down slowly."

He hung onto the hose with both hands.

"What if you get stuck?" I said as I took a hold of the hose.

"Then you'll have to pull me out."

I was thanking my lucky stars that he didn't weigh a hundred pounds but I felt guilty because I knew he was showing off for me.

"Did you hang up your stocking?" he said.

"Be careful, Donny."

I gripped the hose tightly and crouched on the roof beside the chimney.

"Ho, ho, ho," he said and I felt his weight tugging on the hose like a fish on the line.

He slowly disappeared as if he'd been swallowed by the brick. Little by little I let the hose slide through my hands and asked myself if I'd gone bonkers. What if he got stuck? How could I get him out? Myron would be coming home soon. My stomach was in a knot and I was gulping air. Then I heard Donny yelling. His voice sounded as if he were in a cannon.

"I'm down, I made it! I'll let you in!"

I pulled the hose out of the chimney and let it slide off the roof and drop to the alley like a dead snake. I scrambled off the garage, thankful to be on the ground again. No one in the neighborhood seemed to be paying any attention. I stood by the garage door that hadn't been opened in years and waited. Before long I heard Donny banging on the door.

"It's unlocked, pull on it!" he shouted from inside and I grabbed a rusted metal handle and tugged with both arms.

The door opened by folding like an accordion and the accumulated dirt against the bottom made it almost impossible to move. I took the toe of my shoe and scraped away some of the dirt and weeds and finally the door creaked and moved a few inches.

"Just a little more," Donny said.

We pushed and tugged and managed to crack the door not much more than a foot, but as skinny as I was, I wiggled through into the garage.

"Boo!"

He jumped out at me from the shadows and scared the daylights out of me, wearing some kind of a mask like a black knight.

"Jeepers, Donny, you gave me a heart attack. What's that?"

He pulled off the helmetlike thing and I almost fell down laughing. He looked like he'd spent a week in a coal mine, so covered in soot that all I could see were his lips and his blinking eyes behind his wire-rimmed glasses, every inch of him covered in soot.

"Are you all right?" I said and I started laughing again.

"Yeah, there was a damper at the bottom but when I jumped on it a couple times it broke loose and I was standing in the fireplace."

"Look at you, your clothes, what'll you tell your parents?"

"I'll think of something."

"What's that thing?" I said.

"It's a welder's mask, there's some stuff over there."

I stopped laughing and scanned the garage. It looked more like Halloween than Christmas. The shaft of light coming through the partially-opened door exposed hoary cobwebs and floating dust and I sneezed. The garage reeked of mildew, a musty dampness that hung in the filthy air. In the poor light I almost tripped over the frame of a car that sat on the floor with no wheels and what was left of an engine. Someone had been putting it together or taking it apart a long time ago. There was a workbench at the back of the stall and a stairway that led to the second floor.

"What's upstairs?" I said.

"Just some old furniture," Donny said and he smiled with his white teeth flashing from out of the soot.

He hung the welder's mask over two large metal cylinders with gauges on their tops and small rotting hoses looped over them.

"What are those?" I said.

"Acetylene and oxygen tanks, for welding. My dad has those at the garage."

"What does your dad do?" I said, scrutinizing the contents of the dank garage, noticing that everything was rusted or decayed beyond use.

"He's a mechanic."

"Well, it doesn't look like anyone's worked in here for years."

I was breathing fast and I checked my watch. It was five twelve, he was on his way home.

"We can't stay very long," I said and I stepped carefully to the workbench.

Dented cans of oil, jars of nuts and bolts, all manner of other junk congregated mutely in piles on the work bench; fan belts, tire chains, funnels hung on the wall, all of it covered with grime and dust. Mice had been everywhere, chewing and nesting for generations. I spotted an old dog collar on a shelf and I rubbed off the metal tag. BUSTER. Clara's dog! Her hunch had been right. What had her dog gotten into that Myron had to kill him?

Donny pulled a heavy wood box out from under the bench and slid off the top. The cloud of dust he stirred up made me gag. In the box a large food grinder rusted, the kind I hand turned for my mother, though much smaller, when she made relish or hamburger and other stuff.

"What else is in there?" I said, unable to see in the shadows.

Donny lifted something out of the box.

"A meat cleaver and some kind of saw," he said. "I think it's a butcher's saw."

He held them up. Both were badly rusted.

I checked my watch, it was five twenty-three, time was running out. We poked through the discarded odds and ends but found nothing.

"What are we looking for?" Donny said.

"I don't know."

I hurried up the steps and, being taller than Donny, collected cobwebs with my face. There was a kitchen with an old ice box and stove, a living room, a bedroom, and a bathroom that once had running water. I turned the faucet on the sink and it squeaked with rust but nothing came out. We quickly searched through the rooms: mouse-eaten furniture, a few old newspapers and magazines, a large iron frying pan, the floor covered with mice droppings, and then I started to panic.

We hurried down to the garage door. I was afraid Myron could tell someone had been in there, but it seemed he hadn't been in this side of the garage for years. The door to the stall where he kept his car was padlocked from the other side so the only way out was the big door. The problem was we couldn't latch it when we left unless Donny could fly up the chimney. Myron could see that the latch was unlocked if he had the notion to check.

We slipped through to the outside and, with a lot of grunting, shoved the door back in place. I scraped dirt with my shoe and packed it against the bottom in an attempt to make it look as if it hadn't been disturbed. Donny coiled the hose but it was smudged with soot.

"We've got to take it with us," I said. "If he sees it like that he might get suspicious."

He hung the coil over his shoulder and picked up his jacket.

We hurried down Herschel until we were almost to Marshall. The few people we passed stared. Donny looked like a fireman who had been in a house that burned down around him. Three blocks along, I waited while he ducked up an alley and stuffed the hose in a garbage can.

"If I'm wrong about this man I'll buy him a new hose and leave it under his porch," I said.

I noticed Donny had ripped his shirt and one of his black hands had a bloody spot.

"Did you hurt yourself?" I said.

"Naw, I'm okay."

"What'll you tell your parents?"

"I'll sneak in the house and hide my clothes and get in the shower."

"Thanks for your help, I couldn't have done it without you," I said as we reached Selby, "but you could've been in big trouble. You could go to jail for breaking in like that."

Or been killed.

"Aw, that was nothing. Did you find what you were looking for?"

"No."

"What are you going to do with that old dog collar?"

"I'm going to give it to the dog's owner."

"If you need any more help just let me know."

I was disappointed that we found nothing more than we'd find in any old unused garage, except for Buster's collar. I knew now I had to get into the house. It was my last hope. There might be something that the police could use as evidence against him. He kept my mother's letter. What else did he keep?

The streetcar pulled up and Donny stood beside me as if we were married. He smiled out of his happy soot-covered face and smudged glasses and I had to laugh. He looked like a chimney sweep without the hat, holding his clean jacket in his sooty hand.

"You are a sight," I said.

"So are you."

I quickly checked my skirt and jacket.

"Am I a mess, too?" I said.

"No, I mean you're pretty."

I climbed one step into the streetcar and looked down at him.

"Could you get into the house without the owner knowing?"

"Easy, when do you want to do it?"

"I'll let you know. So long, Donny, thanks."

He watched the streetcar carry me away. He thought I was pretty. My head and heart were muddled, but I knew Donny was only helping me because he had a crush on me, and I felt terrible that I'd put that innocent little kid in grave danger. And worse, it really bothered me that I was contemplating doing it again.

Chapter 33

During the following week I nearly wore out my brain sifting through clues and hunches and evidence that pointed to Myron Wilbershy. I felt as if I were suffocating with it, unable to tell friends or parents or the police. And I was scared. I never went anywhere alone. I tried to forget for a time and have fun, but even at the Spring Swing at the downtown YMCA Saturday night with Jim I couldn't quit thinking about what Myron had done to my mother and father, and almost to me. In the movies the murderer is always caught, but he'd gotten away with it for nearly seventeen years, and maybe it was too late to ever prove it. Sometimes I'd realize I was slamming dresser drawers and throwing shoes across my room and kicking over my wastebasket.

Jean thought I was wrong, that there was nothing to show that he'd harmed either of them, and when I tried to convince her I couldn't come up with one solid piece of evidence, only the failing memory of a dying old man in a rest home or the stories of a strange old woman who thought the Commies were destroying the streetcars. I knew I could convince Jean if I told her I was sure that it was Myron who attacked me, but I couldn't prove that either, and I didn't dare tell her for fear she'd let the cat out of the bag.

Jean figured my mother ran away from my drunken father and when he found out where she was he came looking for her. So what. Maybe she ran away from Myron because she was afraid my father would find her. Or, as Myron said, they could be living happily ever after in another city where they chose not to go back to their old life in Mason City. But the refrain that kept repeating itself in my heart was the certainty that my mother would never give me up, never sell me.

Jean was kind, and she was trying to be helpful, but she said it could just be wishful thinking, that every kid that was

adopted wanted to believe that about their mother. Either
my parents found each other and wanted to start fresh, and
that meant without a little baby, or my father never found
my mother and she married someone else and had a whole
new life and they'd both gone on with their lives, just as I
had to. Jean scared me because she made so much sense
and I knew she could be right.

Maybe I'd blown the whole thing out of proportion
because I so badly wanted to believe that my mother loved
me. And sometimes I couldn't help but wonder: Would I be
so driven to find my mother if I had a boyfriend who really
cherished me? But how about Paul Williams in Mason City?
He said he'd bet his bottom dollar that neither of my parents
would give me up. And how about Myron? He said my
mother adored me. It didn't add up. People forget and mix
things up and lie and it seems impossible to sort out the
truth. I was scared and tired and confused. The only thing
stronger than the impulse to give up was the haunting voice
drawing me to what I'd find in that house.

I hadn't forgotten what Mr. Shapiro taught me in the
middle of all my confusion, and on the way to the dance
Saturday I talked Jerry into stopping at the Saint Paul
Home For The Aged for a few minutes to visit my grandparents. They'd tricked me onto the porch of the Runner
thinking I was visiting Scott's grandparents so I figured
I'd use the same ruse.

"I didn't know you had grandparents," they all said.

"Well, they're my adopted grandparents," I said and
laughed. "You know, I'm adopted, so I have adopted
grandparents."

That always held kids off when I'd talk about being
adopted. All eight of us piled out of the car and rough-
housed up to the main entrance. A skinny little nurse smiled
warmly and welcomed us. She wanted to know what church
group we were.

"We're Saint Paul Central's Adopt a Grandparent Club," I said. "We're here to see my grandpa and grandma."

We could see that many of the residents had gathered in the day room, perched precariously in chairs, slumping in wheelchairs, and shuffling unsteadily with canes or walkers.

"Oh, splendid," she said. "Who are your grandparents?"

"All of them," I said and I led the gang into the day room.

I could tell by their expressions that my friends were stopped in their tracks in the presence of so many skeletons and scarecrows and walking corpses. The fun and humor drained out of them and I thought a few would drop their teeth on the floor. In innocent fun Jerry had joked about feeble old men, imitated them, but he'd never seen a gang of them, crooked and crippled beyond repair.

"We were just going to have a little sing-along," the nurse said. "You can join right in."

A younger woman at the piano started playing "Take Me Out to the Ball Game." The kids stood frozen, not knowing what to do. A few of the residents started singing, weakly, creakily, out of tune, while others sat dozing and drooling and staring blankly. I hoped my friends would rise to the occasion and I went over and sat between two tottering old men and started singing loudly.

"Buy me some peanuts and Cracker Jack."

Jerry came through. He kneeled beside a decrepit little woman and joined in the singing, and then Jim shyly sat next to a dozing man. That did it. After the initial shock most of the kids, some with somber faces, mingled with the old people and sang along because they didn't know what else to do. Tom and Lola seemed the most uneasy and they hung back and sat together on the edge of the group but they sang, too, and the old folks seemed to wake up and come alive with new kids on the block. They started singing with more enthusiasm and clapped their bony hands.

"I don't care if I never come back."

We sang for almost a half hour, and by that time my friends were relaxed and having fun, hamming it up with cheerful faces, holding an arm around one of the forgotten. When the singing was done, the little nurse thanked us over and over again.

"Singing is so good for them," she said. "Some of them don't remember their own names but they remember the old songs."

We visited a few minutes and then I picked out a grand-mother the way my family picked out Christmas trees.

"Can I adopt you?" I said to a gloomy stooped woman with gnarled hands and several scabs under her thinning white hair.

"What?" she grumped like Mr. Shapiro.

"Can I adopt you?" I said loudly.

"I never heard of that," she said from her wheelchair.

"Well it's done all the time. I need a grandmother and you're the one I want."

She brushed a hand over her skimpy white hair as if she were looking in a mirror.

"Well, if it's all right with them," she said reluctantly and nodded at the nurses.

"What's your name?" I said.

"Doris . . . Doris Flowers."

"Well, Doris, you're *my* grandma now and when I come to see you I'll bring you flowers."

She lit up a little and put her skeletal hand to her cheek.

"That's what my husband said when he asked me to marry him, said he wanted to keep me in Flowers."

"Where's your husband, is he here?"

"Died in 1932, God rest his soul."

I bent down and hugged her. When I glanced around the room to see what my friends were up to, most of them were adopting a grandparent. Jerry and Steve each had a scrawny old man in a wheelchair and they were drag racing them down the hall while the men were laughing and throwing taunts at each other. Sally was holding a woman's hand and listening to her going on and on about when she was in high school and Jim was reading a letter to a woman who couldn't see well enough to read. I was so proud of them I could've kissed them.

We bustled back to Jerry's car and piled in.

"The guy I adopted," Jerry said, "used to play football for Minnesota."

"Hard to believe," Jim said.

"The woman I adopted reminded me of my real grandma," Sally said. "I haven't visited her for months."

"I got Doris Flowers," I said. "Her husband died eighteen years ago."

"Are you really going back to see her?" Steve said.

"Yep, she's my new grandma."

We laughed and they talked about how scared and awkward they felt at first.

"Make friends with an angel," I said.

"What's that mean?" Sally said.

"I don't know," I said, "but an old man in a rest home told me that a few months ago."

"They're so sad, sitting there, a bag of bones," Steve said.

"Couldn't you hear them shouting to you?" I said.

"No, what do you mean?" Lola said.

"They're shouting at us to live every day with gusto," I said, "while we're young, while we're alive, gung-ho."

No one said anything for a minute as Jerry turned down the hill into downtown.

"I heard them," Steve said.

The musical "Joan of the Nancy Lee" went better than we'd hoped and the audience loved it and stood and applauded for two or three minutes and while I was singing and acting out the story I forgot myself for a time. Donny Cunningham was in the front row and he kept waving at me when we were taking our bows and I'd swear I could still see traces of soot on him. He'd shadowed me in the halls as usual and I talked to him once after second lunch. He told me he'd found a way into the house and I told him to stay away from there, that the owner might notice him hanging around and get suspicious. I wondered if bringing Donny into it was a big mistake.

I hadn't worked up the nerve to try to get in Myron's house all week, but on Wednesday, after choir practice, I stopped at Clara Singleton's and gave her Buster's collar.

"Heavens to Betsy, where'd you get that?" she said, sitting on the veranda steps along the side of her house. She wore her husband's long underwear and bib overalls.

"In Myron's garage."

"You went in his *garage?*" she said in a whisper.

She studied the old dog collar and rubbed it fondly between her fingers.

"That sumbitch, I was right all along," she said. "I let that phony bashfulness hoodwink me, but in my heart I always knew that bastard killed Buster. Buster and that big St. Bernard of his got along swell. Buster must've gotten into something Myron was afraid I'd see."

"I think he killed my mother, too," I said and I waited for her reply.

She squinted at me and slowly nodded.

"You might be right, girl, if Myron was the one who sold you to the lawyer. Or could be your mother couldn't bear to do it and had him do the dirty work."

"My mother wouldn't ever give me up."

Clara chewed on her unlit stub of a cigar.

"That's what we'd all like to think, I suppose."

"*You* convinced me. Myron told Mr. Shapiro that the mother was deathly sick, that's why she was giving up the baby. But you told me my mother was never sick a day when you knew her. Could she have had some weird disease you couldn't see?"

227

"Nonsense! She was robust, young, as healthy as a horse."
Clara buckled the collar into a loop.

"You told me Myron showed you a Christmas card he'd received from my mother," I said.

"That's right, he did."

"Do you remember the handwriting; was it the same as the handwriting on the note my mother left when she ran away?"

Clara paused a minute and studied the dog collar.

"Don't remember," she said, "but I'd guess I'd have noticed if it weren't a woman's writing."

"That's the one thing I can't explain. If my mother sent him that Christmas card, then she was away, safe, in another life and Myron didn't hurt her at all. But what doesn't add up then is how could Myron put me up for adoption? I would've been with her from wherever she sent that Christmas card."

"It's a puzzle, that's for sure, but I knew he killed Buster," she said.

"I know he killed my mother. That's the only explanation that makes sense. He's lying. I believe Mr. Shapiro remembered what really happened. And Myron killed my father, too. A man in Iowa saw my ad and called me. He said my father never came back after he came up here to find my mother. Myron said he never saw my father. He's lying, and you might be the last one who saw my father alive."

"I have a mind to go over and slap him in the face with Buster's collar," she said and she spit onto the greening lawn.

"Please don't, until I've had a chance to search the house."

"You're going into the *house?*"

"Yeah, it's my only chance," I said. "Maybe he's left some evidence, something the police could use to arrest him."

"Better not, girl, no tellin' what he'd do if he caught you."

"Will you help me?" I said.

"Break in his house?"

"No, watch out for me when I'm in the house, warn me if he shows up unexpectedly."

"How am I goin' to do that?"

"Have you got a whistle you could blow?"

"No, don't believe I do . . . got a bugle though."

"A bugle?" I said.

"Yep, was my husband's, got it when he was in the cavalry."

"That would work. Can you blow it, make noise with it?"

She pushed herself up with a grunt and disappeared into the house. When she came back she had a dented old Army bugle that had a soiled gold chord hanging from it. She stepped over to the railing of the porch, put it to her lips, and blew. A warbling tinny blast filled the neighborhood and sounded like Gunga Din, warning his friends of the ambush with his dying breath.

"How's that?" she said.

With her long white hair flowing from under her husband's old felt hat she could be an old Gabriel.

"That's perfect, I'm sure I'll hear that inside the house."

I could've heard that in North Dakota. She settled heavily on the porch steps and hung the bugle around her neck, ready at a moment's notice.

"I'll do whatever I can," she said, looking at the dog collar, "but I wouldn't go sneakin' into that house if I was you."

"I'll let you know when I'm going to do it. It'll be when he's at work so you probably won't have to warn me."

"I won't fall asleep at my post like our politicians. You ever wonder why Truman give half of Europe to the Commies? He's been a card-carrying Commie for years, duped us all. He's the one who gave 'em the know-how to make their atom bomb."

"It's getting late, Clara, I've got to get out of here before Myron sees me," I said, changing the subject. "I'll be back soon. You practice on the bugle."

"You be careful, child, or you'll end up like Buster."

Like one of Buster's bones, I carried that thought all the way home.

Chapter 34

After school Donny and I walked from the streetcar and my legs felt like rubber. He thought I was up to some kind of a prank, puffed up about helping me, enjoying himself. I kept telling myself it wasn't too late to turn around and do it some other day or do it never. It was warm, partly cloudy, a wonderful spring day to stay alive.

We turned up the alley and stood by the garage for a minute, scanning the neighborhood for anybody who might be paying us any attention. I told Donny to hold the fort and I scrambled through Clara's back yard and alerted her. She tried to talk me out of it but then, reluctantly, took up her post with her bugle and immediately squinted towards Myron's house for any sign of him.

Donny told me he could get in through the coal chute door, a small black iron door at ground level that led into the basement. He hadn't actually tried but he was confident he could squeeze through. With a cotton mouth and breathing as if I'd run from Milwaukee, I turned him loose.

The little kid sneaked past the back porch and crept around to the side of the house. Quickly he was on his knees and working with a screwdriver to pry open the metal door that probably hadn't been opened since people started heating with oil. I stood out of the sun under the eaves of the garage and I knew it could all go wrong, that we might not only come up empty but we could come up in jail.

Donny had the metal door open, it swung up on its hinges, and he started into the opening head first. He couldn't hold the door up and it was digging into his back as he tried to worm his way through. I hurried to the side of the house and lifted the heavy door and Donny wiggled through and disappeared. I slammed it and stole around to the back porch, crouching so I wouldn't be seen while I waited.

Quickly, Donny was at the back door, unlocking the latch, and I slipped inside. He looked like he'd been in a train wreck with his wire-rimmed glasses bent and broken and the knee of his pants torn open and another dose of soot all over him.

"What happened?" I said, "are you hurt?"

"Naw, I'm okay. I fell into the coal bin."

"Your glasses are broken."

"I do that a lot," he said, "it's okay."

"Gosh, Donny, I don't know how to thank you, I couldn't have done it without you."

I was trembling and afraid that my chickenheart would show its face and start shouting in my ear.

"Remember what you promised now," I said.

"You sure you don't want me to look around with you?"

"No, stick to the plan. You get away from here and don't come back for any reason. I'll see what I can find and then I'll be out of here fast."

"Okay," he said.

I opened the door and peered out towards the alley. There was no one around.

"I'll pay for your glasses," I said as Donny slipped out onto the back porch.

"Naw, you don't have to, I break 'em all the time."

He dashed out to the alley and disappeared behind the neighbor's garage. I shut the door and locked it. I took a deep breath and turned towards the kitchen.

I was alone, the house silent. I moved quietly, I don't know why, tiptoeing around. The kitchen was large with high cupboards, an old stove and lots of clutter. A pile of dirty dishes sat in a large white porcelain sink. The house had a large pantry and dining room and I sneaked through into the living room where Myron and I had cocoa and cookies. Motley stuffed furniture that looked a hundred years old filled the house, with stacks of newspapers and magazines everywhere. I turned to the other room, the den, with my main objective, the rolltop desk.

I sat in the wood swivel chair in front of the desk and cringed when it squeaked. I opened the drawer where I thought he'd kept my mother's note. It was crammed with envelopes with old stamps, bundled with rubber bands. He was a stamp collector. I dug through the bundles, stacked them on the desk top until I'd emptied the long narrow drawer, but no note from my mother. I stuffed the bundles back into the drawer and tried the drawer below. It had several small boxes and jars filled with canceled stamps and old coins, Indian head pennies, liberty nickels and silver dollars. I rifled through every drawer and nook of the rolltop desk and found old keys, dozens of pocket watches, fancy fountain pens, war bonds, old post cards, but no letters. Had he hidden the note somewhere else?

I kept dropping things and I felt like I was underwater and the pressure was building with every second. I was about to give up on the desk and search other places when I thought about the envelopes. I opened that drawer again and started flipping through each bundle. The addresses were from all over, seldom one with Myron's name on it, covers he'd collected for years. Then, in the middle of a bundle, I found one addressed to Peter Buggs in Mason City, Iowa. My heart skipped a beat.

I opened the envelope and pulled out the letter, written in a woman's hand.

Dear Peter,

I want to come home. Your lovely little daughter is growing like a weed and she needs her father. I want to try again to make our marriage work. I pray you've given up the bottle. If you want me back please send some money to 358 Herschel Street, Saint Paul, Minnesota. Address it to Genevieve, the people here don't know my last name. Under <u>no circumstances</u> come up here, it would only make things much more difficult. I will be home soon.

With my love,
Ginny

It was the letter my father brought with him when he was searching for my mother. How did Myron get a hold of it? There could only be one explanation. He killed my father. Was that enough evidence to convince the police? I wanted to run next door to Clara's and call. Myron must have intercepted my father's letter with the eighty dollars. Was it in the drawer too? I flipped through several more envelopes, trying not to change their order, and I found my mother's note, the note she left when she ran away. It was folded but had no envelope. I laid it on the desk top and continued through the bundle. Bingo. There was a larger envelope addressed to Myron Wilbershy at 358 Herschel, Saint Paul, Minnesota. I pulled out the card. It showed a snowy Christmas scene with the manger. Inside it said SEASONS GREETINGS. Written on the left side was a short note.

> *Dear Myron,*
> *I hope you are doing well and are happy.*
> *I am fine. I'm sorry I hurt you.*
>
> > *With kind regards,*
> > *Genevieve*

My hand was shaking so I could hardly read it. I laid out the three notes and it felt like a punch in the stomach. The handwriting was identical. I turned over the envelope the Christmas card had come in and looked at the postmark. It was somewhat smudged but I could make it out. December 22, 1933. The place was harder to read but it looked like Rice Lake, Wisconsin.

My feelings collided like fireworks, glad and mad, happy and sad, bouncing around in my chest like Roman candle fire balls. I was really happy that my mother had gotten away from him and was safe, but at the same time I was terribly disappointed that I didn't find something that could put Myron in jail. I was more confused than anything, because despite the Christmas card, I still felt that Myron had killed my mother. Maybe she'd come back after Christmas, maybe he'd tracked her down in Rice Lake and killed her there. The mystery grew deeper and I felt lost.

I folded the card and slipped it back in the envelope. I couldn't decide if I should take them or not. Only the letter my mother sent my father was incriminating, but it wasn't enough to prove anything. I slipped them back in the middle of the bundle, hoping to get them in the sequence I'd found them. I figured they were safe there unless Myron suspected I was stalking him. A voice inside my skull was shouting at me to get the heck out of there.

I heard a noise, a bump, a step? I held my breath and was ready to bolt through the front door. I listened for Clara's bugle but all I could hear was my heart thumping to beat the band in my chest. I knew our house would make noises when I was all alone, like it was stretching or sagging, and my father said that when a house warms up in the sun it makes noise because the wood is expanding.

I walked through the first floor quietly, searching in drawers and cupboards but finding nothing helpful. Every time I glanced over my shoulder into another room I expected to see him standing there, watching me. A clock struck five, scaring the buttons off me. I opened the door to the basement and, for some reason, felt I would find what I was looking for down there.

The shadowy basement was divided into several rooms by unpainted wood walls and the grimy flyspecked windows were too small to crawl through. There was no way out of the basement except back up the rickety wooden stairs. The entire basement looked like a pawnshop, although most of the stuff appeared to be too old and rusty to be of any value.

The floor was concrete and there was an area with a large double sink and a washing machine. Clotheslines, with clothespins clinging like wounded wooden birds, ran along the ceiling in the damp basement air and everything stunk of mildew. I got the feeling that Myron didn't go down there often. In one corner, just past the old coal bin that Donny fell into, there was a long narrow fruit cellar with shelves along both sides, filled with jars of pickles and jam and stuff that looked like it had been there since the Civil War. I felt a chill when I saw it had a dirt floor and that dirt had been recently dug up! A shovel leaned against the back wall.

I sat on my haunches and dug with my hands in the loose dirt. Was this the grave he'd already dug when he tried to chloroform me? I was scared. No one would ever find me. Was this what I was looking for? If he was going to bury me here, had he buried my mother or father here?

I forced myself to move. I checked the time, five twenty-four. I felt like I was holding the bottle of hydrogen sulfide in Miss Mauleke's classroom and the seconds were ticking and I didn't know how many ticks were left. I searched the basement, ducking under some of the lower wood beams, brushing cobwebs out of my face, but my mind kept bringing me back to that dirt floor.

Wet with sweat, I could hold on no longer and I dashed up the basement stairs and out the back door, making sure it locked as I pulled it closed. I ran around through the alley and found Clara peering down the street for any sign of Myron.

"Thanks, Clara, I'm out."

"Holy mackerel, I've been a nervous wreck," she said with a big sigh. "Glad that's over with."

She thought *she* was a nervous wreck. She ought to feel the jackhammer banging away in my rib cage. I was so scared I knew if I didn't go back at the first opportunity, I never would.

"I have to go back."

"Are you crazy girl?"

"The Christmas card was from my mother. It was post-marked December 22, 1933. It was her handwriting."

"Well, then, that ends it. She's off somewhere and—"

"He killed my father and I think he's buried in the cellar. I have to go back with enough time to dig. Will you watch out for me?"

"You sound like you're lookin' to get yourself in a heap of trouble. What if he catches you diggin' up his basement?"

"He won't if you watch for me. Will you?"

She looked over at Myron's house.

"You betcha I will. That sumbitch killed Buster and I hope you find enough to put him on ice for the rest of his life."

I'd catch myself walking around at school like a zombie, my mind completely focused on that dug-up dirt floor in that gloomy basement. I'd use a phony pass to get out of school so I'd have several hours to dig and cover my tracks before he came home. I'd have to get Donny out of classes as well. It felt like I was going downhill, faster and faster, towards some mystery, and I could no longer stop or slow down.

On Tuesday, D.B. Sanderson explained the Leyden jar to the physics class, a large, empty glass jar lined inside and out with tinfoil to about two thirds of its height. It had a metal cover with a rod sticking out of it. In theory it was supposed to store electricity, though it looked like an ordinary Mason jar. After demonstrating some electrical principles, D.B. told everyone to join hands, linking the whole class into one human conduit.

"Hold on tightly," he told us.

He asked Steve, at the end of the line, to take hold of the radiator with his free hand.

"Oh, gosh, will it hurt me?" Steve said with a whiny voice.

"No, you'll simply feel a slight tingle move through your arms," D.B. said, "just enough to realize the current has passed through the line and been grounded."

The empty jar looked harmless enough and we held hands, waiting for one more of the bungler's classic demonstrations, most of which had backfired. D.B. cranked up enough electricity so we could all feel a slight tingle and then he asked Hugo Hendricks, who grinned at the head of the human chain, to take hold of the jar's conducting rod.

We were laughing and enjoying that goof-off time and Hugo reached toward the jar and started horsing around.

"Good-bye, cruel world. Good-bye, mother. Good-bye, dear old Central."

D.B. let him play it to the hilt, and then Hugo clutched the jar's rod like he was going down at sea.

Zzzzzzaaaaaaappppppphhhhh!

In an instant we were jolted as if we'd been hit with lightning, blasted back into our seats, and in the uproar of shock and shouts, Steve, hanging onto the radiator, seemed to have gotten the worst of it. The jolt went through my arms so quickly I couldn't tell the direction, and in the middle of the complaints and outcries, I looked at D.B., standing calmly in front of the class. There was something else going on besides demonstrating the Leyden jar.

I watched closely, and sure enough, trembling slightly at the corner of his mouth, the beginning of a smile that, for the first time I'd ever seen, spread across his face. D.B. Sandersen, the Casper Milquetoast of the faculty, stood grinning before his class, and it was a smile of satisfaction and sweet, sweet revenge. He'd slyly nailed all of us, repaying us a little for all the stuff we'd pulled on him, and he'd given Steve Holland a special dose, and he'd done it with an empty jar.

As I walked from the classroom amid the jabbering of the kids, I envied D.B. his revenge. I wanted something like a Leyden jar to zap Myron Wilbershy and I really believed I'd find it under the dirt floor of his fruit cellar.

That night I woke up in a sweat at three forty in the morning, dreaming I was being buried alive.

Chapter 35

Donny acted as if we were going to a picnic as we hurried from the streetcar towards the house. I'd only told him I needed to get back in the house once more, that I didn't have enough time to find what I was looking for. We'd been excused from our two afternoon classes thanks to the phony passes. Rita Reynolds, a sophomore who worked in the office sixth period, would intercept the passes before they got sorted into the teachers' boxes. As we hurried along Herschel I wasn't worried about getting caught skipping school. I was worried about staying alive long enough to serve time in seventh period.

Donny waited in the alley while I alerted Clara. In her husband's work shirt, suspenders and pants, she took up her post with the dented old cavalry bugle.

"This'll have to be the last time for this monkey business," she said, "my heart won't take it."

"If I find what I'm looking for we'll be calling the police on your phone before the day is over."

"Where'd you get the midget?" she said.

"He's a friend from school."

"Kindergarten?" Her laugh was more like a growl.

Donny decided he'd go through the coal door feet first this time and I held the heavy door up while he slithered into the basement. I had a foreboding about doing this again and I'd taken a few precautions. I told my mother I was staying over with Jean that night, in case I couldn't make it home in time for supper. I hadn't told Jean what I was doing because I thought she might try to stop me. I told Jean my mother thought I was staying overnight at her house so she shouldn't call me, that I wanted to watch Myron's house all night and I'd be staying at Clara's. If I got done in time, I could always show up at home for supper and tell my mom I wasn't staying overnight at Jean's after all.

After Donny let me in and I locked the door behind him, I watched him skip down the steps and walk off into the neighborhood as if he'd just pulled a fast one in wood shop or something. I felt a lump in my throat when he went out of sight and I hurried to the fruit cellar and started digging. It was twelve fifty-four. I dug furiously, reminding myself that I was digging up my mother's grave, or my father's, and if I could find them, I'd have the police waiting for Myron when he came plodding home. The digging was easy, that ground had been opened up in the last few weeks. With every shovelful I dreaded what I'd find.

I worked for over an hour, the dirt piling high on the basement floor along with my panic. A clock somewhere in the house chimed the hours. I'd found nothing but an occasional rock in the sandy soil. It was humid, and even though the basement kept a coolness during the afternoon, the sweat was running off my face, my pleated skirt and short-sleeved white blouse were smudged. Twice I stopped digging when I heard something in the house, or heard the house. I'd hold my breath and not move for as long as I could but nothing came of it.

I crept upstairs and got a drink by putting my mouth under the kitchen faucet. My curiosity took me to the window to check the outside and then I tiptoed up the wide stairway that had a worn dark-red runner. On the landing a massive grandfather clock stood with the brass pendulum swinging behind the glass. There were several rooms on the second floor, large and small, and there'd been some remodeling of the old house, rooms made smaller by partitions that had newer paint and wallpaper than the ancient original. It was obvious from the accumulated dust that several rooms were unused.

A large bathroom had one of those huge fancy tubs that sat a few inches off the floor on cast iron feet. There were several bottles of pretty soap and bubble bath and soft fluffy rugs on the floor. The room was fairly neat compared to the rest of the house and had a stack of large pink towels.

The bedroom Myron obviously used had clothes strewn over chairs and the dresser, shoes and socks here and there. A large, unmade bed seemed to sag in the middle from his large hulking body. Several other rooms had beds of various sizes that looked as if they hadn't been slept in for years. One bed with a frilled skirt and flowered pillows and spread had probably been his mother's and appeared untouched since the day she died. Myron preserved his mother's memory by keeping her room as though she were still living in it while Clara kept her dead husband around by wearing his clothes and smoking his cigars. Some neighborhood.

I went through some of the drawers but found only normal clothing and human clutter. I opened a door and found the stairway to the attic. The smoothly worn steps squeaked and complained and as I came up to the third floor the heat took my breath away. The attic was a disappointment, almost empty, except for a few old trunks, piles of magazines, and some forgotten furniture. Rafters slanted in from all directions with dormer windows and I had to watch my head. The attic floor had become a graveyard for other carcasses, moths, flies and shriveled bumblebees that had been trapped in Myron's house as well. Cobwebs, mouse droppings and old hornet nests had taken over the place.

I opened one of the trunks and found souvenirs from the Army: uniforms, bayonets, an old helmet. Another trunk was filled with worn and ragged children's toys, but nothing to incriminate Myron. I knew I was on the right track in the fruit cellar and I fled the stifling dust-conquered attic for the cooler basement.

When I shut the attic door and tiptoed down the hall, I heard a noise. I froze. I listened. Nothing.

I hurried to the basement and continued digging. I was down about four feet and working my way to the back of the cellar. The hardest part was finding a place for the dirt and I started piling it under the bottom shelves that ran the length of the fruit cellar. It was three fifty-six and I hadn't found a trace of anything and I knew I was close to the point of no return, that if I didn't start replacing the dirt in about fifteen or twenty minutes I'd never have it all back by the time he came home.

Then I saw something in the dirt that made me swallow. It was a bone. I dropped the shovel and gently picked it out of the soil, a piece of a thin curved bone, old and fragile and crumbling. I'd been right all along. I sat at the edge of the hole and cradled the little bone in my hands. I thought it must be a piece of one of my mother's ribs. I broke down and cried, at first trying to be quiet and then sobbing out loud. I'd found what I never wanted to find.

I lost track of time, sitting there with my mother's rib bone in my hands, imagining how I'd lived for nine months with that bone sheltering me from harm. But I knew I didn't have to put the dirt back. I'd run to Clara Singleton's and call the police and my sorrow turned into anger and rage. I wanted to wait until Myron came through that front door and take the shovel to his head, I wanted to personally beat him into his fruit cellar graveyard.

I scrambled out of the hole and trudged up the narrow stairway with the sweat running off me. As I shut the basement door I heard the bugle blaring, Gunga Din warning of ambush with his dying breath. In that same instant, the lock on the back door snapped open and Myron Wilbershy lumbered in with several books under one arm, head down. Shocked senseless, I had a split-second to duck into a narrow broom closet and pull the door closed to a crack.

I was trapped! In that instant, I knew full well that if he caught me, I'd dug my own grave, and I'd join my mother and father, disappearing as they had, in that unmarked family plot.

Chapter 36

Scared to death he'd hear my heart pounding, I tried to calm my hysterical breathing. I had to stand sideways, in a crouch, too tall for the narrow space. I tried not to bump the stuff in the closet: a broom and mop, a pail on the floor, a dust pan hanging by a nail on one side. He'd driven to work, home early. I'd been careless, not checking the garage for his car before coming in the house.

I heard him plop down the books and sigh. I felt his heavy step as he passed only inches from the broom closet door. I was sure I could smell him, his hot breath, muttering quietly to himself.

"I'm home again, daddy's home again."

It struck me at that moment that the man was crazy, insane. Without knowing it he had snared me. As far as I could tell he went into the front of the house and I dared take a hold of the towel rack on the inside of the door and pull the door tightly shut. In a moment he was back in the kitchen, running the water, drinking thirstily. He kept muttering on his way to the front of the house. I strained to listen. I thought I could hear the stairs creak. Did he go upstairs?

I wanted to make a break for it, through the kitchen, unlock the door, and dash away. In the open I knew I could outrun him. Myron was no match for the Runner. But I didn't know where he was. I opened the narrow door an inch and listened. He was talking, or was it a radio. A radio. The upstairs toilet flushed. He was upstairs. Now was my chance. I tried to work up the nerve to bolt from the closet when I heard the stairs creak again. I pulled the door shut. In a moment he was back in the kitchen. I eased back against the wall, avoiding the broom and mop handle. Sweat dripped off my face and ran down my legs. He was talking to himself.

"Make a nice dinner, a nice dinner, you'll enjoy a very nice dinner."

I was shaking with chills. What if he needed something from the fruit cellar? I'd never know for sure where he was. I'd have to stay in the broom closet all night and wait until he left in the morning, take my chances that he wouldn't go down in the basement. I'd outsmarted myself. No one would be looking for me. Jean thought I was spending the night with Clara; my mother thought I was spending the night at Jean's. Donny promised he'd leave the neighborhood and not come back until I talked to him at school.

Myron was making his supper, banging pans and washing things in the sink and stirring something. With the clatter of dishes you'd think he was making supper for an army. He went on and on until I thought my legs would give way. The pain shot through my thighs and back. I didn't think I could stay in that position another minute. Finally, he gathered his food and left the kitchen. Maybe on a tray. Was he eating in the formal dining room, sitting alone at the large mahogany table, visiting with imaginary guests? Had he gone upstairs with his supper? I could still hear the radio from time to time and it sounded like he was talking to himself.

I slowly allowed my body to slide down the wall until I was sitting on the rim of the pail. My knees were jammed against the side. The relief to my legs and back was ecstasy but I realized I wouldn't be able to stand, only tumble sideways out of the closet. My mouth and throat were parched. I kept telling myself I could make it through the night.

Occasionally I could hear the radio, hear him talking to himself. He was even more of a fruitcake than I'd thought. I thought of Donny Cunningham in the custodian's locker in the girl's lavatory. He'd foolishly gotten himself trapped, too, had to decide to stay or run. I was in a lot more trouble than Donny and I couldn't make up my mind.

I couldn't believe it! There I was, squatting on a pail in a broom closet, clutching a piece of my murdered mother's rib bone, fearing for my life, and wondering how I'd ever gotten into that terrifying mess. I thought of Mr. Shapiro; he'd been right all along. I couldn't help but think that if he hadn't hung on, if he'd died before I got to the hospital, I'd be home safely eating supper with my parents, never would've found out what happened to Genevieve and Peter Buggs. Would that have mattered? Was it so important to end up dying for it? What was I *doing*?

Myron was thumping down the stairs. I closed the closet door. He rattled around in the kitchen, running water, washing dishes, opening and closing the refrigerator, humming to himself and talking out loud. I couldn't make out most of what he said but he was in a good mood and talking about the lovely evening and something about the moon and love.

Suddenly it hit me; dishtowels were hanging on the towel bar on the inside of the closet door. I was doomed. Crunched as far back and down as I could, I was measuring my life in seconds. It was stifling and dark. I wanted to crack the door, but he was right there, only a few feet from me.

The door opened a foot. His hand reached in and snatched a dishtowel, and he went about his work. I tried to swallow, afraid to breathe. I recognized what he was humming and it surprised me. "Someone To Watch Over Me." I had to run for it. Out towards the front door. Maybe if I threw a chair in his path I could get the door open before he grabbed me. It was my only hope, because he'd have to look to put the dishtowel back. And worse, he might sweep the floor as I always had to after I did the evening dishes. The narrow closet was closing in on me like a coffin. I'd decided I'd try to bust out and run, hoping that the surprise of it would throw him off guard for a few seconds.

I tried my legs. I gently lifted my fanny off the pail but I couldn't straighten up. Panic was filling the closet like a well and I was sure I'd drown in it. I prayed. I fought against crying. Would they ever catch Myron when I disappeared? The bustling in the kitchen suddenly stopped. The light went out.

Myron lumbered towards the front of the house. I caught my breath. He wasn't tidy. He didn't sweep the floor, didn't put the dishtowel back. I felt a tingle of hope. Maybe I could make it through the night.

I closed the closet to within an inch and listened. As the night wore on I heard the toilet flush and the water running for a long time, maybe filling the bathtub. Every time I was sure he was upstairs, I'd hear him close by, in the pantry, out to the back door, roaming around the house like a restless bear. He talked to himself and hummed and sang a few words now and then without much tune.

I'd hear the radio, faintly, in and out. It sounded like a baseball game, the Saint Paul Saints. The grandfather clock chimed, nine o'clock. It felt like I'd been in the closet for a lifetime. He seemed to be settling down, no longer back and forth, up and down the stairs. I heard something like a muffled shout, music from the radio, and him mumbling.

Then, after a while I realized I hadn't heard a sound for a long time. He was asleep. Could I get out of the closet quietly, without falling onto the floor and tipping over the pail? I didn't think so, my legs were numb, my feet asleep. Could I sneak to the back door and slip out without waking him? Voices argued inside of me. Go! Stay! What were the chances that he'd open the broom closet in the morning. Maybe he'd be in a hurry and not spend much time in the kitchen. But even if I could only pile out of the closet with a clatter, I'd still be able to make it out the door before he could come downstairs. Go while you can!

I fought the paralyzing fear. I swallowed hard, took a deep breath. I started to push the door open. He was standing there, in the kitchen, getting something out of the refrigerator. I caught myself. I almost tipped out onto the kitchen floor. I froze. Gently pulling the door closed a few inches, I tried to still my body like a stone. I hadn't heard him or felt his weight on the floor. I didn't know if he'd left or if he was in the back entryway. I decided I had no choice. I'd have to stay in the closet until he left in the morning. I leaned back on the wall and tried to quietly adjust my rump on the pail without rattling the handle. I figured that before morning I'd have to use the pail. Already I had to go and I was glad I hadn't had anything to eat or drink since noon.

The old grandfather clock prolonged the night, faithfully announcing the hours through the peaceful house. I heard a police siren or fire truck around four in the morning and I wished they were coming to 358 Herschel. My body screamed at me and I managed to pull up my skirt and go in the pail, hoping what sounded like Minnehaha Falls hitting a tin roof didn't carry upstairs. After awhile that sweet smell filled the closet. In the end, would that be what betrayed me?

I must have dozed off and on because suddenly daylight flooded the kitchen and Myron came lumbering down the stairs, singing little tunes and talking to himself. He kept try-ing to sing "Oh What A Beautiful Morning," but he couldn't remember all the words. I was shocked that a man who murdered and buried two people, and tried to kill me, could be so light-hearted and cheerful. I wanted to stab him in the heart with my mother's rib bone.

He clattered around in the kitchen. I could smell coffee and bacon. I hoped the aroma of the food would cancel out the smell I was sitting on. After what seemed like an hour, Myron took his food into the other room or upstairs. Exhausted and with a craving thirst, I kept telling myself it wouldn't be long now. I could hear a radio and his babbling and the traffic of the waking city. My lower body was with-out feeling, my blouse and slip were damp with sweat, and my back, with an excruciating voice, was pleading with me to move. I began to think I couldn't outwait him, that I'd have to roll out of the closet and let him do with me what he wanted.

Finally he came back into the kitchen. I prayed he wouldn't go into the basement. The clatter of cups and plates sounded as if he were piling them in the sink, the way they were yesterday. He did dishes at night! Hope came roaring into my heart. I told myself I could sit there another hour if I needed to. Suddenly he came through the kitchen, muttering.

"It's a lovely day, enjoy a beautiful day."

I held my breath. I heard the back door shut. The house went silent. I'd done it. I'd crawl over to Clara's if I had to. I pushed the door open a few inches and looked at my watch. It was seven twenty-one. He opened the pawn shop at eight thirty. I hesitated. Wait a few more minutes, in case he forgot something. Seconds seemed like hours until I couldn't wait another heartbeat. I pushed the door open and rolled out onto the floor with the bucket clanking beside me.

I lay there with my legs pulled up and slowly tried to straighten them, avoiding the spreading puddle. Pain shot through my back and legs. I wanted to cry. Little by little I was able to straighten my legs and sit up. I hung onto a counter and pulled myself to a standing position, momentarily crippled. The sun was shining, I was alive! I clutched my mother's bone and stumbled towards the front door.

I heard something. Was it the old house making noises? I stood perfectly still and listened. Only my heavy breathing. I wanted to escape that nightmare, dash out the door and shout to Clara. But something drew me up the stairs like D.B. Sandersen's magnetic fields, something stronger than the urgency to escape. An inner voice shouted at me to *run*, before it's too late! Still, I crept up the stairs and prowled along the hallway, glancing in the rooms. They were the same, nothing seemed to have changed.

I paused at the bedroom I'd guessed was Myron's mother's. The closet door was open. That seemed different. I inched in for a closer look. The closet was stuffed with fancy old-fashioned clothes, musty dresses and coats, dozens of shoes, but nothing unordinary.

I turned to abandon ship, to dash wildly out of that scary stone morgue into the freedom of sunlight, when something caught my eye. One of the dresses was caught in a crack in the back wall, as if caught in a *door!* I knelt and pulled at the dress and a small door opened a few inches. It startled me. I knelt there a moment, transfixed. Then I pulled it open and crawled in.

Chapter 37

I came out in a beautifully furnished windowless room, lit by an old fashioned standing lamp with a fringed shade. I was kneeling on a plush Persian rug, completely dumbfounded. Expensive framed paintings hung on the four walls: land-scapes, ocean, a farm with golden cornfields. Bookcases along the wall bulged with books and magazines, framed photos stood on top of the bookcases and hung on the wall. A small rocking chair and table stood by the lamp.

Suddenly my heart skipped a beat. In a far corner I hadn't noticed a *woman* sitting motionless on a mattress in the shadows. Like startled deer we peered at each other. Thin and pale, she drew me in with large blue eyes. I could see she had nothing on but a man's partially buttoned white shirt. Her black hair hung to her waist. Only then I realized she wore an iron manacle around one ankle and it was attached to a chain. The chain was anchored in the middle of the floor to a large iron loop coming out of a metal plate. She was chained like a dog.

Astonished, I couldn't make my voice work. I sat on the carpet and straightened my aching legs. She gazed at me as if I were intruding on her private world. Finally she spoke with a timid voice.

"What a surprise," she said matter-of-factly, "he didn't tell me you were coming."

"He doesn't know I'm here," I managed to say, catching my breath.

The mattress she sat on had lovely flowered sheets and brightly colored quilts and pillow cases.

"He promised he'd bring you for a visit before you graduated."

"What!"

"He tells me all about you, Laura, so when we get married and become a family, you'll come and live with us."

She spoke slowly, without emotion, as if in a trance.

"What on earth are you talking about? My name is Sandy."

"Oh, I know all about you, you're a senior at Central and live with Myron's friends until we can all be together."

I felt like Alice in Wonderland, nothing she said made sense.

She pointed at the photos on the bookcase. I scooted on my knees over to where I could see them. I was going crazy! They were of *me!* The pyramid on the Ramsey playground with my grade-school friends, my picture in the paper for winning the scrap drive, a little girl in front of the bear cage at Como Zoo, a shot of Jean and me, maybe when we were freshman, standing on a street corner.

I thought I was losing my mind. Was I dreaming?

"Who *are* you?" I said.

"Why, hasn't he been showing you *my* pictures? I'm your *mother.*"

I felt a throb of the heart, still clutching my mother's rib bone in my left hand. Her words came bursting into my head, colliding like great Roman candles and skyrockets, the wonder of it, the horror of it, the joy of it!

"Mother?" I said. "Oh my gosh, oh my gosh, I thought he killed you, I thought you were dead." I held out the bone. "I thought this was one of your bones."

"Didn't he tell you? He was always bringing me messages from you. Wasn't he giving you little messages from me?"

"No, he's lied to you. Oh my gosh, oh my gosh, I've been searching for you, I found you on my own, two months ago I'd never heard of Myron Wilbershy."

"That can't be," she said and a cloud of confusion appeared on her face. "That just can't be."

"I'm getting you out of here, calling the police."

"Oh, I can't leave, he'll hurt you," she said as if she were dazed, "he'll hurt you."

"He can't hurt me, I got away from him," I said.

"I can't leave, he has people watching."

"What people?"

"You can't see them, but they're watching, they'll tell him and he'll hurt you . . . and punish me."

She talked as if she were hypnotized, or that she couldn't understand that she'd been rescued.

"He can't hurt either of us anymore, I'll get you out of here where we'll be safe from him forever."

I was up on my knees at the edge of the mattress.

"Laura!" she said, gazing at me with her fearful blue eyes.

"Was that my name?"

"Yes, Laura, oh Lord, my baby girl, you're all grown up."

I crawled up on the mattress and hugged her. I laughed and cried but she hesitated, stiffened, unresponsive. I held on and felt a sob shudder through her body. Then, slowly, she put her arms around me and started bawling, weeping with a sorrow and joy that had been chained up for seventeen years. We were a mother and daughter who found each other across a generation of loss and horror and separation. We clung to each other, sobbing, for a long time, letting all the pain and fear and loneliness pour out. Then I realized it was time to call the police!

Laura Buggs, how do you do,
All my life, I've looked for you.

She took me by the shoulders, swished her long hair out of her face, and looked me in the eye.

"Let me *look* at you," she said with tears running down her thin face. "What a beautiful girl you've grown up to be."

She studied my face and I couldn't find any reply.

"I'm going to go and call the police now—"

"No, no, don't, he'll hurt you."

She still spoke without feeling, everything about her muted. It was like something in her spirit had been murdered.

"He's not going to hurt anyone ever again, he's going to jail. I'll just call from the window."

She bit her lip and gripped my arm.

"It'll be all right," I said, "I won't leave you, the police will be here in minutes. Okay?"

She took a deep breath and began to tremble.

"I'll hurry."

I stood for the first time in that room. Pain shot through my legs. I ducked out through the low door and rushed to the window that faced Clara Singleton's house. I couldn't grasp the immensity of the bizarre story she'd told me. Had Myron kept track of me ever since the adoption? I felt creepy, dirty, he'd been watching me and my life, that pig! I wanted to take a shower.

I unlocked the window and tried to open it. It wouldn't budge and I could see that it was nailed shut. I wished the boys from D.B. Sandersen's physics class were there. I tried the window next to it but it wouldn't budge either. Suddenly I felt the terror again. What if Myron came home right then and caught us both? I picked up a wood chair and slammed it into the glass, shattering both the inside window and the storm window. It sounded wonderful in that stone dungeon, like something breaking out. It felt so good I wound up and smashed the other window and then I looked around for something else to smash. I threw the chair across the room and hollered across the yard.

"Clara! I've found her, my mother's alive! Call the police! Call the police!"

Clara appeared on her porch in bib overalls and waved at me.

"My mother's alive! Call the police, quick, tell them there's been murder and kidnapping!"

I'd never seen Clara move so fast, into the house and out of sight. It was a bright spring day and I felt an uncompromising joy overwhelm me and fill me. I spotted a crow atop a telephone pole in the alley, calling wildly, *caw-caw-caw.*

Chapter 38

I ducked and crawled through the closet, Alice in
Wonderland, entering a world of make-believe and fairy tale.
The mother I believed was dead and buried huddled in the
corner, shaking. I scrambled over and hugged her. She was
gulping air and felt cold.

"I'm back and I won't leave you again until we're out of
here."

"He'll catch me," she whispered, "he'll catch me."

"No . . . you're safe now, you're safe."

I let go of her and sat back on the mattress.

"Is that what happened when I was a baby and you were
going to leave him, he caught you?"

"Oh, yes . . . that was so long ago."

She stared blankly.

"What happened?" I said.

"He came home early, before I had you ready, and he read
the note I'd left on the kitchen counter. He begged me, said
he loved me, couldn't live without me. I told him my mind
was made up. All that night he guarded us and wouldn't let
us leave . . . wouldn't let us leave. I thought we'd get away in
the morning but he tied me up. He told me if I yelled or
made trouble he'd hurt you."

"How horrible," I said.

"For several days he worked, and most of the nights,
building those walls, making this room. He chained me to
the floor and warned me that you would disappear if I tried
to get away. He took you somewhere during the day when
he went to work and I didn't dare try to escape . . . didn't
dare try. Then one day he didn't bring you back. He told me
some nice people were raising you and if I obeyed him you
would be safe and happy, but if I tried to get away, you'd be
badly hurt."

Myron Wilbershy was a monster! and I realized with horror that, like a zombie, she was even talking like him.

"Did you try?" I said.

"At first, no . . . I *believed* he would hurt you and I did what he wanted, thinking it was my punishment for leaving my husband and taking you from your father. But after a year or so I was going crazy and I tried. I felt guilty about what might happen to you, but I tried. I pounded on the wall and screamed until I lost my voice but nothing came of it . . . nothing came of it. He turned the radio up full blast in this room and then took me out and closed the door and right in the next room I couldn't hear a sound. He'd made the walls very thick, the floor and ceiling; it was soundproof. He'd take me out of the room at night and once I ran but I couldn't get out the locked front door before he grabbed me. He punished me."

"What did he do?"

She turned her face away.

"He punished me."

I could feel my blood boiling.

"After that he kept me on the chain most of the time when I was out of the room. One time I tried to set the room on fire by pulling the cord out of the lamp and sparking the two wires but it blew a fuse before I could get a fire going. I shocked myself, burned my hand. He made me live in the dark for almost a month after that. Seemed like a year. Took away the lamp, put a light on the ceiling that I couldn't reach. Only gave me a lamp back a few years ago."

"I hate him!" I shouted, "I hope they hang him!"

"I tried a few other times over several years, told him I thought he'd killed you, that I wanted to see a recent picture of you. Hit him with the iron once, I did his ironing with him sitting close and reading the paper. It glanced off his head and hit his shoulder but it didn't knock him out. He had a huge bruise and a gash in his shoulder. I paid dearly for that . . . paid dearly."

"I don't know how you survived," I said.

"One day I gave up, knew I could never get away, believed he would kill you if I escaped. I tried to kill myself a few times, but I wasn't any good at any of it. He'd won. I was glad he hadn't hurt you and I accepted my fate."

Her voice carried such resigned despair I choked up.

"Well, you're free now," I said, "and he can never punish you again."

She gave a little laugh.

"He told me that after I fell in love with him, we would fetch you and be a happy family. He's insane, batty. He really believed I'd fall in love with him. I tried that for a while, too, called him sweetheart, kissed him and hugged him and told him how much I loved him, but he saw through it, I'm not much of an actress."

"It must have been horrible for you, *all those years*."

"He treated me like his sweetheart, always wooing me, bringing me presents, flowers, books to read. I read seven or eight books a week, it was a way to get out of this room."

"How did you . . . what did you do when you had to go to the bathroom?" I said.

"It's only difficult when he's at work, he leaves me a potty. When he's home he takes me to the bathroom . . . he fills the tub with bubble bath for me, he loves lilac, and he bathes me and brushes my hair and rubs my body with lotion, aquamarine lotion. He pampers me and carries me to his bed like newlyweds."

She quit talking for a moment and stared at the small open door that led out of her captivity.

"He was very careful not to give me a baby, said that would ruin everything. The thought of it terrified me, I knew he'd never allow a doctor to help me."

I was embarrassed, didn't know what to say.

"One time I made it to an open window on a summer night and screamed. He left me in the room for weeks, wouldn't empty my potty until it was overflowing . . ."

Her voice trailed off.

"Did he beat you?" I said.

"No . . . if I obeyed him he treated me kindly, spoke to me kindly, played his little game of romantic illusion. He let me listen to the radio every night, didn't want me to fall behind in time like some recluse. I'd listen to the reports every night through the war and pray for all those men. He brought me whatever books I wanted, magazines, the newspaper. Just last month I was stunned. There was an ad in the paper, someone was looking for *me*."

"That was *me*," I said.

"That was *you?*"

"Yeah, I've been looking all over Saint Paul for you."

"I'd lost all hope that anyone remembered that I ever existed. And then I saw *that ad*. I took that page of the want ads and put it under the pile of old newspapers so he wouldn't see it. But one night he asked me if I'd seen it and I told him no, that I never looked at the want ads . . . never looked. I could tell he was mad, or scared, or both, and for many nights he would go out for hours, until ten or eleven and never tell me where he was."

"He was out stalking me. I think he figured it out, that I put the ad in the paper. He tried to kill me about three weeks ago, but a friend chased him off."

"He promised me he wouldn't harm you if I obeyed him," she said.

"He lied, he's a born liar."

"I'd given up," she said, "I was planning ways to kill myself when I saw that ad. It made me want to keep on living, someone out there remembered me, cared about me, and hope, like a white dove, came back and landed in my heart.

Hope is the thing with feathers,
that perches in the soul.'"

"You know that poem!" I said.

"It's my favorite, he gave me a book of Emily Dickinson's poetry."

"We had to learn that very poem in school this year."

We held hands and recited the poem together. By the time we reached the third verse I choked up and I listened to my mother's muffled voice.

"I've heard it in the chillest land,
And on the strangest sea;
Yet, never, in extremity,
It asked a crumb of me."

"You didn't give up on me, you didn't forget me," she said and she squeezed my hand.

I thought of all the times I just about did and I felt so proud and good and thankful.

"What happened to my father?" I said.

"Oh, Peter . . . he was a wonderful man. Impulsive, strong-willed, stubborn, but wonderful, God rest his soul. I couldn't hear him at the door, but he came to the house one summer evening in August, a few months after I'd sent him a note telling him I wanted to come home. But he shoved his way past Myron, wouldn't take no for an answer, insisted on searching the house, that he knew you and I were here."

"The neighbor, Clara Singleton, told him," I said.

"Myron had been giving me a bath and he locked me in the bathroom when he went to answer the door. I heard Peter charging up the stairs calling our names, 'Ginny! Laura! Ginny, are you here?' I shouted to him, 'I'm in here, Peter, in here!' and my heart leaped with joy . . . leaped with joy. I got out of the tub just as he kicked the door open. He hesitated a moment, just a moment. I think he was shocked to see me naked in this man's house, and for that split second, when he was trying to sort it out, Myron hit him in the head with a hammer."

"Oh golly, was he—"

"Peter slumped to the bathroom floor and never moved. I always felt so horrible that his last thought was of me living with another man, unfaithful to him."

"Oh gosh, how awful, how sad, I'm so sorry."

"I couldn't tell for sure, but from what I pieced together, he fed Peter to his St. Bernard, piece by piece, ground up and fried."

"What!"

She said it as if she were giving a weather report.

"He cut Peter's car into little hunks of scrap and got rid of it piece by piece, took him several years. Not a trace of either the car or Peter . . . either the car or Peter."

"How ghastly," I said, "that's why he killed Buster, Buster had one of my father's bones."

"And he thought I could fall in love with him."

I felt nauseous, faint, I had to change the subject.

"So it *was* you who wrote in the Christmas card?"

"Yes, he had me write in it and then he went somewhere out of town to mail it, in case anyone ever asked about me." She embraced me with her large blue eyes. "But no one ever did, until you."

My heart wanted to run up a flag and celebrate and I was tickled pink that I hadn't given up. I could see that she didn't have a stitch of underwear on under the big shirt.

"Would you like to get some clothes on before the police get here?"

"Oh . . . yes . . ." she said indifferently, as if she'd lost all concern for modesty.

"Where are your clothes?"

"In the dresser and closet in the far bedroom. Bring me the lavender dress."

I scooted out through the hidden closet door and hurried to the back bedroom. I grabbed a slip and bra and panties from the dresser and a lavender dress from the closet. It wasn't a dress from 1933 but right in style, new, he'd been buying her things right along. I brought her the clothes.

"He didn't want me wearing panties, wearing much of anything," she said and averted her eyes.

I told her I'd be right outside the room. I knew she couldn't get the panties on until she was unchained and

while she dressed I flew down the stairs into the basement
to get the axe I'd seen the day before. I kept wondering who
was buried in the fruit cellar?

My name was *Laura*. I loved it. I saw the movie *Laura*
when I was thirteen and never forgot it. Gene Tierney and
Dana Andrews. They still played "Laura," the theme song
from the movie, on the radio. Of all things, the story was
about a creep who'd kill a woman he loved rather than let
her love someone else.

Back upstairs with the axe and breathless, I called to her
at the closet door.

"Are you changed?"

"Yes, come in."

I ducked through the door and stood up with the axe
in hand. She took my breath away, standing there in her
lavender dress with her long black hair hanging below her
waist. She had high cheekbones, a large mouth and those
captivating eyes that reminded me of Betty Davis. She was
as tall as I was.

"You look beautiful," I said.

She looked at me with a frown and I realized I was
scaring her with the axe.

"Oh, this, I'm going to cut the chain."

I had her move as far back as she could and stretch the
chain tightly over the metal plate on the floor. I got down
on my knees and choked up on the handle the way my
father taught me. I figured the chain was not as tough as the
padlock. I swung with all my might at that stinking chain. It
made a horrendous noise. I'd put a dent in one link, but that
was all. I swung again and again, attacking the chain that had
made my mother a slave for seventeen years. Sweat flew off
my face and I felt good, happy, astounded. I swung away,
steel against steel, my will against Myron's, sparks flying. I
shouted with each blow.

"That . . . filthy . . . pig . . . will . . . never . . . touch . . . you
. . . again!"

I was exhausted, but the chain, though badly wounded, still held my mother captive. I was sucking air, my chest was heaving, and I was terribly disappointed. I wanted to be the one to break that repulsive chain, to set her free.

Then we heard pounding on the door. The police had arrived.

Chapter 39

The police were good men, super kind and gentle with my mother, who seemed bewildered with all the commotion in the house. Squad cars and detectives kept arriving and it seemed, even with all their experience, they couldn't get over what had taken place at 358 Herschel, right under their noses for seventeen years. They cut the manacle off my mother's ankle and I heard more than one of them curse Myron under their breath.

Captain Powers showed up and seemed to take charge. He asked me a lot of questions and I showed him the three notes in the rolltop desk. I told him how my mother saw Myron kill my father and how she thought he got rid of his body and car. That stopped him in his tracks for a minute. Clara wandered through the swarm of people, still wearing the bugle around her neck, shaking her head, shocked that Genevieve had been right next door the whole time.

They were taking Genevieve to a hospital for a checkup and when they asked for our family preference, I told them Dr. Hartfiel and Miller Hospital. I could imagine having two mothers in the same hospital room. I was ready to go with her when Captain Powers and another detective led me towards the kitchen.

"Did you know this guy was the man who attacked you in front of your house?" Captain Powers said as we stood in the kitchen.

"Yeah, but I never did see him so I wasn't really lying. I didn't want to sic you on him yet because I thought he killed my mom and I wanted to prove it before you scared him off."

He just shook his head and the detective standing behind him smiled.

"Can you positively identify this man?" Captain Powers said.

"Oh boy, can I."

"Do you think you could go with us and point him out so we can arrest him?" Powers said.

I couldn't believe it. They could've found him on their own. They were as outraged and disgusted as I and they knew how I felt. I wanted to kiss them.

"I insist on it," I said

Captain Powers smiled and almost stepped on the pail that was still lying on the kitchen floor with a puddle beside it.

"What's this?" Powers said.

"That's where I hid all night, in the broom closet. I tipped it over when I fell out of there this morning."

The odor drifted up to our nostrils.

"There'd be a lot more in it if I had to hide in there all night," he said and we laughed.

I rode in the passenger seat of the unmarked squad car next to Powers and the other detective rode in the back. He pulled out fast and squealed the tires turning onto University. He flipped a switch and the siren began to wail and the lights were flashing and I started to cry. I was speeding through traffic to get the man who destroyed my family; murdered my father, made a slave of my mother and stole seventeen years of her life and all I could do was bawl. Captain Powers glanced over and saw the tears streaming down my face and I tried to wipe them on the sleeve of my dirty blouse.

"Listen, kid, you go ahead and cry. Some damn bad stuff came your way, but you nailed him. You nailed that slimebag and if it hadn't been for you, we'd have never caught him, he'd have kept your mother like that until one of them died."

The detective in the backseat patted me on the shoulder.

"You got him," he said and I was bawling out loud.

My mind was a jumble and my body was running on empty. I realized I hadn't eaten or slept in twenty-four hours, but the anticipation of bringing Myron Wilbershy down had my heart thumping.

We zoomed through downtown Saint Paul with all the traffic pulling over and letting us by, as if they were celebrating my mother's freedom, as if they were cheering us on to catch that monster and lock him up in the Stillwater penitentiary until his teeth fell out.

We flew across the Robert Street Bridge and down Concord Street and he turned off the lights and siren. I pointed out the pawnshop and he pulled to the curb a few doors up. There was a squad car across the street, watching the place.

"Go around back," Powers said to his partner and we got out of the black Ford. I walked to the front door with Powers and he hesitated.

"I'll give you a couple minutes," he said and I knew instantly what he meant. I liked him a lot.

I pushed through the door with the detective a few steps behind me and I felt joy and triumph and hatred well up in me, my mother's and father's blood. We passed a grandma-like woman on her way out, clutching a few dollars in her grubby hand, and I saw that there were no other customers. I could feel the blood pumping through my body and face, hot, raging, and I had no fear.

Myron was behind a glass showcase in his vest and shirt-sleeves. He had a jeweler's lens clipped on his glasses and he was examining a watch. When he glanced up and saw me he was startled. He quickly caught himself and picked up his shy polite manner.

"Oh, hello, what brings you all the way down here on this lovely day . . . this perfectly lovely day?"

I had to admire his acting ability, he could *be* Charles Laughton. He'd known me all along, but when I first knocked on his door he never showed a flicker of surprise or recognition.

"I have one more question," I said and I was trembling.

"I've asked you nicely to quit bothering me," he said and he glanced at Captain Powers who was looking at guns in a glass case. "I've told you over and over I don't know where your mother is or what happened to her . . . what on earth happened to her."

"And she broke your heart, right?" I said with as much sarcasm as I could spread on it.

"Yes, it torments me to think about her, so please—"

"The mosquito has one more question, then I promise I'll fly away," I said.

He glanced quickly at Powers and then back to me. He was sweating. He pulled out a hanky and dabbed at his forehead.

"Very well," he said and sighed, "one more . . . only one more."

"What did you give my mother for breakfast this morning?"

He stared at me blankly and I could see the confusion and panic colliding behind his eyeballs.

"I don't know what you're talking about, you must be crazy, please leave now so I can wait on my customers."

"How is it that you don't know where my mother is when you've got her chained like a dog in your house," I shouted, "you dirty, lying, filthy creep!"

I wanted to smack him in the face. He started to reach under the counter when Powers moved up beside me.

"Keep your hands on the counter," he said with a steely voice.

I glanced over and saw his big black pistol pointed at Myron's chest.

"Please give me an excuse," Powers said.

Myron moved back a few steps, frantic, his eyes darting.

"Were you reaching for the hammer you killed my father with?" I shouted.

I felt brave with Powers standing there with his gun drawn.

"I should've drowned you," Myron said with a curl to his lip.

"I don't drown easily," I said and my nostrils flared.

Then, suddenly, Myron sagged like a balloon that was losing air. The other detective came into the shop and they arrested him. Handcuffed, he slogged to the squad car like a whipped dog, looking at the ground, without a word. I wanted to kick him as they led him past me but something inside me wouldn't allow it.

I smiled when it occurred to me that, after all, it was *greed* that brought Myron down. If he'd drowned me no one would have ever found him out. But he couldn't pass up the $970, and how could he have ever dreamt that that little baby girl would grow up to hound him into that police car.

Another squad car delivered me to the hospital to wait for Genevieve. I fell sound asleep in the waiting room and they woke me around three o'clock in the afternoon. They brought me food and I ate like a horse. I wanted to call my mom and break it to her gently, but I didn't know where to begin. She wouldn't be worrying, thinking I was at Jean's overnight and still in school today.

They found Genevieve in good health but said she needed lots of exercise to get her muscle tone back. She'd require some dental work, but nothing serious. Mentally, they said it would take time for her to readjust to normal living and that sometimes that was very difficult for someone who's been kidnapped or held captive for a long time. The police offered to put her up in the Saint Paul Hotel until she could contact family in Iowa but I wouldn't hear of it. The evening papers would be full of the story and I could no longer hide what I'd been doing from my parents.

"I'm taking my mother home with me," I told the policeman. *"I'm* her family."

They drove us in a squad car and I talked the policeman into using the lights and siren and wheeling down Summit Avenue. He laughed and flipped the switch. I felt like I was in a movie or a beautiful dream. I was sitting beside my mother, who I'd believed to be dead, and we were roaring down Summit Avenue with the lights flashing, announcing to the world that our love had won, that we hadn't given in to the Myron Wilbershys of the world, and that we had the incredible gift of life to share, to live with gusto.

In my heart I thanked Mr. Shapiro. And I thanked Fred and Donny Cunningham and Clara Singleton and I thanked God for giving me my mother back. I suddenly realized it wasn't my need to know why they didn't keep me that drove me, but it was my mother's spirit drawing me towards her, willing me to find her.

We didn't talk, as if we were both soaking up the wonder of that moment. I was smiling and waving out the window at the people who watched us go by. Then my mother started waving too. It was her parade, her welcome back into the world, her homecoming, and I could sense that she was relishing the sights and sunshine and sweet aromas of Summit Avenue on a gorgeous spring day.

We roared around the corner at Cleveland and drivers made way for us. I didn't know how Gladys Meyers would take this incredible miracle, or Howard, but I was hoping that they'd be warm and kind and welcome their daughter's real mother back to the world. Gladys would have a cow with any unexpected hitch in our routine lives. With this she'd have a whole herd.

The cop pulled up to the house and doused the siren. Gladys stood in the doorway with her hand over her mouth.

Chapter 40

My mom was flabbergasted when I told her what had happened and where I'd been all night. We settled awkwardly in the living room and we were both talking at the same time while Genevieve sat quietly on the sofa with her legs curled under her, observing us with piercing blue eyes. Gladys was shell-shocked.

"You *found* Arnold Shapiro! I can't believe it," she said. "But I didn't think you cared . . . I mean you showed no interest . . ."

"I know, Mom."

I changed the subject and told her about the house and how Genevieve had been chained for seventeen years and from time to time Genevieve would shyly add her incredible part to the story.

"That's horrible, you went through what Amelia Earhart is going through right now somewhere," my mom said.

I rolled my eyes for my absent father.

"I always wondered about her," Genevieve said. "You don't hear anything more about her in the news."

"You remember Amelia?" my mom said.

"Oh yes," Genevieve said with a touch of excitement in her voice, "I was pulling for her all along."

I couldn't believe it, but I hoped their interest in Amelia would be something they'd have in common.

"What a wonderful woman she is," my mom said, "an example for us all. I've told Sandy many times, when she's down and things aren't going well, to just say to herself What would Amelia do?"

Then, as if it were the unforgivable sin, Gladys suddenly realized it was dinner time and she wanted to start cooking. I could tell she was in a lot of pain and I told her I'd call Dad and have him bring Chinese. Genevieve startled and

cringed when my father blustered in the door with the
steaming cartons and I could see the fear in her face.

We ate in the dining room with full regalia and my mother
was a showcase of motherhood, treating me like an angel
who'd just arrived from heaven. It was comical and sad. She
was doing her best to be a perfect mom but I could tell she
was having a hard time with my real mother suddenly dropping into our life out of the blue. The more my father heard
of the story the more he kept muttering under his breath
how he'd like a few minutes alone with Myron Wilbershy.
He kept smacking one fist into his other hand and then
apologizing to Genevieve for startling her.

My dad insisted that she stay with us until she got her feet
under her.

"That would be swell," I said.

"Oh . . . maybe Genevieve would like more privacy in a
place of her own," my mother said.

"Seems to me," my dad said, "she's had enough privacy."

I was bubbling with joy but I caught myself restraining
my exuberance when I recognized the hurt in my
mother's eyes.

My mother cheerfully insisted that she needed no help
with the dishes or anything else in the kitchen and she
retreated there to be alone and get a grip on herself. I felt
bad, knowing how hard a second mother would be on her,
so abruptly, without any time to get used to the idea.

Genevieve was anxious to call Iowa and find out how
many of her family were still alive and my dad said he'd help
her with the operator. I lay down on my bed for a few
minutes and instantly fell asleep. They woke me at eight
fifty-five to answer the phone. Jean had seen the paper and
was so excited she could hardly talk. I filled her in briefly
and told her I'd see her in the morning and she whispered
that she and Dave had their blood tests.

I tried to spend the rest of the evening with Genevieve,
hearing about my first year of life and the father I'd never

know, but the phone started ringing off the wall. When I wasn't talking to friends and telling them I was all right, I found out I had a grandmother in Iowa, and an uncle and aunt, and five cousins.

Genevieve's father had died and he never knew what happened to her, always convinced that if she were alive she would've let them know. Her mother was still alive, and her sister and brother. Her brother was working the family farm and her younger sister married a mailman who lived in Waverly. They were ecstatic with joy and were driving up to Saint Paul in the morning. Genevieve showed the most emotion and excitement yet in anticipation of seeing her family.

My dad had a disliking for reporters from something in his past and he shagged several of them who showed up at the door. I didn't know how they found us so quickly. Genevieve said she wouldn't talk to anyone.

My mother let Genevieve help her make up the bed in my mom's bedroom and I hoped they'd like each other. My dad signaled me to follow him and then ducked out to the garage. By the time I got there he was already polishing the station wagon.

"What, Dad?" I said.

"Sandy, now that you know about how we got you, I want to explain something."

He furiously rubbed in the wax.

"We gave money for you because we couldn't go to a regular adoption agency. I committed a crime when I was young, stole some money from—"

"I know, Dad."

He stopped buffing and looked at me with his soft hazel eyes. His mouth opened slowly in disbelief.

"You *know?*"

"Yeah." I shrugged.

"How long have you known?" he said and went back to polishing the hood with less vigor.

"Awhile."

I knew how hard this was for him.

"And it doesn't make any difference?"

He spoke without looking up.

"No, I'm proud of you, Dad. You paid for your mistake and you've lived a good life. You've become a good person and I'm darn lucky to have you for my father."

He didn't look up, fighting back tears, but I saw a few of them fall onto the hood and get polished into the wax finish.

The following day it seemed strange to be in school. I was so charged I couldn't sit still, but life flowed on as if my mother hadn't been chained like a dog. Several teachers told me how shocked they'd been to read about it in the paper or hear it from Cedric Adams on the radio and they were so glad I wasn't hurt. Donny tagged along behind me in the hall after second period. I waved him on and invited him to eat lunch with me. You'd have thought I gave him the world.

"Did you know your mother was in the house?" he said.

"No, Donny, and I'd never have found her if it wasn't for you."

Donny beamed like a headlight all through lunch, the only boy at a table with me and a bunch of Debs.

I got out of Miss Bellows' English when I agreed to talk to a reporter from the *Pioneer Press*. I figured they'd pester me until I did. We sat in a little room off the principal's office as if I were some kind of celebrity. He had huge ears and never took off his hat. Maybe his ears made him a good reporter, they looked like they could hear someone whisper in Duluth. Every time I told him something more about that day and night, he'd whistle through his teeth and make his pencil dance. I wouldn't tell him much about Genevieve, especially the private stuff. I told him he'd have to talk to her about that. The guy said that besides the local papers and radio, *Life Magazine* was onto the story. I could hardly believe him, but that would be up to Genevieve anyway, when she got her bearings.

I raced home from school, running the block from the streetcar, anxious to see how it was going with my mom and Genevieve. My dad was home early; he'd taken Genevieve to see a psychologist at the University the doctor at Miller Hospital had referred her to. They were fairly optimistic she could eventually recover from the horror she'd gone through and live a somewhat normal life.

Captain Powers called and left word that the bone I found wasn't human. It was the rib bone of a dog, I figured Buster's. So far they'd found no trace of Peter Buggs although they identified the frame in the garage to be that of a 1932 LaSalle coup. Myron had been indicted on one count of murder in the second degree and one count of kidnapping. He was being held in the county jail without bail.

My mother told me the relatives had come from Iowa, nice people, and they had to get back to milk. In a few days they were coming to get Genevieve and she'd live with them on the farm for a while, just what they said she needed. My mom looked relieved, though I could tell she was in pain.

"Where is Genevieve?" I said, always being careful not to call her mother in Gladys' presence.

"I don't know," she said, "I haven't seen her for a while."

I chugged upstairs and called.

"Genevieve! Are you up here?"

She wasn't in my mom's room, not in my room. The bathroom door was shut. I knocked.

"Hello, are you in there?"

No answer. I tried the door. It was locked!

"Genevieve, are you in there?"

I could faintly hear a voice muttering. "He'll find me, he'll get me."

"Genevieve, it's Sandy. You're safe here, he can't ever touch you again, he's in jail! Please open the door."

"He'll find me . . . he'll get me . . ." she said over and over.

My mother came up the stairs.

"What are you shouting about?" she said.

"Genevieve, she's locked herself in the bathroom and won't come out."

"Genevieve, it's Gladys. It's okay to come out. Sandy and I are here, everything's okay. You want to open the door?"

We could hear her repeating herself as if she were hypnotized. I felt panic grip me; what if she killed herself after coming so far. I'd heard of people doing that, killing themselves after they were through the worst.

"Quick, go find your dad," my mother said.

I ran downstairs and found my dad in the back yard.

"Dad, Genevieve locked herself in the bathroom and she won't come out!"

We hurried upstairs where my mom was talking softly through the door. My mom and I took turns talking to her while my dad tried to take the door handle hardware off. He didn't want to kick it in and frighten her worse. Then he thought of the bathroom window, we kept it open an inch or so this time of year. As long as Genevieve was mumbling he felt no need to break in quickly.

He put up a ladder, removed the screen, lifted the sash, and climbed through. He quickly opened the door and let my mom and I take over. Genevieve was curled up naked in the tub, shivering violently in water that had turned cold.

While my mom helped her dry off and get dressed I realized how wounded my beautiful mother really was, how her years with that brute had crippled her mind. I was terribly afraid that, in one sense, Myron would hold her captive the rest of her life.

Chapter 41

We all walked on egg shells the next few days. I'd get home from school as quickly as I could to relieve my mother and spend time with Genevieve. My dad hung around in the morning more than usual and he drove Genevieve to the University for her hour with the psychologist. When he'd get back with her he'd go off to work for a few hours. I knew how hard it was for Gladys, fighting her own pain and nausea, but she was kind and very understanding with Genevieve. They were like two kids, desperately hanging on to their swamped canoe in the midst of a wind storm and I wanted to throw them a life jacket but I didn't know how. I was proud of both of them, lucky to have two brave mothers who loved me.

I tried to get back to normal at school and leave my worry at home. Before baseball practice Monday afternoon Jim talked more than I'd ever heard him. The Junior-Senior Prom was that coming week and he told me he always went fishing that weekend with his father and uncle and cousins, up around Ely when the ice was out. I told him it was okay, that I had an uncle and cousins now, too. He'd talked to Steve, the perpetual bachelor of our gang, and Steve called and asked me to go.

The afternoon of the prom I had two mothers doting over me. I'd traded formals with Marlene Hill, a junior Deb who was skinny like me and about the same height. We figured old formals on new bodies might not be recognized. Hers was a beautiful orchid-white strapless with small waist and fluffed skirt to the floor. I couldn't wait to wear it. I sat in front of my dresser mirror while Genevieve worked on my hair and my mom watched from a chair, enduring the way Amelia would and assuring us she was just fine.

"I was skinny like you when I was your age," Genevieve said.

"You were?" I said with sweet surprise.

"Yes, I didn't bloom until I was almost twenty."

After being around Genevieve I had renewed hope that I wouldn't be flat-chested all my life. Despite her tall, slim figure she was well endowed, and unless my father, Peter, sabotaged the mix, I looked forward to being a late bloomer.

While she fussed with my hair the doorbell rang. Gladys insisted on going to the door and Genevieve and I kept at it. She said she was going to cut her hair to shoulder length, and I figured she wanted to cut away all remembrance of those horrific years as if she could cut the memory out of her brain.

Sometimes I'd look at Genevieve with awe and be overcome with emotion. Life's greatest tragedy is to be unloved. The love my mother had demonstrated for me was beyond my comprehension, a kind of love I'd never heard of, that for much of that torturous time she'd make no attempt to free herself for fear of harming me.

Gladys came staggering into my bedroom with an envelope and an open letter.

"Sandra, you're *rich!*" she said, out of breath. "You're rich!"

She handed me the letter. I read it, sitting in front of my dresser mirror, and I couldn't believe my eyes. The estate of Arnold Shapiro had been settled and I had received $33,000! There was a cashiers check in the envelope. The amount didn't hit me at first and I opened my top drawer. In the hodgepodge of stuff I spotted the marble, the blue and red marble I'd been afraid to let go in Whalmen's study hall so long ago. I had to smile.

I shuffled through the clutter and found the picture of Mr. Shapiro and me playing Chinese checkers. He was looking into the camera, stubbornly defying Elsie and the crazy world around him. I looked at the check and smiled. We crossed paths in 1933 and the check was for $33,000, a fortune.

"Who is that?" Genevieve said, looking over my shoulder.

"An angel," I said, "a tottering old angel."

"You're rich!" Gladys said, still gasping.

"No, mother, we're all rich."

The prom was beautiful and a happy relief after the past weeks. We doubled with Cal and Gretchen and those two were a mystery. I thought Cal was sweet for taking her. I figured that Cal's going to jail had something to do with Gretchen, but I didn't know what. I'd never seen Gretchen looking so good and normal, after all the years she walked around in those terrible clothes like a zombie. Someone told me her father had been put in jail. I laughed at the thought of Mr. Luttermann and Myron in the same cell.

Steve was flying high and goofing around as usual and he fast danced with me once when we were the only couple out on the floor. I knew he secretly loved Katie and I still loved Scott and Cal loved Lola and I wondered if life was always this mixed up. I knew I was lucky to be alive and I couldn't help thinking that this dance would have gone on just as it was without me and I'd be buried in Myron Wilbershy's fruit cellar.

We drove across Minneapolis to the Hasty-Tasty and along Lake Street I could see myself clinging to life out on the running board, hearing my friends screaming, scared to death. That seemed a lifetime ago. I couldn't help but think about Mr. Shapiro and the people at the Sunset Home For The Aged And Friendless. I'd decided I'd start college in the fall with my friends and maybe I could take nursing or something that would let me work with old people. I'd pay off the medical bills my parents had hanging over their heads and I'd help Genevieve get started wherever she chose to settle. She was going to Iowa in the morning.

A sadness overwhelmed me while we were eating cheeseburgers and fries and malts and I didn't know where it came from. I'd found my mother, alive, and that brute was behind bars forever, I hoped, and I had a family in Iowa and I was filling up with sadness. Was it because my high school days were over? Was it because Scott didn't love me? Was it for my murdered father?

As I rode home across Minneapolis, sitting next to my good friend Steve in his father's faithful old Chevy, I realized this was the deal: That in the end it doesn't matter a hoot who your real parents are or if you ever know them or how they treat you. The deal is we've been given the gift of a life, and we get to decide what we're going to do with it. In the end, that's the only thing that really *matters*, what we *do* with that gift!

On May 30th, Memorial Day, Myron Wilbershy hung himself in his jail cell with his shirt. He was fifty-two. He left a note: *I can't live without my one true love.*

Even though I knew he was insane, a mentally ill man, I couldn't feel sorry for him, couldn't work up any compassion. Maybe in years to come I'd be able to.

My mother called Dr. Hartfiel on the first day of June and my dad took her to the hospital. I wondered how much of it was Genevieve showing up in our life so unexpectedly and all that had happened in the past weeks. It was just my dad and me again at home for a while. I caught the Selby-Lake for downtown after school and surprised my mom in her hospital room. She shared a room with another woman with only a curtain separating them but I wasn't going to let that stop me.

I found her dozing in the high hospital bed, looking exhausted. I woke her gently and we said all the usual stuff. Then I took a deep breath and went ahead.

"Mom, I don't know how to say this but I want to try."

She pulled herself up into a sitting position against the pillows. She had that expression on her face she had when she told me I was adopted.

"You're the mother who raised me, who cared for me and worried over me and saw to it I did the right things, and that's the way it will always be. No one else can ever do that for me, I'm grown up. Genevieve is a stranger to me. She's the woman who gave me birth and took care of me that first year, but I don't even remember that. I think we'll be more like good friends than a mother-daughter thing. I pray that she'll recover from her horrible experiences. But you're the only *mom* I'll ever have."

I got it out just in time because we were both choking up.

"Oh, Sandra," she said, "thank you. I think I've always dreaded this day would come. But you know, now that it has, it's not so bad, it can't change our seventeen years together."

I swallowed.

"What would Amelia do?" I said.

She managed a thin smile.

"What would Amelia do?" she said.

The next day I ran into Sally after third period. Our year-book, the *Cehisian*, had come out and we were passing them around and signing them. I gave her mine to write in and she gave me hers.

"I haven't seen you in weeks," she said, "where have you been?"

"Finding Laura Buggs," I said and I sailed up the hall in the stream of kids. I knew my remaining days at Central were few and I intended to live each of them with gusto. I was going to visit Doris Flowers on the way home. I repeated it to myself so I'd never forget.

Mr. Shapiro, you're my hero,
You helped me discover, I was never a zero.

༄ THE END

Author's Note

Although the main plot and characters are fictitious, I have
incidentally used the names of actual students who were
present at Saint Paul Central in 1949. All public events, dates,
scores, news items, and locations are historically accurate.
The murder of Mary Kabascka in Saint Paul on January 16th,
1950 is fact. The demise of the streetcar in the Twin Cities is
factually chronicled.
—Stanley G. West, September 1999

Saint Paul Central as it appeared in 1949.

Saint Paul Central no longer exists as it did in 1949. The
building was demolished in the 1980s and a new school
building erected. All that remains of the past is the name . . .
and the memories.